MW00929386

STORM'S RUIN

AMELIA STORM SERIES: BOOK FOUR

MARY STONE
AMY WILSON

DESCRIPTION

The road to ruin is paved with deception...

U.S. Senator Stan Young has more skeletons in his closet than a centuries-old graveyard...and more power than a nuclear blast. When Ben Storey, the city councilman running against the incumbent senator, uncovers damning evidence against Young, he decides to take the information to the only person with the resources to pursue it—Amelia Storm.

Between looking for the case that will finally take down the Leóne mafia family, the abrupt reappearance of her troubled sister, and her search for a rat within her own agency, the military veteran turned FBI agent's plate is full. But when Ben Storey sends Amelia an urgent request to meet him, how can she say no?

Ben is playing a dangerous game, and Amelia soon becomes a pawn. In the greatest fight of her life, who can Amelia trust when everyone turns against her...and her opponent hides behind a cloak of deception?

From the wickedly dark minds of Mary Stone and Amy Wilson comes Storm's Ruin, book four of the Amelia Storm Series, where you'll realize that your home might not be as safe as you thought.

1

Ben Storey wanted to enjoy the short trip from his house to his children's school, but a nagging suspicion he couldn't explain prickled the hair on the back of his neck. His focus alternated between the rearview mirror and the sides of the street.

How long had that white car been behind him? Was it following him? For what reason? And why?

Stop it!

He was driving himself crazy.

Besides, who in the world even knew he'd left his office early enough to pick up his kids? His chaotic work schedule rarely allowed him the opportunity to do the school run for Dylan and Janis. Classes ended at three-thirty in the afternoon, and Ben was normally stuck at the campaign office until way past dinnertime most nights.

He'd made a special effort to pick them up today, knowing his wife would be in court all afternoon, but his grand plan for family time had been thwarted thanks to a surprise call from FBI Special Agent Amelia Storm.

She'd caught him just before he'd stepped out of the office

and adamantly insisted they meet in an out-of-the-way location...tonight. If the FBI was contacting *him* for a time-sensitive meeting, he couldn't refuse, even though he doubted the news was good.

Maybe that was the reason for his feelings of unease.

Yes, that was it.

The digital clock in his car's center console read three-twenty as he circled the school and pulled up in the back of what felt like a mile long line in what his wife lovingly called "school zone hell."

Thankfully, both his kids attended the same public school. He couldn't imagine waiting in lines like this twice. He didn't know how parents with more than two kids did this every single day without going out of their minds.

As he waited, he slumped back against the headrest of the driver's seat and tried to calm the worry in his mind.

Maybe his wife had been right. Iris usually was.

Maybe he should have stuck to local politics. Ben had sought his seat as a city councilman to help represent the lower-income portion of Chicago—people like him and his wife—but lately, he'd wondered if pursuing politics on a national scale had been a mistake. He'd never cared for the divisive, partisan nonsense that dominated Washington, and his aspirations to bring a reasonable mindset to D.C. seemed more farfetched as each day passed.

Challenging an incumbent senator as entrenched as Stan Young came with a laundry list of risks and obligations, not the least of which was Ben's ridiculous work hours. Still, any time he thought to take his name out of the race, he was reminded of who Stan Young was.

Sure, Ben's personal history wasn't squeaky clean. He'd made plenty of decisions he wasn't proud of...mistakes too.

But Stan Young existed on an entirely different level. Ben hadn't dug deep, but in just scratching the surface, he easily uncovered more skeletons in Stan's closet than a centuries-old graveyard.

According to Iris's most recent candid observation, Stan Young's secrets were like a carrot on a stick, and Ben was the horse. The horse never got to eat the carrot unless the person with the stick showed mercy. Ben doubted Stan Young was capable of that.

Iris had always been the one to keep him grounded in reality, but Ben couldn't leave a job half-finished. As the son of two blue-collar parents, he'd been instilled with a healthy work ethic that had served him well during his five years in the military as well as his time in law school. Wanting to continue the race no longer mattered. He'd made commitments and invested himself into this. Giving up was not an option.

The school bell sounded, calling Ben from his introspection. He put his car into drive and rolled forward about five inches as the first wave of kids rushed out from the tall double doors.

Some students walked with friends while others took off at an outright sprint. At the sight of the kids and their eagerness to get as far away from the school as possible, his glum thoughts loosened their hold.

Ben was forty-three now, but memories of his youth didn't feel that distant. Back then, he'd have been first out the door when the bell sounded at the end of the day. He and his friends would race to their favorite neighborhood comic shop, pool their spare change, and buy one of the cheapest comics they could find.

Times had changed more than Ben could have imagined. He and Iris, thankfully, had far more financial stability than their parents did. And rather than rush off to some comic store in a sketchy Chicago neighborhood, Dylan and Janis hurried home to finish their schoolwork so they could play virtual reality games with their friends.

As he continued to inch forward, Ben caught sight of Janis taking the stairs two at a time. Her hair bobbed and whipped in the wind as she skipped along the sidewalk. He waved at his daughter to get her attention, and she threw her arm up to return the greeting. Dylan was a few steps behind, too cool to acknowledge his dear old dad, but he kept pace with Janis as they headed toward the car.

Ben smiled to himself and threw the car back into park before stepping out to wait for them on the sidewalk. Judgy moms might look on with disgust as he acted as chauffeur, welcoming his kids and opening doors for them, but Ben lived for these innocent memory-making moments with his children.

Sometimes, he got a great big hug from Janis. Other times, Dylan would nod as he dove into the back seat of the car. He was at that tender age where being seen with "the old man" wasn't considered cool. But whether he got the greeting he wanted, Ben knew his kids would remember that dad was there, waiting with a smile and open arms.

At least sometimes.

A rush of unseasonably warm November air blasted through his hair, bringing with it a hint of ozone. The sky was partially cloudy, but forecasts promised a cold front would roll through Chicago, drenching the city in a series of back-to-back storms.

"Dad, Dad, look!" Janis held out her smartphone for Ben to see. "Look! That's Emma's dog, Frank, and he's wearing a tie."

Kids could find joy in everything. A lesson adults too often forgot as the years stretched on.

Ben relished every available chance to soak up some of their enthusiasm. And just as described, the phone showed an image of a golden retriever wearing a blue and black tie around its neck.

"He sure looks happy." Ben chuckled at the good boy sitting so pretty for his picture. "Someone just gave him a promotion. Head butt sniffer."

Janis rolled her eyes at his *dad joke*, but she couldn't hide the amused grin. The one that revealed front teeth that were still too large for her face. "Frank *always* looks like that. He's always happy."

"That's because he's a dog, honey. Dogs are always happy. They don't have responsibilities, jobs, or chores." Ben turned to clasp Dylan's shoulder. "Hey, buddy, how was school today?"

"Fine, I guess. Pretty boring, like usual." Dylan answered in monotone with a casual shrug and turned toward the car. "Where's Mom?"

A woman in the minivan behind him blasted her horn, her face a mask of anger that he dare hold up the line for even a few seconds. He gave her a friendly wave instead of the middle finger salute before gesturing for the kids to climb into the back seat of the navy-blue sedan.

He glanced at his watch. "Well, based on the time, I'm guessing she's still in court. There're a couple big trials going on this week, so she's pretty busy."

Dylan's head bobbed as he climbed into the car. "We just started a unit about the courts in social studies. I don't think my teacher knows that Mom's a judge yet, though."

Janis climbed in next, shoving at her brother to get him to make room.

"No, I'd imagine they don't." Ben was about to close the door when he noticed a shadow of trepidation darkening Dylan's face. "You okay?"

Dylan's gaze dropped to his backpack. "My teacher

knows who you are, and I don't think he likes you very much."

Janis popped a piece of gum in her mouth and held out the pack for her brother. "Why doesn't he like Dad if he's never even met him before? That's not very nice."

The mini-van's horn blasted again, much longer this time, and Ben gently shut the door and walked around to the driver's side. Ignoring the angry driver, he took a moment to breathe, not wanting to appear anxious around his kids. Politics was not a popularity contest in the real world. Most politicians, even those trying to do good, made enemies faster than friends.

And he had painted a giant target on his back after sharing information with the FBI.

Ben sent up a silent prayer. He needed the meeting with Amelia to bring more good news than bad. But for the moment, he needed to focus on what was important. Spending what little time he had with his kids and reassuring them that their dad was bulletproof when it came to the haters was priority one.

With one final breath, Ben opened the driver's door and took his seat. He put the car into drive and rolled forward about three and a half feet before having to stop again. He wanted to throw his hands up and ask the biddy behind him if she was happy now.

He didn't, of course. Not that he would have been rude before his half-cocked senatorial plans, but now, his every word and gesture and facial expression were studied and dissected to death.

Just like his daughter was studying him now.

"I wouldn't worry too much if someone doesn't like your old dad." He added a chuckle to soften the message and smiled back at Janis through the rearview mirror. "It's not his fault. He's never met me, so all he knows about me is what he reads in the news and what he sees on television. He might just really like Senator Young too. I'm running against him, so in a sense, that makes me the enemy. You know, like the Rebels and the Empire."

Janis laughed, a high-pitched giggle that made him smile. "Which one are you again?"

He narrowed his eyes at the reflection in the mirror and deepened his voice. "Search your feelings."

Janis threw her head back and nearly choked on her gum. To Ben's surprise, Dylan cracked the smallest of smiles at Ben's poor impression of Darth Vader.

It was all fun and games now, but in reality, Stan was so much worse than a Sith, maybe even worse than the Emperor. But the kids didn't need to know that. They needed to hold on to their innocence for as long as possible because the world would do its damnedest to strip them of it in due time.

Dylan's anxiety seemed to dissipate as he set his backpack by his feet. "Yeah, lots of my friends think Senator Young is a jerk anyway."

Replacing the pack of gum in the pocket of her backpack, Janis settled into her seat. "Haters gonna hate."

Twisting around, Ben held his hand up for a high-five. "That's right. They're just doing their job. Pay 'em no mind."

After a hearty laugh and a round of high fives, Ben found himself smiling, all the worries of the day having lifted...for now.

When they were finally able to go faster than a snail, he zigged and zagged through residential neighborhoods, avoiding traffic that gridlocked the major streets. Even as he listened to Dylan and Janis chat about their classes that day, Ben kept one eye on the clock and one on the road.

Though he wanted to be more active in the conversation, to enjoy the time with his kids and away from work, his mind kept wandering. Ben threw in the occasional comment or question to keep the small talk alive, hoping that it might hold his stress and worry at bay.

It wasn't working.

Ben had gone to the Bureau a couple months ago with a heap of information he'd amassed about Stan Young's finances, as well as records from the man's agricultural business, Happy Harvest Farms. There was no doubt in Ben's mind that Stan and Happy Harvest were colluding with a shady labor contractor, Premier Ag Solutions. Premier's ties to human trafficking had been swept under the rug more than once, but Ben didn't have the means to track down the money trails or corroborate the accounts of employee abuse.

But after his and Iris's friend, Vivian Kell, had been killed in the middle of an exposé about Premier's misdeeds, Ben knew the time had come for him to act. Vivian's article might never see the light of day, but Ben wouldn't let her death be in vain.

He'd scraped together every bit of remotely useful information he had, including what he'd provided Vivian during her research. Armed with his evidence, he'd gone to the people who had the resources to confront a business the size of Premier Ag Solutions or Happy Harvest Farms. He'd gone to the FBI.

It was the right thing to do, he knew, but his cooperation with the Bureau had made him a Federal informant.

He was playing a dangerous game, which he'd elected not to share with his wife or family. If Iris knew Ben had taken potentially damning information about Stan Young to the FBI, she would...

Don't think about it.

His hands tightened on the steering wheel, and he knew he could think about nothing else. He couldn't predict how she'd react. Maybe she'd understand, or maybe she'd kill him before Stan Young had a chance.

No. She wouldn't kill him. She'd knock some sense into him and insist on protection for their family, something he should have already done.

Federal informants required Federal protection. And a little extra protection would help to alleviate the stress he'd been under. He made a mental note to address that during his meeting with Agent Storm. She would surely understand. She was probably wondering why he hadn't already made the request. And that would also solve any need for meetings in out-of-the-way locations.

The clock ticked closer to the agreed meeting time of 4:45, but Ben felt a little more confident now that he had a plan going forward. Good news or bad, he would solve at least one problem this evening. He breathed deep, filling his lungs and exhaling all the pent-up stress that had been weighing on him as he pulled into the two-car garage of his modest suburban home.

Iris's sister, Sharon, arrived a few minutes after they had settled in. She'd agreed to watch the kids while Ben was "taking care of business" and ushered him out the door with assurances that they'd be sugared up and bouncing off the walls by the time he returned. Despite her teasing, he knew the kids would be well looked after.

With a quick "thank you" to Sharon and a kiss each for Dylan and Janis, Ben set off.

Agent Storm's message had suggested they meet at a house in Englewood. Ben had looked up the address and confirmed the residence was vacant.

Since Stan Young was a member of the U.S. Senate's Intelligence Committee, Agent Storm had expressed concern that the man might listen in on a phone call. Even though Ben hadn't directly expressed the desire to keep his relationship with the Feds hidden, Agent Storm had picked up on the unspoken request.

He glanced up to the darkening sky as he slowed to a stop in front of a two-story house and turned his gaze outward, searching for any sign of Agent Storm or her partner, Agent Zane Palmer. He'd spotted a couple vehicles farther down the street but doubted any of those rusted junkers belonged to an FBI agent.

The area had seen better days, and the windows of nearby houses were boarded over, with orange warning signs plastered over battered front doors.

Tree branches rattled overhead as a gust of wind swept its way down the street. At least the tall oaks and maples had persevered where men had failed.

So many of the houses in the neighborhood had been left to rot. They showed signs of attempted remodeling with the intent of attracting higher-income folk. The cold truth was that people who could afford nicer homes didn't want to live in Englewood.

That, coupled with the litany of sub-prime mortgage loans in 2008 and then the housing bubble burst, and these overpriced homes never stood a chance. They'd probably been left empty for years.

Ironically, the government's mismanagement of the recession of 2008 was part of what had propelled Stan Young forward to the U.S. Senate.

Ben snorted and pulled onto the driveway. How apropos that he'd come to one of the affected areas to discuss Stan Young's alleged criminal activity.

Tightening his grasp on the steering wheel, Ben focused on the house. He doubted Agent Storm would risk parking in the ramshackle garage, but maybe she'd left her car in the lot of a convenience store a few blocks away. Aside from the impeding storm, the weather that day had been pleasant. Ben hoped their meeting would end before the wind and rain kicked up.

He rubbed his temple, wondering if he should also park on a different block. A flicker of movement inside the house stopped him from putting the car in reverse.

"Just get this over with and go back home where you belong."

The sooner he did just that, the sooner he'd get the hell away from this veritable graveyard of houses.

With another glance to the splintered shutters and pock-marked shingles, Ben leaned forward to pull open the glove compartment. He pushed aside a pair of woolen mittens and grabbed a matte black handgun.

Before this damn campaign, he'd rarely made use of his concealed carry license, but since he'd dug up Stan Young's dirty laundry, the precaution seemed necessary.

Granted, he was supposed to meet a Federal agent today, but that fact didn't silence the nagging paranoia in the back of his mind.

Before his thoughts could wander off to another pit of anxiety, he opened the car door and stepped into the cool breeze.

A shiver ran down his back as he peered at the shadowy porch. The window to the side of the door flickered with warm light.

With a shack like this, there probably wasn't any power to the property, and while he watched, the light just beyond the window seemed to shift rather than flicker. Ben reasoned that, if he had been stuck waiting with the threat of rain in a powerless home, he might have made use of the abundant kindling all around the deserted neighborhood to light a fire in the hearth too. Maybe Agent Storm had come early and needed the welcoming warmth.

Just to be safe, he kept his gun in hand and crept closer

for a peek through the window before announcing his presence. Better that than to barge in on some squatter. Who knew what kind of reception that might earn him.

Leaves crunched underfoot as he followed the worn sidewalk up to a precarious porch that groaned in protest as his weight tested its splintering planks. He was surprised to see that the window's glass was still intact. Through it, Ben caught sight of the living room fireplace. Flames licked up from the burning wood within the hearth like fingers crooking to call him inside.

Though the fire provided light enough to see the room, it appeared to be empty, leaving Ben to wonder what his next move should be. Chances were good that Amelia was in there, maybe exploring other rooms in the old home while she waited.

With his phone in one hand and his gun in the other, Ben debated whether to go inside or give Amelia a call. His phone told him the time was quarter 'til five, but storm clouds had blotted out the daylight like the sun had already set.

A stiff breeze rushed through the neighborhood, and with it came the sharp smell of ozone and the first sprinkles of what would definitely become a deluge. That was enough to make his decision. Ben pocketed the phone and reached for the door. He needed to get this meeting done quickly, or he might be swimming home.

A few chips of paint flaked off the wooden door as Ben twisted the knob, pushed it open, and stepped into the skeleton of what had probably once been a welcoming family home.

"Hello?" Blinking to adjust to the change in light, he let the worn door swing closed at his back. "Agent Storm? Agent Palmer? Is anyone here?" He held his breath, listening for a response.

Nothing.

With the door shut to block out the scuttling of leaves and the drone of distant traffic, the only sounds were the steady rhythm of his pulse, the faint scratch of tree branches against the roof, and the crackling of the fire.

The floor creaked as he made his way toward the welcoming fire. "Agent Storm? Hello? Are you here?"

Pop.

Searing pain ripped through his knee.

A cry of surprise escaped him, but he barely heard the sound over the overwhelming red-hot pain. Fire traveled up his leg in a series of explosions, and as he toppled forward, his brain fought to put together the pieces of what had just happened.

He wondered if he'd stepped on a mine or run into a sharp corner, but he didn't have to ponder the assumptions to know they were ridiculous.

His phone landed atop the carpet with a *thud*, followed by his gun. Ben threw out a hand, catching himself just before his face hit the floor. The force of the collision reverberated up his arm, but the sensation barely registered over the fire in his knee.

Gasping for breath, he attempted to tuck his good leg underneath himself so he could stand and figure out what in the hell was happening. He clenched his jaw and reached for his weapon.

The scrape of shoes on floor was as loud as nails on a chalkboard, and he closed his eyes against the invasion of sound.

"Amelia?"

The world moved in slow motion, like a video that had been turned down to a quarter of its normal speed. Every movement was as sluggish as if he were underwater, no matter how much he willed himself to go faster.

Pop.

When he caught the faint disturbance, the pieces fell into place. The sound was quiet, more like a paintball gun than a weapon capable of real destruction.

A fresh inferno tore through his lower back, and in that moment, his brain registered little else aside from the pain. As his head bounced off the floor, the force of the blow jerked him away from where he'd perched at the precipice of shock.

Pressing a hand against the dingy carpet, he almost forgot why he wanted to shift to his back in the first place. His presence of mind was leaving him as surely as the blood pooling all around him.

Who?

He wanted to know who hated him this much. He had to see.

The effort to roll over was Herculean, and darkness nibbled at the edges of his vision by the time he made out his assailant's figure. Or maybe his vision was fine, and the darkness was just this damn house.

He never should have opened that door, never should have stepped into this pervasive gloom.

Right now, he should have been at home, helping Dylan and Janis with their homework. He should have been breaking down a math problem for his little girl, not bleeding out on the floor of some decrepit living room.

Was Iris home by now? Was she stuck in traffic on her way out of downtown?

He'd been so terrible to his beautiful wife, and as he stared down the barrel of his own mortality, he didn't know why. He wished he could apologize. A real apology. Not the platitudes he'd offered in the past. He wished he could let her know that none of what he'd done was her fault. That he was the only one to blame.

But he already knew he wouldn't leave this house.

His teeth chattered as he squeezed his eyes closed, hoping to clear the haze from his vision, but opening them proved an even more difficult task.

A shadowy figure stood at his feet, and even as he focused the remainder of his energy, he couldn't make out any details. They might have been a man, a woman, or the angel of death.

The person—the entity—spoke, but Ben was already on his way out. He was cold, tired, and just wanted to rest. Maybe he could see his family one last time, even if they were only figments of his imagination.

As his angel of death raised the handgun for the lethal shot, he hardly noticed the movement. The late-afternoon gloom gave way to rays of warm sunlight, and the dusty living room was transformed into the breakfast bar at the edge of his kitchen. Janis looked up from her waffle to flash him a lopsided grin. To her side, Dylan said a cheery "good morning" as he combed his unruly hair with the fingers of one hand.

Iris emerged from the walk-in pantry with a jar of raspberry jam. She smiled. A soft, genuine expression of contentment, the likes of which he hadn't seen in over seven years.

He opened his mouth to tell her he loved her and to tell her he was sorry…

Pop.

2

S moothing both hands down the fabric of her black slacks, Special Agent Amelia Storm swiveled her office chair to face the man at her side.

Agent Zane Palmer's slate-gray eyes were fixed on a sheet of paper on the table. The fabric of his ebony suit was tailored to his lean, muscular frame, and his sandy hair was styled with a slight part to one side with the rest brushed forward—a look that straddled the line between professional and fashionable.

At a glance, Amelia could almost fool herself into thinking he worked for a large bank instead of the FBI. Agents at the Bureau were compensated well, but Amelia doubted someone with their salary would opt for a timepiece quite as expensive as the silver watch on Zane's wrist.

Then again, he was thirty-four, single with no children, and had a mother who'd made a fortune as an investment wizard. With her help, Zane likely tripled his salary each year. And aside from the expensive watch and suit, he lived well within his means. His silver Acura was sleek but not overly expensive. Chances were good that his watch cost almost as much as the car.

As the thought crossed Amelia's mind, she bit her tongue to stop herself from laughing.

Zane's head jerked up, and he met her eyes with a quizzical expression. "What? Is there something on my face?" Even after more than a half-year in the Midwest, his words were still tinged with a hint of his native Jersey accent.

"No, your face is fine." Waving a dismissive hand, Amelia slumped down in her chair. "I was just spacing off, and I thought of something funny."

"Uh-huh." Zane's tone dripped with sarcasm as he leaned to the side and propped his arm on the table. "It's already three. When does your sister's flight get here again?"

Why did he have to remind her? Amelia had made a valiant effort to keep herself focused on work, but with his question, her thoughts wandered right back to her sister, Lainey Storm.

Amelia had been eighteen when she escaped from Chicago to join the military and hadn't been there to protect little Lainey from falling in with a sketchy group of friends. Binge drinking and late-night raves turned into cocaine, and eventually, Lainey was introduced to heroin.

Though Amelia couldn't be sure when her younger sister began shooting up, she assumed it had to have started after Lainey turned eighteen. After all, a crippling addiction like that would have prevented her from graduating high school.

Lainey came by her propensity for addiction honestly. For seventeen years, their father had been consumed by alcoholism. Jim Storm's downward spiral came on quickly after Amelia's mother lost her year-long battle with cancer. Bonnie's death cut Jim Storm off at the knees. He crawled into a bottle to numb the pain and had only recently emerged from it in the last three years. Rehab helped him to turn his life around, but only after he'd been willing to take the steps.

Whether it was witnessing Lainey's fall from grace or finally being able to move on from the pain of his lost love, Jim had found the strength to get clean. Amelia wasn't entirely sure which had been the trigger. Truth be told, she tried to avoid any emotionally charged discussions with her family.

Hell, she tried to avoid emotionally charged discussions with *anyone*.

Between her father's absence and ten years of military service, she'd had to fend for herself for so long that she'd started to view feelings as a luxury for people whose heads were screwed on straight.

As far as she was concerned, her brother was the only one of their family to append some sense of normalcy to his life.

At least until Amelia dug beneath the surface.

From the outside, Trevor had a loving wife, two kind children, honorable military service in the Marine Corps, and served his home city as a homicide detective. Taken at face value, he was the best of all the Storms. But underneath the spit and polish, he had skeletons of his own.

Normal people didn't wind up facedown on the streets of Chicago with two slugs buried in their back and one in their head. But dirty cops did.

Trevor had sold out to the D'Amato Family.

And when his demons had caught up to him, leaving him facedown, dead in a ditch, Amelia was forced to leave her military career, come home, and help the family pick up the pieces. Lainey was the last of those pieces she'd been struggling to put in place.

Lainey had reached out to Amelia almost a month earlier, and after three weeks of continuous contact, she'd assured Amelia that she wanted to return to Chicago to get clean.

"Earth to Storm."

Blinking a few times, she forced her focus back to the windowless room in the heart of the FBI field office and smiled brightly at her partner. "Her flight's supposed to be here at four-thirty. Do you think I should have just driven to Milwaukee to pick her up?"

Zane waved off the suggestion. "No. It's a short flight, but the drive there and back still would've taken most of your day. And…"

Amelia blew out a breath so long and hard that her lips fluttered with the inhale. "And there's no guarantee she'd even be where she said she was. I'd probably have wound up driving to a heroin den, getting into a heated argument with someone, and spending the trip back to Chicago stewing with rage."

"Or you could fork over a hundred-fifty for a plane ticket and leave work early." Zane flashed her one of his patented smiles. "Which means you get to bail on more of this." He gestured to the sheets of paper strewn across the table.

Amelia rubbed her temple and held back a groan. "Old Leóne cases. Don't remind me."

Feigning a stern look, Zane waved a document at her. "No, Agent Storm. These aren't Leóne cases, not according to the law."

"Right, right, I'm sorry." She fake gagged herself. "I meant to say possible RICO case fodder."

With a snort of disgust, Zane let the paper drift back down to the table. "There's nothing in any of these statements about the assholes working for the Leóne family, except for a few minor drug trafficking cases."

Propping an elbow on the armrest, Amelia dropped her cheek into her hand, weary to the bone.

The Racketeer Influenced and Corrupt Organizations Act had been established back in the seventies in order to combat the Italian Mafia. Rather than prosecute each individual member of a criminal syndicate, RICO allowed the Federal government to use past and present cases to establish a pattern of activity. The result was harsher penalties, as well as the ability to charge those who had given orders to commit crimes and not just the foot soldiers.

The problem with prosecuting a RICO case was that it was subject to the same criteria as any other criminal charge —proof beyond a reasonable doubt. And over the last couple weeks, reasonable doubt had been the name of the game. They'd dug around for old Leóne cases, but like Zane had said, only a few of the defendants had provided statements indicating they'd committed their offenses at the behest of the family.

Unsurprisingly, none of the three men were alive. Two had committed suicide, and the third had been killed in prison.

Amelia stretched both arms above her head until she felt a light pop in her back. "You know." An involuntary yawn stole her breath for a moment. "The Leónes have been around since the days of Al Capone. They were small fish back then, but I think it's safe to say that they've learned a few things from all the families that've come and gone in other cities."

As he reached for his stainless-steel thermos, Zane's gaze shifted to her. "Learned a few things, as in how to run a criminal syndicate without having any of their people tried for being part of the syndicate."

She had half a mind to call him Captain Obvious but didn't know whether he would have taken the joke or seen it as an insult. He wasn't wrong. But his regurgitation of the facts offered little in the way of hope. "The Leónes wouldn't be the first to figure out how to dodge RICO, and I doubt they'll be the last."

Zane's gaze darted to the clock on the wall. "Shouldn't you be leaving soon?"

Amelia forced her back to straighten. "Yeah. In the next fifteen minutes. I'll probably be way early, but I hate driving around the damn airport, you know?"

"Oh, I know." Zane snorted. "Midway is a zoo at this time of day."

"Still…" Amelia hated being torn between work and her family, "I feel like I should be here for that three-thirty meeting with the Assistant U.S. Attorney."

With a dismissive wave, Zane shook his head. "Don't worry about it. It's probably bad news anyway. I'll call and fill you in once it's over." Zane took a gulp of coffee. "Oh. Were you able to get Lainey a spot at that rehab center you told me about? New Horizons, wasn't that what it's called?"

Amelia spun a piece of her newly blonde-tipped hair around her finger. "That's it, yeah. And yes, I did. They're holding a room for her, so all I have to do is bring her in. I talked to a few people around the office about it, and everything I've heard sounds good. It's not one of those expensive resort rehab centers in Malibu or Miami, but it's nice."

"Good. It's a lot less stress on you to have that all sorted out ahead of time."

She wished that was true. Even with the arrangements made, her shoulders felt like a series of knots. "I guess. I just can't help but think that something'll get screwed up and that this whole thing's going to be a disaster."

As he tapped an index finger against the table, Zane tilted his head, appearing deep in thought. "Well, until now, that's been the going rate whenever you've interacted with your sister, hasn't it?"

"You could say that." Glancing down at her hands, Amelia resisted the urge to pick at her burgundy nail lacquer. She had little hope for this meeting, though deep down, she was rooting for her sister to finally pull out of the tailspin her life had become. "She usually asks for money, though. I can't figure out what she'd even be able to do with a plane ticket. It's in her name, so it's not like she can sell it to someone. And I paid for it with my credit card, so she can't ask for a refund and run off with the cash."

"So, what's the worst that can happen? She doesn't show up, right?" Zane shrugged, but the way he averted his eyes said he wasn't entirely convinced of the line of BS he was feeding her.

Amelia could think of a thousand different ways for things to go south. But she understood the sentiment Zane was trying to relay. *Stop being so damn negative.* And again, he was probably right.

"Yeah, I guess so."

His eyes settled on hers, and his expression softened. "I don't want this to make me sound like an asshole, but try not to get your hopes up too high, okay?"

From what Amelia had gathered during their half-year friendship, he was just as guarded as she was. To see him let down the carefully polished veneer made her stomach flutter in a way she hadn't felt since…since she'd met Alex Passarelli.

Which was a name she wished would stop popping into her mind, almost as much as she wished her traitorous libido would settle down when she was with her current partner.

Dammit.

Now wasn't the time to ponder her feelings about any man, let alone Zane Palmer. Once Lainey was safely behind the doors of New Horizons Rehabilitation, then maybe Amelia could stop to mull over the stupid butterflies she got every time Zane smiled.

As for Alex, well, she wasn't sure a time would ever come to consider her standing with him or the D'Amato family. And not just because of her history with them. The D'Amatos were long-time rivals of the Leónes, and though a ceasefire between the two families had held steady for five years, there was no way to tell when the feeble truce would crack.

What would happen then?

What choices would she have to make?

"You okay?"

Amelia snapped to attention, cursing herself for letting her mind wander again. "Sorry...what did you say?"

Worry wrinkled his forehead. "I said something stupid to the effect of not getting your hopes up too high, but I should have just kept my mouth shut."

Emotion burned into her sinuses, but she forced that shit back down and smiled instead. "No shutting of the mouth necessary because you're right. It'll suck if something goes wrong, but I don't think it'll surprise me." She paused to rub the bridge of her nose. This conversation was dragging up too damn many emotions, and she simply wasn't equipped to deal with them. Especially not now. "I'm just not great at stuff like this."

"You're doing fine." He gave her shoulder a friendly nudge. "Honestly, I don't think anyone's good at stuff like that. Dealing with addict relatives isn't easy. Not for anyone. Just take it one thing at a time, and seriously, don't worry about missing this meeting."

The calm tone of his voice, coupled with the sincerity behind the words, was usually enough to keep Amelia's anxiety at bay. Inhaling and exhaling through her nose in a slow, steady stream, she nodded. "Okay. Yeah. Like you said, it's probably just bad news anyway."

Zane clapped his hands together and shot her another of his trademark grins. "See? That's the spirit."

She couldn't resist that face. Or the genuine care reflected in his eyes. But before she could reply to Zane's half-sarcastic comment, a metallic click drew their attention to the heavy wooden door.

The room was locked with a keypad and a six-digit code known only to four people in the office. But unless they figured out a tactic that would salvage their failing RICO case, Amelia suspected the pint-sized, remodeled closet would return to its former glory as a chair graveyard.

Shoving the door open with an elbow, Glenn Kantowski's honey-brown eyes flitted between Amelia and Zane as she fumbled into the office. "Hey, Storm. Are you about to head home for the day?"

"Yeah, I was just about to head out." Standing, Amelia scooped her handbag off a chair that was missing both armrests.

Agent Kantowski was a transplant from the FBI's Public Corruption Division, and she'd been assigned to the Leóne task force to lend her expertise. Though the Special Agent in Charge, Jasmine Keaton, had personally vetted Glenn, and the team got along like old friends, Amelia wasn't eager to reveal the true reason for her early departure.

As far as Glenn was concerned, Amelia was about to leave so she could go lay on the couch and watch the *World Series of Poker* while she ate a family-sized bag of potato chips. Just because she'd become more comfortable opening up to Zane didn't mean the sentiment extended to any of her other friends.

Amelia headed toward the door. "Was there anything else you guys needed before I leave?"

Zane had already turned back to his computer. "No, I don't think so. I'll get ahold of you later and let you know how this meeting goes."

"That works for me. I'll see you guys tomorrow." Amelia offered a parting mock salute before taking her leave.

If Glenn hadn't been in the room, she would have been tempted to hug Zane goodbye.

So far, he was the only person she'd told about Lainey's abrupt reappearance in her life. She didn't want to give the news to her father only to have Lainey flake out or to learn that the whole request was a misguided effort to steal money.

Only after Lainey walked through the doors of New Horizons would Amelia update her father. Not a second earlier.

Amelia passed a couple familiar faces on her way out to the parking garage, but as soon as she spotted Joseph Larson, she was ripped from the cloud of thought like a bird shot in mid-flight.

Joseph Larson's pale blue eyes were fixed on the phone in his hand, and he hadn't noticed Amelia on the other side of the glass and metal double doors. Hand hovering above the lever, Amelia gritted her teeth.

Some days, when she arrived at the FBI office, she wondered if that not-so-distant night had even happened or if the whole ordeal was a vivid nightmare. Joseph had dared to use Alton Dalessio's death to blackmail her into sleeping with him. The whole situation was asinine. Worse still was the fact that she'd almost given in.

Guilt over her own uncertainty in the Alton Dalessio incident had nearly tipped the scales. She'd come within inches of giving Joseph what he wanted, to satiate whatever carnal need had compelled him to take an interest in her. But she hadn't been able to go through with the deed, and she'd had the strength to walk away.

How many women hadn't felt they had that option? How many had the bastard manipulated and gaslighted into doing whatever he wanted?

The thought made her sick to her stomach, and she'd

added taking Joseph Larson down to her laundry list of those she'd vowed vengeance against.

According to Zane and the members of the building's cleaning crew with whom he liked to chat and gossip, Larson had become quite friendly with the Assistant U.S. Attorney, Cassandra Halcott. Amelia hated to admit that she'd been relieved when Zane gave her the news, and she could only hope that Cassandra and Joseph's physical relationship was consensual.

But she refused to worry about that now.

Right now, she needed to get to the airport, and the smarmy agent wasn't going to get in her way.

Lifting her chin, she readjusted her handbag and shoved open the door. Eyes fixed straight ahead, she painted an impassive expression on her face and strode past Joseph as if he didn't exist.

He knew what would happen if he touched her again. She'd made sure there was no potential for him to misinterpret or twist her words.

If Joseph Larson ever laid another finger on her, Amelia would kill him.

3

A s Zane and Glenn's discussion about her eleven-year-old son's most recent video game of choice ended, a light knock drew his attention to the door. Three-thirty had come and gone, and Zane was glad Amelia hadn't tried to stick around for what would undoubtedly be another dose of disappointment.

Tapping a ballpoint pen against the notepad he'd been using to make a grocery list, Zane pushed to his feet. "That must be our guest of honor."

Glenn straightened a stack of papers and set them beside her laptop. "Good timing. Another ten minutes, and I'd have had to leave to pick up my son from his band practice."

"Band, huh?" Zane scooted around the table. "What does he play?"

Glenn beamed with pride as if she'd been waiting for a moment to reveal this information. "Saxophone. It's what his dad, my ex-husband, used to play when he was in high school and college."

"Sax, that's pretty cool. I played trumpet for a couple years, but I was terrible at it." Pausing in front of the door, he fixed Glenn with a stern look and held up a finger. "Don't tell Storm about that. She doesn't know, and of all the stupid middle school stories I've told people around here, that's one that I keep to myself. I don't even want to know how many ridiculous jokes she'd come up with if she found out."

Though her shoulders shook with laughter, Glenn pursed her lips and mimicked a zipping motion along her mouth. "Your secret is safe with me."

"I appreciate it." He pressed down on the lever handle and pulled open the heavy door.

Cassandra Halcott offered them an apologetic smile. Her glasses, charcoal slacks, shiny black heels, and understated accessories lent her an air of competency and class that was well suited to her position as an Assistant U.S. Attorney.

The professional attire was a far cry from the t-shirt and jeans she'd worn when he first met her via an online dating app. At the time, he'd only lived in Chicago for a total of two weeks, and aside from a few acquaintances at the FBI office, he didn't know anyone in the city. A friend of his—an old CIA contact, Nate Tennick—had recommended that Zane try out a popular dating app. Even if he didn't meet Mrs. Right, a few dinner dates would be a good way to get a feel for Chicago's social scene.

As luck would have it, the first and only "date" he'd had was with Cassandra. Her profile hadn't revealed her profession as an Assistant U.S. Attorney, and he hadn't known her job title until after they'd slept together for the first time.

After a couple more dates, their little fling had ended on amicable terms. Neither of them had been in the market for anything long-term, and they'd both agreed that their relationship didn't need to extend beyond a few nights of harmless fun.

To be sure, he liked Cassandra as a person, and after the past few weeks, he'd come to appreciate her work ethic.

How she'd wound up with a piece of work like Joseph Larson was beyond Zane's understanding. Maybe there was a redeeming aspect to Joseph's cactus-like personality that Zane was too jaded to see. For Cassandra's sake, he hoped so.

"Afternoon, Agents." Cassandra blew out a sigh and stepped over the threshold. "I'm so sorry I'm late. I was at the office and got caught up in some paperwork. I kept telling myself I'd be able to make it here in time, but…"

"Chicago traffic," Zane finished for her.

Smoothing her windblown auburn hair, Cassandra nodded. "Yeah, exactly. You know, I looked it up not long ago, and according to a bunch of different websites, Chicago has the second-worst traffic in the country."

"I believe it." Zane stepped around the table and stood by his chair. His mother would have spanked his backside if he'd taken a seat first. "I was in D.C. for ten years before Chicago, and before that, I was in Jersey City. Now, D.C.'s traffic is awful, don't get me wrong, but it doesn't hold a candle to Chicago."

Only half of his recollection was untrue, or maybe only a third. He had grown up in Jersey City, and he *had* spent a little time at the Washington, D.C. field office, but nowhere near ten years.

The life of an FBI field agent was often a dangerous one, but for Zane, a career at the FBI was a reprieve from the constant peril he'd faced as an operative for the Central Intelligence Agency.

His decision to leave the CIA had been a long time coming, and a near-death experience in the frigid wasteland of Siberia had pushed him to turn in his resignation. He'd had his eye on the FBI, and the U.S. government had concocted a backstory for him in case any curious coworkers thought to investigate his history.

The days of stalking Russian government officials and

infiltrating the country's aristocracy were over. Fortunately, aside from a couple scars, all he had to remind him of the experience were a handful of easily hidden tattoos. He'd considered laser removal, but a sentimental part of him had never been able to follow through with the idea.

A metallic squeak pulled him from the thought as Cassandra took her spot in the rickety office chair across from him and Glenn. She scooted closer and folded her hands on the table. "I'm afraid I don't have much news for you, Agents, and what little I *do* have isn't good."

Zane eased himself down to his seat in an effort to minimize the squawk of protest. At six-foot-three, deftly situating himself in a half-broken office chair was no small feat. He and Amelia had been stationed in this repurposed storage room for a few months, and he'd learned to work around the quirks of their collection of busted chairs.

To his side, Glenn closed her laptop and leaned forward. "All right, let's hear it."

As Zane took a drink of bitter, black coffee, Cassandra's gaze dropped to her hands. "Based on my most recent review of the Leónes' RICO case, we've lost a lot of ground." Her eyes shifted from Zane to Glenn. "I know that you've been searching high and low for new cases to add to the investigation, but so far, none of them are sticking. We don't have any Leóne-specific charges outside of Emilio Leóne's prostitution ring, and even that one is shaky."

Glenn waved a hand at the manila folders and scattered papers. "What about our recent cases? The Enrico case, or the Strausbaugh case?"

Cassandra shook her head. "Without the testimony from the corrections officer who facilitated the hit on Enrico, we've got nothing that'll stick. The U.S. Marshals *still* haven't found a trace of Russel Ulmer, and the inmate who actually committed the murder doesn't know anything about why Ulmer wanted Enrico dead."

While the news wasn't unexpected, Zane still wanted to punch his fist through the drywall. Where had Ulmer disappeared to? He'd been in the wind since Amelia and Larson questioned his ex-wife.

"What about the ex?" Glenn opened a folder and tapped on the photo of Wendy Truesdell. "Would she have tipped him off?"

Zane snorted. "Not a chance. She'd have arrested him herself if we'd let her."

"Agent Palmer's right." Cassandra laced her fingers together, and Zane could tell she was trying not to fidget. "Wendy Truesdell didn't have anything to do with Russel's disappearance. Chances are, Ulmer caught on that we were after him, and he disappeared. If he'd truly been working with the Leónes, then he'd have been prepared for the eventuality. He's probably not even in the country anymore."

Glenn pushed the folder aside and opened a second. "Which brings us to the Ian Strausbaugh case. And, by proxy, Alton Dalessio. How is it that we can't include any of that, Counselor?"

From fidgety to cool and collected, Cassandra's demeanor flipped one-hundred-and-eighty degrees at the question. The woman was apparently more comfortable addressing a skeptic than an agreeable peer.

Just like Amelia.

Zane looked to the clock. Ten 'til four. Lainey's flight would touch down at Midway in less than an hour. For Amelia's sake, Zane hoped Lainey had been truthful and would actually show up.

Cassandra patted the air with a hand, and her steely gaze warmed just a touch. "I've been over Cliff Allworth's statements about Ian Strausbaugh, and the bottom line is that he killed Ian to cover up a personal secret. Not as a direct order from the Leóne family."

Leaning back in her seat, Glenn rubbed her temple. As quickly as the moment of scrutiny had arrived, it was gone. "I was afraid of that. And with Dalessio, I assume it's because our forensic accountants couldn't trace any of the funds from his child exploitation videos back to the Leóne family coffers?"

"Unfortunately, that's exactly right. And with Dalessio dead, there's no telling if we'll ever even find that money."

Zane tapped an index finger against his thermos. "Not to mention that Allworth wasn't able to point us in a tangible direction for any of that. Even with everything he told us about what he and his partner did to cover up for the Leónes, there's nothing to corroborate it. You know, since he killed his damn partner."

Glenn scoffed. "So, we're back at square one with approximately zilch, is that right?"

Cassandra offered him and Glenn an apologetic look. "I'm sorry, Agents. Unless we find something that we can work with soon, this will be another case that gets pushed to the back shelf. Legally, there's just not anything I can do."

Zane recalled Amelia's words from earlier. "The Leónes do some brash stuff, and they're definitely prone to over-reaching, but they *have* been around since the days of Capone. You don't last that long as one of Chicago's top criminal syndicates without learning a thing or two, you know?"

Glenn lifted a shoulder a half inch before letting it fall. "They run their business like it's a business, which means they'd actively avoid anything that would bring them harm."

Zane couldn't disagree. "RICO's been used to take down Italian crime families in other cities, and I'm sure the head of the Leóne family took notice. Same for the D'Amatos."

"Exactly." Cassandra turned to the whiteboard. "Even if the Leónes didn't know that we were building a RICO case against them, they'd operate like we were. They know that if the money doesn't all go to one place, or if it can't be traced to one person, the odds of us tying it all together in a courtroom are slim."

In the silence that followed, Zane wondered what his and Amelia's work lives would look like without their focus on the Leónes. Would they even work cases together, or would one of them wind up stuck with Joseph Larson like Amelia had been during the Enrico investigation?

They had become such a central part of their time at the FBI office, Zane had trouble when he tried to picture a day without a case that involved the Leóne family.

Then again, their task force *had* inched a little too close to a certain U.S. Senator, one who happened to be a member of the Senate's Intelligence Committee. Stan Young's security clearance was one of the highest in the country—only a step behind the CIA operatives and analysts who gathered and compiled the information.

An all-out inquiry into a criminal conspiracy that involved Stan Young was too reminiscent of Zane's days in Russia. Some things never changed. Here he was again, tracking down dirt on yet another wealthy politician.

Readjusting her black-rimmed glasses, Cassandra cleared her throat to end the spell of quiet. "The U.S. Attorney told me to let you know that the timeframe here is up to the Bureau's discretion, but right now, our office has done all it can."

Zane managed a reassuring smile. "You have, and we appreciate the legal guidance. We'll pass all this on to SAC Keaton and let you know where we end up."

Rising to stand, Cassandra's expression showed no hint of

any hopeful optimism. With a curt nod, she gathered her things. "Best of luck, Agents."

As much as Zane wanted the retirement of their RICO case to be the end of his dealings with Stan Young, his experience told him otherwise.

With men like Stan Young, the end only came when they were dead.

4

If Amelia never drove to another airport again, it would be too soon. She'd lost count of how many times she'd been cut off, nearly sideswiped, and been flipped off by another driver.

The next time a friend or family member arrived at the airport in the middle of the day, Amelia was getting them a damn bus pass. Hell, she'd pay for a personal helicopter ride if it meant she didn't have to deal with near-rush-hour traffic and the confusing tangle of roads leading into Midway.

After finally locating a parking spot in the overcrowded concrete garage, Amelia pulled out her phone to check the flight tracker. A dull rumble overhead drew her attention to the sliver of skyline visible from the third floor of the parking garage. The sun's rays diffused through a layer of gauzy clouds, and a darker mass was moving in from the west. Weather forecasts had predicted severe thunderstorms would start in the next hour. Amelia prayed the inclement weather would hold off until her sister was safely on the ground.

A red indicator flashed on the screen as she pulled up Lainey's flight information.

Delayed. Dammit.

Slumping down in the driver's seat, Amelia blew a raspberry. The clock had just ticked over to four, leaving a solid half hour before Lainey's plane had been scheduled to arrive, but it hadn't left the ground yet. The delay indicator showed it was scheduled to take off in a half hour.

Amelia, however, was more than familiar with the airline's half hour delay tactic. They were prone to pushing back in these small increments to avoid pissing off travelers with the truth. And with the storm coming in, the real delay could be hours. Hell, Lainey might not even make it out of Milwaukee at all if the storms lasted too long.

Amelia closed the flight tracker and pulled up her text messages. Right at the top of the list was a message from her wayward sister.

Hey, Amelia. My flight was delayed because of all these storms. They say to stay close. We will take off as soon as the storm passes. Maybe an hour or so. I'm going to grab some junk food and wander the gates until takeoff.

A second text followed, this one complete with a picture of a television that displayed the weather radar. *Holy shit, this storm system is huge. At least there aren't any tornadoes.*

Amelia tapped out a response. *Text me when you're boarding. I've got the flight on my tracker app.*

Between Lainey's text and the picture of the airport coffee shop, Amelia had no reason to doubt her sister's sincerity.

The storms bearing down on Chicago were part of a much larger system that ran from Springfield, Illinois, all the way up to Canada. The boomerang shape of the incoming cold front had closed in on Milwaukee already. With any luck, it might catch a warm front over Lake Michigan and blow straight past Chicago.

The thought had Amelia chuckling at her own pathetic hopefulness. She was never that lucky. Since she was already parked and there was a possibility that the flight from Milwaukee could leave in the next half hour, she had no choice but to stay put. The flight was only an hour hop down the coast. It would take her longer to make the roundtrip home and back now that rush hour was in full swing.

"Great." Amelia let her head loll backward.

She'd been in such a rush to get to Midway early that she hadn't even stopped to fuel her car or grab a snack or drink. Midway was full of coffee shops and food vendors, but her father had raised her and her siblings to shun overpriced meals at airports and movie theaters. Even though Amelia had disposable income now, old habits were hard to break.

Another fifteen minutes ticked by as Amelia went through the rest of her email inbox, exchanged a couple more texts with her sister, and sent Zane an update.

When her stomach growled like a lion needing to be fed, she sent a silent apology to her father and grabbed her handbag. Within seconds, she was striding for the airport entrance. Once inside, she stopped at a familiar chain café near baggage claim. After ordering a cinnamon roll and a small coffee, she made her way to a booth in the backmost corner of the dining area.

With a quiet sigh, she set down the paper cup and plate before plopping onto the thinly cushioned seat.

Well, guess this is home for the next who knows how long. She wanted to mutter a string of four-letter words but stuffed them down with a bite of the gooey roll.

Amelia disliked watching television shows or movies on the small screen of her phone, but she was hard-pressed to come up with a better alternative to pass the time. Outlets were easy to find throughout most of the airport, so at least she didn't have to worry about battery life.

When the smartphone buzzed in her hand, Amelia wondered if she and Zane had some bizarre psychic connection. Before the device could vibrate again, she swiped the screen to answer.

"Hey, how'd the meeting go?" The eagerness in her voice was painfully obvious, but she didn't care. Amelia was desperate for any friendly interaction to stave off boredom.

"Not great. About like we expected." Zane's tone matched her sour disposition. "How's the airport?"

Amelia poked the last chunk of cinnamon roll with her fork. "It's great. Exactly where I wanted to spend my night."

"It's my preferred hangout spot on Mondays and Tuesdays."

"Great, today's Monday. When are you going to get here? We can huddle together and watch *Battlestar Galactica* on my phone while we eat falafel that costs three times more than the place down the street from work."

"That sounds perfect. I'll be there in five or six hours, depending on traffic." Sarcasm rolled off his tongue with such ease, he almost sounded serious.

Of all the partners she'd been assigned during her time with the FBI, Zane definitely ranked as her favorite. Amelia wouldn't admit it out loud, but she kinda wished he would come and keep her company. Short of that, office gossip would have to suffice. "Okay, real talk, though. What did you guys go over in that meeting? What did Cassandra say?"

As Zane sighed, the faint creak of an office chair followed. "Not a lot. It's more or less what we've been thinking. Unless we find something groundbreaking soon, then this case is dead in the water. I ran everything by SAC Keaton, and she's giving it another week. If there's nothing new by then, then we shelve it and go back to our regularly scheduled programming."

Amelia sipped her coffee. She had to remind herself to watch what she said in a public location, even if she'd chosen the most isolated seat. "A week, huh? We've been digging through those records for a lot longer than that and haven't found anything that a good defense attorney wouldn't rip apart in a few minutes. I'm not real optimistic about what kind of magic we're supposed to conjure in another week."

"Honestly, neither am I. I don't doubt we'll have to deal with the Leónes again, but I think this is the end of the road for RICO. At least for now."

Amelia wanted to pound her forehead into the table or maybe order another gooey treat and drown herself in sugar. "Is there anything else we could've done? This just feels... anticlimactic. It's like we were on a road trip headed for a concert, and we turned off on the wrong exit and wound up at a Cracker Barrel instead."

"That is..." Zane chuckled, "painfully accurate. But to answer your question, I don't know. I don't think there is, though. It'd be different if we'd found Russel Ulmer or if Matteo Ricci hadn't shot himself in the head before the Marshals found him in Kansas."

Before Amelia could respond, a short beep cut in over the line. She pulled the device away from her ear and spotted an email notification. Swiping down on the screen to preview the new message, her eyes widened. "What the hell?"

"What?" Zane's voice was tinny, and Amelia returned the phone's speaker to her ear.

"I just got an email." Glancing around the area, she lowered her voice to just above a whisper. "From Ben."

"Really?" Zane's attentive tone echoed the surge of intrigue that flooded Amelia's thoughts. "What about?"

"Hold on." Amelia held up the phone to scan the message.

Agent Storm, sorry for the short notice, and sorry to drop this on you out of the blue. I know that you were Vivian's confidante at the FBI, so that's why I'm coming to you. I've just learned something today, and it's urgent that I pass it on to you ASAP. I have an address where we can meet to talk discretely, and I'll post it at the bottom of this email.

Please, come alone, and please, let's not talk over the phone. Stan Young can't access my email, but I'm not so sure he hasn't bugged my office. He has people everywhere, and I've learned the hard way that I can't trust anyone.

"It's short. He wants to meet with me to talk about something. I don't know what, but he says it's important, and he's pretty specific about only meeting with me. Something about how Vivian Kell came to me, so he knows I'm trustworthy."

Zane blew out a low breath. "Yeah, that sounds important. Where does he want to meet?"

As she checked the email again, Amelia tugged at the end of her long ponytail. "Englewood. I know the area, or at least I used to."

"Why Englewood?" Skepticism had mingled with Zane's curiosity.

"He didn't say. It's a pretty short message. I can forward you the email if you want."

"If you don't mind."

"Yeah, no problem." A couple taps and button presses later, and the message was on its way.

In the moment of quiet that followed, Amelia could almost picture him scratching the side of his face as he mulled over Ben's request.

Amelia took the opportunity to eat the last bite of her food, and she chased the sweet roll down with a swig of coffee that had cooled off far too quickly for her liking. Wiping her fingers on a napkin, she pushed the paper plate away. "What do you think?"

"It's out of nowhere." His chair creaked again. "But I guess most of our communication with that guy has been out of nowhere. Informants giving the Bureau dirt on the mob and a sitting U.S. Senator can't really keep a consistent schedule."

"He wants to meet as soon as possible, and right now, it's only..." she looked at her watch, "ten 'til five. My guess is that Lainey won't be here until quarter to seven, at the earliest. Englewood's a bit of a drive, but I think I can make it there and back in time as long as Ben doesn't want to talk my ear off."

"Are you sure?" A hint of concern tinged Zane's voice. "It's supposed to start storming pretty soon. It doesn't look like something you want to be caught driving in."

She drummed her fingers against the wooden table. "I know, but this seems worth it. Especially if it's something that can get us back on track."

"You mean away from Cracker Barrel and back to the concert?"

Amelia brushed a couple crumbs off her pastel blue dress shirt. "Exactly. And, besides, it beats the hell out of sitting around Midway watching stuff on my phone for the next who knows how long."

"You have a point. Just watch your back, okay?"

She was already heading toward the door. "Of course. I always do."

RAIN POUNDED against the roof of Amelia's car as she pulled to a stop behind a dark blue sedan. In the downpour, she could hardly make out the color, let alone the make or model.

As she looked to the shape of the two-story house, uncertainty prickled at the back of her neck. Despite only being about seven miles from the airport, weather and traffic extended Amelia's commute to nearly an hour. If she hadn't been familiar with side streets, she'd still be on the road.

After sending a quick text to advise Zane that she'd arrived at the meeting address, she double-checked her service weapon, pocketed her phone, and tugged the canvas jacket tighter around herself. If nothing else, she was grateful for her foresight to stash the coat in the back seat.

Amelia gritted her teeth, counted to three, and sprang out into the torrent. As she hurried over the curb to the sidewalk, she could barely hear the splash of her footsteps over the rush of the storm. Her flats were soaked through by the time she reached the front porch.

Streams of water worked their way through cracks in the awning, and the wooden beams groaned in protest as Amelia strode to the ancient-looking front door.

Why the hell did Ben Storey ask me to meet him at an abandoned house? No, not even just an abandoned house. A foreclosure that the city had condemned.

Glancing over her shoulder to the shape of the navy-blue car, she peeked through the window next to the door.

Inside, the place looked abandoned except for a fire in the hearth that was in desperate want for new wood to keep it going. There was something in front of the fireplace, but since the fire was almost burned out, Amelia couldn't quite see if the shape was a heap of rags or maybe a squatter trying to shelter from the storm. She hoped it was the former.

Either way, she couldn't see Ben Storey. His car was in the driveway. At least, she hoped that was his car.

Amelia reached for the battered doorknob.

To her relief, the door swung inward with a creak.

Though the leaden clouds of the storm had blotted out most of the daylight, the darkness of the house's interior was disorienting.

"Ben? Are you here?"

Amelia blinked to adjust her vision and held her breath, awaiting a response. All that greeted her was the monotonous patter of raindrops against the roof, the distant rumble of thunder, and the *drip-drop* of a leak in the siding.

Amelia froze. Goose bumps rose along her forearms as her pulse rushed in her ears.

The nagging sensation of eyes on the back of her head was so pervasive, she turned around to check that no one had crept up behind her.

I'm not alone. I'm supposed to meet someone here. This is a creepy abandoned house, and it's storming. That's why I feel like this.

She hated empty houses. The desolate structures were too reminiscent of bunkers in the Middle East. Of clever, improvised explosive devices waiting for a hapless passerby to walk too close. Of ankle-height wires rigged to the pins of fragmentation grenades. Of stinging sand and burning sun, the dull pop of gunfire in the distance, and the faint cries of the wounded and the dying.

She didn't recall the action, but her service weapon was in one hand when she pried herself away from the memory. With a slow breath in, she swept her gaze over the shapes and shadows cast by the dying fire at the end of the living room.

Flexing her fingers to chase away the faint tremor, she patted her coat for a flashlight but only felt her phone.

"Shit," she murmured.

She kept a mini flashlight in the glove box, but she had no desire to brave the torrential downpour. Her phone would work just fine. Now that her eyes had adjusted, the shadows weren't as oppressive.

Squinting at the brightness of the screen, she tapped a button to bring the front flash to life and flicked the beam of her phone's light to the floor to light her path. The formerly beige carpet was colored a shade darker by matted dirt and grime, and she couldn't tell if anyone had walked through the area within the last decade.

The thundering rain drowned out the sound of her footsteps. If Ben had been exploring the depths of this decrepit house, he might not have heard her come in with the storm raging outside. The explanation was flimsy at best, but Amelia didn't want to lean into her paranoia and desperately clung for a reason to remain positive.

Amelia cleared her throat. Calling out for the man went against every instinct she'd honed over the years, but she wasn't in a combat zone. Ben had contacted her with this address. There had to be a reason he'd chosen it. She couldn't creep around and sneak up on a Federal informant—a man who was also a military veteran—just because she'd been overcome with a bout of paranoia.

"Ben Storey? This is Agent Storm. Where are you?"

Stepping over the exposed tack strip, she swept the phone's light along the right side of the room. A set of musty curtains shivered as the wind slipped through cracks in the wooden planks that covered the narrow, broken window. The cloudy glass of the second window, the one beside the porch, was still intact, but more of the same tattered curtains blocked out the meager light from outside.

Though the drywall was marred with dents and holes, and though the carpet had worn through in spots, Amelia was surprised to see the place in one piece. On the drive here, she'd noticed that other abandoned houses in the neighborhood were in far more dire straits.

"Ben, hello? It's me, Agent—"

As she shifted the glow from her phone to the left side of the room, the words died in her throat.

The white light caught the syrupy blood that pooled

around Ben Storey's head like a macabre halo. Beneath his dark suit jacket, his white dress shirt had been stained almost entirely red.

"Shit." Amelia sucked in a breath through her teeth and brought her service weapon to bear. Adrenaline's chill rushed through her veins as her body tensed, preparing for a fight.

The illumination from her smartphone barely reached the stairs beyond Ben's body, and for the second time, she cursed herself for neglecting to bring a proper flashlight.

Swinging her aim to double-check the entrance to the dining area, Amelia half-expected to find that a masked assailant had snuck up behind her while she was busy calling out for Ben.

To her relief, what she could see of the room was still vacant. Oscillating the sights of her weapon from the direction of the kitchen to the looming stairwell, she edged around Ben's body to peek at the second-story landing.

Gritting her teeth, she tapped the screen of her phone to turn off the flashlight. After letting her vision adjust to the low light, she pulled up Zane's number. For what felt like an eternity, she looked back and forth between the stairs and the open living area, listening intently for any disturbance that might have been inconsistent with the storm raging outside.

Nothing stirred.

Swallowing the dryness in her mouth, she squinted down at her phone, pressed the button to dial Zane's number, and raised the device to her ear before the harsh glow could dull her night vision.

The line clicked to life before the second ring had finished. "Hey, what's up? Any update on the meeting with Storey?"

"Special Agent Zane Palmer, this is Special Agent Amelia

Storm." Unsure if she was alone or if Ben's killer might be hiding somewhere in the house, she kept her voice level. If anyone was listening in, she wanted them to know that the Federal Bureau of Investigation would be up their ass in minutes.

"Hold on." Like a switch had been flipped, Zane's tone went from friendly and amiable to focused. When he spoke again, his breathing was heavier. "Sorry. I was in the parking garage, and you know how you lose service in there sometimes. What's going on? What's wrong?"

"Ben's dead." Amelia didn't see any reason for a preamble. "Shot, once in the head, once in the torso, and possibly a third time in the leg. It's hard to tell. Most of the windows here are boarded over, so it's pretty dark."

Zane spat out a slew of four-letter words that could have brought a flush to a sailor's cheeks. "Hold on. I'm video calling you." The line went dead, but only for a second. She swiped the screen and Zane's face appeared. "You're at the address from the email you sent me, right? Is anyone else there?"

Amelia's head had been on a swivel from the moment she'd stepped into the house, but once again, she looked to the top of the staircase and then to the shadowy doorway that led to the dining room. "I don't know. I haven't seen anyone since I got here. Well, other than Ben." She turned the camera so that Zane could see everything she did.

"Get the hell out of there and wait in your car. I'll call it in to the CPD, and then I'll get someone and head over there."

"Yeah." Amelia flexed the fingers along the grip of her nine-mil.

"I mean it, Storm. Get somewhere safe until backup arrives."

Still on high alert, she stepped toward the door. "Believe

me, I don't want to be in this house any longer than I have to."

Before Amelia reached the handle, a series of pronounced thumps cut through the drone of the storm like the explosion of a mortar. Heart in her throat, she jumped back in time to avoid being knocked down as the door swung toward her.

Despite the whirlwind in her head and the adrenaline searing her nerves, her movements were fluid and measured as she swung the Glock toward the shape of a person barreling into the foyer.

A flashlight cut through the shadows, almost blinding her. She winced as the hellish illumination stung her sensitive eyes.

"This is FBI Agent Amelia Storm." The words exploded from Amelia's mouth on pure instinct. "You have entered an active crime scene. Identify yourself and keep your hands where I can see them. This is your only warning. If you do not comply, I have the authority to use deadly force."

Zane was shouting too, but Amelia was too focused on the barrel of the other person's gun to pay attention to what he was saying. He spoke so frantically, it was as if he were giving sound to the heart racing inside her chest.

"Officer Cynthia McAdam, Chicago Police Department." The officer lowered her light, but her other hand holding the gun was steady. They both stood frozen as they aimed their weapons at each other. "I'd like some proof of that."

Gun still raised, Amelia backed up a few steps, increasing the distance between herself and the officer. "I'm going to grab my badge. It's in my jacket pocket." In situations like this, it was always better to err on the side of caution. Anyone could claim to be an agent or officer, so she couldn't blame Officer McAdam for her show of caution.

"That your partner on the phone?" Cynthia asked, her

eyes flicking to the screen that had somehow managed to stay in Amelia's hand.

Before Amelia could answer, Zane did. "Yes. I'm Special Agent Zane Palmer with the FBI. You're pointing your gun at Special Agent Amelia Storm. Lower your weapon."

As a show of good faith, Amelia began to lower her weapon too. Neither she nor the officer seemed to breathe until both barrels were facing the floor. Amelia repeated that she was reaching for her badge, and the tension abated even more after McAdam examined her credentials.

The officer nodded. "Sorry. Needed to be certain."

When McAdam began to tuck away her weapon, Amelia held up a hand. "I've not cleared the house yet."

McAdam stiffened, her eyes darting between the stairs and each door of the room. She reached for a radio at her shoulder and called in her arrival as first on scene, noting that the FBI had beaten her to the punch.

Weapon lowered but ready, McAdam moved farther into the room. "What's going on? Why were you here?" Suspicion darkened the woman's blue eyes.

"I was here to meet an informant when I found..." She waved a hand toward Ben's body.

"Lucky for you."

Was that meant to be sarcasm? Amelia couldn't quite tell with McAdam's monotone delivery.

"Yeah." Amelia watched the officer closely. Maybe this was her first dead body? If so, the officer might very well soon lose the contents of her stomach. "Lucky me. Just what I needed today."

As she spoke, another car pulled up in front of the house, red and blue lights flashing. CPD was thankfully quick on the scene. The officer moved back to the front door as the squad car door opened. A younger officer with close-cropped blond hair sprinted into the house. Another squad car followed shortly, and McAdam tasked the newcomers with going room to room, securing the scene.

When only McAdam and the younger officer were left in the room, McAdam holstered her gun and lifted a notepad from her pocket. "Give me the details."

When Amelia glanced toward Ben again, she was sickened by how quickly death had taken over his eyes and face. She looked away. Not because she hadn't seen all manner of violence in her days but because of the guilt she felt for not arriving in time to protect the man.

"I got here a few minutes before Officer McAdam. The vic was an informant on a case my partner and I have been working. I assumed that was the reason for meeting in such an...interesting location. Unfortunately, he was dead when I got here."

The younger officer's eyes went wide as he studied the body, and he took a step closer. Light caught his name badge —J. Kavin. "Holy shit. Is that...is that Ben Storey?"

Jaw clenched, Amelia nodded. "Yes. I was on the phone with my partner at the Bureau when Officer McAdam arrived on scene."

Zane!

She looked down at the screen and relaxed a little more to see that the video call was still connected. It was always good to have someone to corroborate information with cases like these.

"Zane...sorry." She grinned wryly. "Got a little distracted there for a minute."

"I'm on my way." When she looked more closely at the screen, she could tell that his phone was in the holder fitted on his dash. "I've notified Corsaw. He wants to ride along with me to your location. You good with CPD until I arrive?"

Amelia watched the officers working on securing the

scene and smiled. "Yes. We'll hold down the fort and wait for your arrival. Thanks."

McAdam's expression darkened as yet another patrol car came screaming up the road. "I'm going to have someone secure the perimeter before this place turns into a circus. Then we'll sit down and try to figure out what the hell happened."

Though a sense of relief rolled over Amelia's tense muscles, the nagging voice in the back of her mind still told her that part of this scene was wrong. That the timing of the CPD's arrival was too convenient. Who in this desolate area would report gunfire? Squatters tended to mind their own business.

Amelia never banked on luck or circumstance. In fact, both set her on guard.

This house, this scene.

It was all wrong.

5

Plan A is a no-go. Implement Plan B.

The text message had caught me by surprise. The evening had gone according to plan so far. Disheartening as it was, I'd prepared for this contingency. Murphy's Law was always in play, but I had hoped to avoid overcomplicating what should have been a simple job.

Still, there was work to be done, and I was never one to shirk my responsibilities. Donning the coveralls of a maintenance worker, I gathered my gear and headed toward the target's apartment.

As I eased the heavy door closed, I set my toolbox down beside one booted foot. I hadn't encountered anyone on my way up to the second-story apartment, but in case any nosy neighbors had been inclined to check their peepholes, my disguise would give me invisibility. No one paid attention to service staff.

Pocketing my lock pick, I listened for signs that another human being might be in the apartment. With Plan B initiated, I was certain the homeowner was gone, but I always preferred to be thorough. A last-minute visit from a relative, an old friend swinging through town, or even an old friend who'd been kicked out by their spouse were all minor details that could easily derail my plan.

I waited a moment longer before grabbing the metal toolbox and strode down the short hall that led out of the foyer. As I stepped into the living area, I inspected the shadowy room by the faint glow of a nightlight illuminating the kitchen. Muted streetlights shone through the closed blinds of an expansive window, but the glow was barely enough to make out the shape of the furniture.

I scanned the nearest wall for a light switch and flicked it on. A floor lamp cast soft white light all around the room.

A pair of luminescent eyes stared out at me from the dark hall. My body went rigid. But just as soon as the visitor had appeared, they were gone.

A cat. I'd been spooked by a damn cat.

Scowling, I pulled a pair of shoe covers from my pockets and slipped them over my boots. I'd wiped my feet thoroughly as soon as I'd stepped into the building, but I knew the soles would still be wet. Knowing that the next people to step into this apartment would probably be carrying a search warrant, I needed to ensure I left no traces of my visit.

Amelia Storm was about to lose everything, and if I was very lucky, she might even end up in prison. I was going to make damn sure of it.

I double-checked my watch as I strode across the living room. I had enough wiggle room if a problem arose, but I wanted to be in and out of this apartment as fast as I could manage. The less time I spent here, the less likely any of the neighbors might notice.

A furry shadow sprinted toward the master bedroom, but I wasn't spooked this time. The little animal was harmless. Thankfully, Amelia was a cat person. This operation would be a lot harder if she had a German shepherd or Rottweiler.

As I reached the bathroom at the end of the hall, I swiped one gloved hand against the wall to turn on the overhead light. Scanning the room, I looked for the most opportunistic place to hide my surprise. It had to be somewhere obvious for the FBI to find, but not so obvious that anyone walking in the room would notice it. Couldn't frame Amelia with too obvious a plant.

My eyes landed on the perfect target, an air vent near the ceiling. I set my toolbox atop the vanity. The whole apartment was neat and orderly, so I was careful not to knock anything too far out of place.

Better safe than sorry.

With one more glance at the vent, I opened the toolbox to retrieve Amelia's surprises. Rather than wrenches, screwdrivers, or drill bits, I was face-to-face with a wood and steel finished Colt handgun and a silver sound suppressor. The man who'd hired me had paid a small fortune for the weapon, and I was almost sad to leave it behind.

But the forty-caliber had fired the shot that ended Ben Storey's life, and as much as I would love to add a beauty like this to my collection, there was no way in hell I wanted to be caught with it in my possession.

When news broke of the beloved councilman's death tonight, tomorrow, or whenever the press got ahold of the information, I wanted my hands to be clean.

The job was to place the blame as far away from my boss and me as possible. Framing Amelia Storm was the best decision, both professionally and personally. Two birds with one stone, as people often said.

In the end, she might not go down for Ben Storey's murder, but she'd be persecuted by the media and would most likely lose her job. Jail sentence or not, stripping Amelia of her badge would be fine with me.

She'd protest, of course, but with what I had in store, she

and the entire FBI would be chasing their tails long enough to ensure both the boss and me remained safely off the radar.

I wished I could be a fly on the wall when the Feds found the murder weapon hidden in her bathroom vent. And all the other treats I had in store for them.

I stood on the toilet to reach the vent, but my taller than average height made the task easy. Once the Colt was tucked inside, the grip just barely in view, I moved quickly to return the grate and then to wipe down the lid of the toilet and vanity.

Next was Amelia's personal laptop and then her closet. With one eye on my watch, I went through the apartment once more to ensure I hadn't accidentally moved a book or a table lamp.

With plenty of time to spare, I'd finished wiping down the ceramic tile of the foyer. As I returned the towel to the tool-box, I took one last look at the still darkness of Amelia's apartment.

This was going to be fun.

Pulling up the hood of my jacket, I kept my gaze on the floor and strode with purpose into the cold rain.

No one would ever know I'd been there.

ZANE HAD ASSURED Amelia he'd be in Englewood as soon as possible, but the digital clock of his car had just ticked over to 6:04 when he pulled to a stop in front of the address from Ben Storey's email. Traffic had been hell.

"Do you always drive like that?" Spencer Corsaw let go of the "oh shit" handle and dramatically shook out his hand.

Pulling the key from the ignition, Zane shot the Supervisory Special Agent a matter-of-fact glance. "Yes."

As he straightened his dark blue FBI jacket, Spencer

shook his head. "Then I'm never riding with you again. These are city streets, not the Indy 500."

Zane grabbed his coat from the back seat and opened the door. "Excuse me. I was rushing to help an FBI agent who was in danger."

Spencer's dark brown eyes widened, and he jabbed an index finger at one of a handful of black and white squad cars. "What danger? Half the CPD is here."

Zane shrugged into his coat. "Yeah, but still. It's the principle of the thing."

"Oh, okay." Spencer's voice was heavy with mock enlightenment. "The principle of the thing. I hope they'll put that on my death certificate the next time I have to drive somewhere with you."

Zane was tempted to tell him where they could stuff his death certificate but decided that silence was the smartest option and stepped out into the steady rainfall. The torrential downpour had subsided for the time being, but from what Zane had seen on radar, there was plenty more still to come. Droplets pattered against the fabric of his jacket as he hopped off the curb to avoid the swollen stream rushing toward a storm drain.

After flashing their badges to the young officer who was cordoning off the front of the house with yellow crime scene tape, Zane and Spencer hustled toward the back entrance.

His effort to dodge the puddles was for naught. They veered off to the sunken sidewalk that looped around the house, and Zane couldn't help but cringe as he splashed through an inch of icy water.

Should have worn rain boots.

Not that he'd had time to stop to consider his options for footwear. He'd had a front-row seat with the showdown between Amelia and the first officer on the scene. For a sickening moment, Zane had thought his friend and partner was going to take a bullet right in front of him…virtually, at least.

The twist in his gut when he thought of Amelia being hurt or killed wasn't surprising—she *was* his friend, after all—but the intensity of the sensation had taken him aback. He knew better than most that Amelia Storm could handle herself, but she wasn't a Terminator or one of the superheroes Amelia doodled when she was bored.

She was human, and sometimes humans needed help.

Though Zane's dress shoes were well-made, they weren't crafted to slosh through inch-deep puddles. By the time he and Spencer reached the back patio, water had seeped into his socks.

When he spotted Amelia huddled under the blue tarp that had been raised as a makeshift shelter while they awaited the medical examiner and the crime scene unit, he felt like a baby for lamenting his damp foot.

Her cheeks were flushed from the cold, and her damp ponytail hung lower than usual. The rain had rendered the tan color of her canvas jacket almost the same dark shade as her hair. Shoulders hunched, she shifted her weight from one foot to the other as she conversed in hushed tones with a police officer. A sergeant, according to the gold patch on his uniform.

Reflexively, Zane reached into his suit jacket to produce his badge. He'd just shown his identification to the younger man in the front yard, but he had to do something to keep himself from fixating on Amelia. The sight of her, so cold and miserable, was like a little pinprick to his heart.

When yet another officer handed him the crime scene book, he scrawled his name before thrusting it to Corsaw.

As Amelia's forest-green eyes met his, she straightened her back and gestured in their direction. "Speak of the devil. Here they are."

The sergeant turned and extended a hand. "You must be Agents Palmer and Corsaw. Glad to see you. I'm Sergeant Karasek from the Seventh Precinct."

Stuffing his badge back into his jacket, Zane accepted the handshake. "Sorry to be meeting you like this." He couldn't help it. His gaze drifted to Amelia of its own accord. "Thank you, Sergeant. You and the other officers from the Seventh for backing up Agent Storm."

The stiffness in the sergeant's stance seemed to subside as he dipped his chin. "It's our pleasure, Agent. We're all on the same team here, despite what some of my colleagues at the Seventh might think."

A little puff of vapor accompanied Zane's quiet snort. "Yeah, I've met some of them. Maybe not from the Seventh, but in the city."

When most Chicago Police Detectives saw Zane's FBI badge and heard his faint Jersey accent, they immediately went on guard. To them, he was an outsider. A foreigner, even.

Fortunately, Sergeant Karasek wasn't one of the skeptics he encountered so often when he worked with the CPD's detectives.

To Zane's side, Spencer brushed the lingering raindrops from his clean-shaven cheeks. "We're waiting on the M.E. and the CSU before we go back into the house, right?"

"Right." Amelia retrieved her phone from her black slacks. "Here, Corsaw. This is the message I got from Ben Storey about an hour and a half ago."

As Spencer scanned the glowing screen, Zane returned his attention to Sergeant Karasek and Amelia. "Did you or any of the other officers find anything while you were clearing the house? Any signs that another person had been here?"

The sergeant stuck both hands in his pockets. "No.

Nothing obvious, anyway. Our priority was making sure the area was safe. I've got a couple officers keeping traffic to this area to a minimum, not that it's going to be much of a challenge. Doesn't seem like anyone's lived here in a while. No signs of a squatter or anyone else. Just the mice and the dust."

Spencer returned Amelia's phone. "Why did Storey want to meet with you?"

A muscle ticked in Amelia's jaw as she tucked the device away. "I don't know. You saw the message. You know as much as I do."

"Shit." Spencer spat the word like an old, flavorless piece of gum. "The press is going to be all over this. We'll have to work fast before that *Gong Show* starts up. Storm, you're *sure* you don't know why Storey wanted to meet you at an abandoned house in Englewood?"

Zane fought against laughter as Amelia shot Spencer an unimpressed stare. "If I did, I wouldn't have had to meet him at an abandoned house in Englewood."

Spencer studied her for a long moment. "Okay, fair enough. That was a stupid question. Maybe we need to be thinking about who might've known what Storey wanted to tell you."

"Right." Zane pulled out his phone and began making notes, wishing he had his iPad. "I doubt we'll be able to tell that from the crime scene, but I think that's a good place to start. Along with the usual stops, like the spouse, exes, business competitors..."

He paused as unease churned in his gut.

Ben Storey wasn't just another Tom, Dick, or Harry who'd been in the wrong place at the wrong time. Englewood was a tough neighborhood, but Ben was a six-one military veteran who'd lived in Chicago all his life, at least according to his campaign website.

But Ben *did* have a powerful political rival. Sitting U.S. Senator Stan Young.

Don't get tunnel vision.

A guy in the public as much as Ben Storey probably had all kinds of people who hated him.

Ideological extremists on both ends of the political spectrum, for instance. For all Zane knew, they could be on the verge of discovering a new breed of domestic terrorism. He had to keep his mind open to all the possibilities, not just one.

Truth be told, he didn't *want* Stan Young to be involved in Storey's murder. A criminal billionaire senator was one encounter with a radioactive spider away from becoming a full-fledged supervillain. Zane had dealt with his fair share of corrupt government officials in Russia, but there was something different about Stan Young. Somehow, he felt infinitely more dangerous.

Zane, Spencer, Amelia, and Sergeant Karasek discussed the neighborhood and the house while they waited for the medical examiner and the CSU. The abandoned houses were the sites of drug deals, heroin dens, and squatters of all shapes and sizes. Bodies had turned up in other addresses, but none were homicides of prominent candidates for the upcoming spring's senate primary.

The steady patter of rain had intensified to the verge of another downpour when the forensic team arrived. In accordance with standard FBI procedure, Amelia's hands were swabbed for gunshot residue, and her service weapon was taken to examine and rule her out as a suspect.

Though she appeared calm for the entire process, Zane noticed her movements were jerky and her shoulders were tense. He'd been with Amelia at plenty of crime scenes, including murders, and this was the first time he'd witnessed a crack in her professional veneer while they were in the field.

Being here rattled her, but besides the obvious, Zane wasn't sure why.

Sure, the location was straight out of a horror film, but the place was swarming with Chicago police officers and FBI personnel. Maybe she was still shaking off the close call with death. And not just with the face-to-face she had with the responding officer. They still didn't know when Ben had been shot, so Amelia could have walked into the house only minutes after the killer fled.

Intuition told Zane there was more to her paranoia than a mere brush with mortality.

Rather than pull her aside to ask about the behavior, he made a mental note to circle back to the topic once they were warm and dry at the FBI office.

Since the front porch wasn't structurally sound, the CSU techs worked quickly to process the kitchen and dining room to give themselves a base of operation. Zane hadn't kept track of the time well enough to tell for sure how long the process had taken, but the temperature had dropped another ten degrees by the time he, Amelia, and Spencer finally set foot in the house.

While Spencer stayed with the lab manager to discuss the findings so far, Zane double- and triple-checked the booties that covered his shoes before following Amelia into the living area. The harsh white glow from a pair of industrial work lights highlighted the years' worth of dust and dirt that darkened the once-beige carpet. Heavy traffic spots had been worn down to the tarnished wood beneath, and tack strips were exposed alongside the splintery wooden baseboards.

The iron-rich scent of blood hung thick in the damp air. A cleaning crew would come through the house after the FBI had thoroughly processed the scene, but they'd never be able to mask what had happened here today. Partly coagulated blood pooled around Ben's ruined head, and darker splotches marked where the lethal gunshot had splattered brain matter along the floor.

Decomposition had strange effects on the human body, but Zane couldn't tell if the bizarre contentment on Ben's face was the result of the body's lividity or if the man had died that way.

Amelia pointed to the faint shape of footprints—each of which had been marked with a triangular yellow sign—that circled Ben's final resting place. "Those are mine. I saw him when I was in the doorway, over there." She waved at the foyer. "I kept as much space between me and the body as I could."

Zane followed the prints to other parts of the room. "Did you go upstairs before you called me?"

"No. I was heading back outside when I was on the phone with you, then I stayed down here with Officer McAdam while the officers cleared the second floor and the basement at the same time." Her wary eyes met his as she patted herself on the chest. "They had body armor, and I didn't."

He held her gaze for a beat longer than normal to silently convey that he'd noticed something was bothering her. When she dropped her gaze to look at the floor, and then to the woman crouched beside Ben, he knew he'd been successful.

Fighting the urge to reach out and touch Amelia, he cleared his throat and turned to the medical examiner. "Evening, Dr. Ackerly."

Dr. Sabrina Ackerly rested both arms on her knees as she peered up at them. With her pale blue eyes, taller than average stature, and platinum blonde hair, the woman could have passed for Zane's sister.

Maybe that's why I've always had a thing for brunettes.

As the thought crossed his mind, he couldn't help but glance at Amelia.

With a push to her legs, Dr. Ackerly rose to her full height. The back of her navy-blue jacket read "Medical Examiner" in yellow block letters. As one of the youngest appointed medical examiners for Cook County, Zane figured there was a good chance the city cops and Feds alike would have trouble identifying her without the coat.

"Evening, Agents. I would say it's nice to see you again, but..." She left the comment unfinished and pulled a notepad from her pocket. "I'm guessing you want the details I've gotten so far?"

Careful to avoid any crime scene markers, Zane made his way to Dr. Ackerly, Amelia close at his side. "Anything you've learned will be more than we know right now."

She offered a faint smile in response. "That's why I'm here."

"What can you tell us about his time of death?" Amelia's tone was somber, but there was the faintest twinge of apprehension that he doubted anyone else would have noticed. "I got to the house at 5:40, and his car was here, but he was already dead when I came inside."

Sabrina flipped back a couple pages in her pint-sized notepad. "Right. That matches up with the body temperature. On average, a human body loses about one point five degrees of heat every hour until it reaches an equilibrium with the air temperature around it. In the case where someone dies in an environment that's warmer than their body temp, then they'll gain one point five degrees per hour."

Zane couldn't remember the last time he'd been at a crime scene that was new enough for the deceased's temperature to be used as a gauge for their time of death. "But that's just an average, right?"

"Yes," Sabrina replied. "It's a good rule of thumb, but there are exceptions, and it isn't perfect. Ninety-eight-point-six is the average person's temperature on any given day, but again, that's an average. It can be affected by environmental factors too. Things like hormones and stress can throw it off, and when we're talking about narrowing the TOD down to within an hour or so, you can see how the one point five rule can be cumbersome." She nodded at the fireplace. "It also appears there was a fire burning, so the temperature in the room at time of death could be quite different than it is now."

Zane looked to Ben's pale, contented face. "And that's exactly what we're trying to accomplish here."

Pushing up her black-rimmed glasses, Sabrina held up a hand. "It's not all bad news. Actually, the sooner we get to the scene, the more accurate our estimate is. Agent Storm, you said you got here at 5:40?"

Amelia blinked repeatedly, as if she'd just come out of a trance. "That's...yeah, that's what time I pulled up in front of the house. I'm not sure what time I got inside, not exactly."

Zane reached into his pocket to grab his phone. "Agent Storm called me after discovering the body." He swiped to his phone log to confirm. "Yeah, I have 5:43."

With a reassuring smile, Dr. Ackerly pocketed her notepad. "That's really helpful. By my best estimate so far, taking into account the air temperature in here, plus the fact that rigor mortis hasn't set in yet, I believe Mr. Storey died somewhere between four-thirty and five-thirty."

Though her voice was barely a whisper, Zane stood close enough to Amelia to catch the slew of obscenities she murmured under her breath. A few seconds passed before he pieced together why the swear words sounded so strange.

She'd spoken them in Russian.

What the hell? He flashed Amelia a puzzled look.

During their investigation into a Leóne run labor trafficking ring, he'd learned that he and Amelia were both fluent in Russian. Amelia's mother had been an immigrant from the Soviet Union, and she'd taught Amelia and her siblings to speak the language from the time they were toddlers.

Zane, on the other hand, had learned Russian through a combination of college classes and friendships with exchange students. Well, that and his time spent in the CIA. Though he was fluent, he was still sure his Russian was better when he was drunk.

The slight headshake he received in response was enough to tell him that Amelia wasn't interested in discussing the reason for her break away from English. At least not right at that moment.

Zane made another mental note to circle back to the topic once they were away from this house. For now, he had to pay attention to Dr. Ackerly. "Cause of death is the shot to the head, I'm assuming?"

"As best as I can tell right now, yes." She nodded. "There's significant bleeding around the head, which tells me that he was alive when that shot was fired. When we rolled him, we noticed a lot more blood under his body, from a shot to the lower back." Pivoting to the side, Dr. Ackerly pointed to the approximate location of her kidney, if Zane remembered human anatomy correctly.

As Zane scratched the side of his face, he noticed the blue vinyl glove and dropped his arm back to his side. "Three shots?"

"Mm-hmm." Ackerly pointed to one of Ben's legs. "One in the side of the knee, one to the lower back, and then one to the head. No defensive wounds that I can see so far, and his phone was on the floor beside him before the CSU bagged it as evidence."

"He was either surprised, or he knew his killer." At the sound of Spencer's voice, Zane, Amelia, and Sabrina all turned to where the SSA stood in front of the arched door-way. "Or both."

Glancing to where the shadows gathered in the corners of the room, Zane tried to imagine where a killer might have lurked as Ben entered the house. With the work lights gone and with all but one window boarded over, the gloom of a cloudy afternoon would have offered the gunman plenty of options.

The killer hadn't fired the three shots in a rage or a moment of passion. Whoever they were, he was sure they had knowledge of their environment before tonight.

Had the killer stoked the fire in the fireplace to make the place more welcoming? Or had Ben lit the wood to stay warm while he waited for Amelia?

Another question to solve.

He returned his focus to Spencer. "They planned this."

Amelia had received a message from Ben asking her to meet him at this address. What had the killer planned for her? Had Amelia been the real target, or had Ben?

Or were they both targets?

Had the responding officer actually saved Amelia's life by arriving so quickly?

As the realization dawned on Zane, the paranoid glint in Amelia's eyes, the edginess in her voice, and the faint tremor in her hands made more sense. She'd already drawn the conclusion that the person who'd shot Ben Storey three times may well have wanted to kill her too.

Spencer gestured to the crime scene tech, who was busy photographing the stairwell. "We've done about all we can here. Come on, we've got some evidence to take back to the field office. Namely, Storey's phone. We'll do more good there than we will here."

"Right." Amelia's trepidation had given way to a hint of eagerness. She clearly wanted to escape, and Zane couldn't blame her. "Too many cooks in the kitchen here. This isn't a big house."

"Exactly." Spencer beckoned for them to follow. "Let's go do our jobs and let these guys do theirs."

After they thanked Dr. Ackerly for her expertise, Amelia and Zane headed back out into the rainy night.

They needed to do their jobs, and they needed to do them soon.

If Storey's killer had failed to eliminate Amelia tonight, then there was no telling what they might have planned for her.

6

No matter the grief her coworkers gave her for keeping a spare pair of shoes locked up in the bottom drawer of her desk, Amelia was grateful for the foresight. Her toes had been like little blocks of ice for the past...how long had it even been? Long enough that the fresh socks and canvas slip-ons were like walking on a cloud.

Upon their return to the FBI office, Amelia, Spencer, and Zane had claimed a conference room for their investigation. Special Agent Layton Redker, a seasoned agent from the Cyber Crime Division, had joined them. Along with gathering all the available digital photos of the crime scene, they'd put in a request for a clone of Ben Storey's smartphone. Hopefully, something in those digital records would point their team toward the killer.

Amelia had excused herself to the ladies' room while the team was waiting on the clone to be sent up. The ETA was down to a couple minutes.

She passed a hand over her face and met the weary stare of her reflection in the bathroom mirror.

You look like shit.

Her inner voice could be a salty bitch at times, but this time Amelia couldn't argue. All those hours spent huddled under a tarp in the midst of a November storm had done a number to her usually polished look.

And despite her fatigue, the day was far from over. Lainey's flight had been delayed a second time, and before she could find some rest, she still had to make a trip back to Midway.

Blowing out a sigh, she reached for the elastic tie that bound her ponytail. The makeshift shower she'd taken on the way into the abandoned house had given way to frizz, and Amelia couldn't stand when her hair was frizzy. She'd dealt with her fair share of bad hairstyles in middle school, and she'd be damned if she wound up in the same trap as an adult.

Her nails scraped against her scalp as she forced her fingers through the strands. When she was satisfied that it was smooth and professional, she wound the elastic band into place.

Based on the way Zane had looked at her—looked *through* her—back in Englewood, he'd caught on to the pervasive sense of unease that followed her like a hunter stalking its prey. No matter the amount of logic she used, Amelia couldn't get past the nagging sense that there was a huge piece of Ben Storey's murder they were missing.

A piece that involved her.

Why else would she have received a message from Storey to ask her to meet him at such an out-of-the-way location? Until tonight, she'd never interacted with the man outside of the FBI office.

So, why the hell did he suddenly decide that he wanted to meet with her, and *only* her, in the heart of Englewood?

Had he even sent the email? Or had he sent the request only for it to be intercepted?

Squeezing her eyes closed, Amelia rubbed her temple. "Why me, Storey? What the hell did you want to tell me?"

Unless she could channel the spirits of the dead, she'd never know. And right now, conducting a séance was the last way she wanted to spend her night. She wanted Lainey's flight to land so she could walk her sister through the front doors of New Horizons Rehabilitation.

Once she saw Lainey delivered safely into the hands of trained professionals, she'd go home, take a long, hot shower, and curl up next to her cat. Hup was used to Amelia returning home by now, and the longhaired calico would be displeased to see the bottom of her food bowl.

Before Amelia could dream up any more pleasantries to add to her make-believe night, her phone came alive, vibrating against the counter with a clatter that echoed all around the bathroom. She jolted upright with a gasp that would have embarrassed her had there been anyone to witness her surprise.

The phone buzzed a second time, and in her anxious state, she snatched at the device, nearly tossing it across the room. Thankfully, her iron grip kept it grasped between her fingers as she jerked it toward her.

A Milwaukee area code?

Though logic told her that she was probably being spoofed by some dipstick trying to sell her some car insurance, her stomach twisted, and she swallowed the invisible cotton balls that had been stuffed in her mouth.

Maybe Lainey's phone had died. Maybe she'd...she'd what? Changed her number in the last hour?

Amelia growled as she answered, "Hello?"

"Hello." The man on the other end of the line was calm and professional. "Is this Amelia Storm?"

She took an absentminded step away from the sinks and

double-checked to ensure all the stalls were empty. "Yes. May I ask who's speaking?"

"Evening, Ms. Storm. My name is Pablo Menendez. I'm a Special Agent with the Drug Enforcement Administration."

Oh, fuck me.

Amelia's heart sank. "Agent Menendez. What can I help you with?"

"Well, Ms. Storm, we've got your sister, Lainey Storm, in custody here at the Milwaukee airport. She...she asked me to call you, and she told me you work for the FBI. Is that correct?"

For the love of everything good and holy.

"Shit!" She clenched her jaw and tried again. "Sorry. Yes. I'm a special agent with the Bureau's Organized Crime Division in the Chicago Field Office. You should be able to look me up in the Federal directory."

"Believe me, I've heard worse." He cleared his throat. "As I said, we have your sister in custody here at the Milwaukee airport. She was passing through security on the way to board a flight, and the TSA discovered a baggie of heroin in her handbag. It's not enough for a trafficking charge, but, well…"

"It's enough that there's no way she's going to skate on it," Amelia finished for him. As the rush of adrenaline receded, a mixture of betrayal and anger took root in her heart. She should have known. Should have known that Lainey had no intent to change her stripes, that she'd been using Amelia as a means to an end. And that end wasn't rehab.

At least I didn't tell Dad or Joanna about this and get their hopes up.

"Well, we can't look the other way, but we can look at leniency for the charge. Possession of a Schedule One drug substance means she's facing the potential for jail time, but we could consider rehab and probation as an alternative if you—"

"No." Amelia jumped in before he could continue. Biting her tongue to hold back the wave of melancholy that threatened to drown her, she blinked against the pinpricks in the corners of her eyes.

"No?" Agent Menendez echoed.

"No. She's on her own." Amelia let out a mirthless chuckle. "Do you know why she was flying to Chicago today, Agent Menendez? I bought her a plane ticket and booked her a spot at the best rehab center I could afford. I paid a three-hundred-dollar deposit, but at least I can get the rest of it refunded."

"I'm...I'm sorry."

She wasn't sure if Menendez was empathetic with every pissed-off family member he contacted, but the twinge of sympathy in his voice seemed genuine.

Amelia reminded herself that she was upset with Lainey. Agent Menendez was just doing his job, and to his credit, he *was* trying to help.

But Amelia was through with helping her sister. Maybe jail time would be Lainey's rock bottom, or maybe she still had to sink deeper before she faced reality.

Maybe she'd never face reality.

"It's not your fault, Agent Menendez." Amelia rubbed the bridge of her nose. "I appreciate your call and offer to help, but Lainey's FBI agent sister isn't going to bail her out. You can tell her I said she's on her own. She can get a public defender like everyone else, and she can deal with it like an adult."

The words sounded harsh, even to her own ears. But as she and Agent Menendez ended the call, she had no regrets about her decision.

Amelia hoped that the prospect of prison time would be Lainey's rock bottom moment.

As she slid the phone back into the pocket of her slacks, she made a vain attempt to swallow past the sudden tightness in her throat.

Eleven years earlier, Amelia had failed her little sister. Trevor was already a member of the Marine Corps, and Amelia had followed in his footsteps when she'd joined the Army. At the time, all she'd cared about was getting as far away from Luca Passarelli as she could manage. After Luca had wrapped one broad hand around her throat and listed off all the depraved sex acts he'd subject her to if she didn't leave his son and Chicago, she hadn't stopped to consider the effect her departure might have on Lainey.

She'd just run. Like a coward, she'd tucked her tail between her legs and taken off to a military base in North Carolina.

Lainey had been on her own.

Where Amelia had Trevor to help her cope with their father's constant string of bad decisions and shady friends, Lainey had no one. So, she'd followed Jim Storm's example and sought comfort in controlled substances. First alcohol, and then when the booze wouldn't numb the pain anymore, she'd turned to heroin. Amelia wasn't even sure she could blame her. If she'd been in Lainey's position, she doubted she'd have done any better.

If she'd stayed in Chicago, then maybe Lainey's story would have a different ending.

Clenching one hand into a fist until her nails bit into the sensitive skin of her palm, Amelia squeezed her eyes closed before the newest round of tears could form. She wouldn't cry here, not at the FBI office.

Ever since she was a kid, she'd dreaded the thought of another person witnessing such a display of vulnerability.

The idea that shedding tears meant weakness was ridiculous, and she'd never viewed another man or woman as weak after seeing them cry.

So far, in her near thirty years of life, she hadn't been able to extend the sentiment to herself.

She would cry, but she'd save her sorrow for when she was alone. Just like she always had.

IT HAD BEEN fifteen minutes since Amelia excused herself to change shoes. Zane had spent that time with the team, waiting for the cloned copy of Ben Storey's smartphone to be delivered. Amelia's initial edginess seemed to have subsided by the time they returned to the field office, but he doubted her paranoia had truly faded.

He'd wanted a chance to speak to her alone before they forged ahead in the investigation, but with Spencer beside him at the circular table, Cassandra Halcott en route, and Special Agent Layton Redker from the Cyber Crime Division in the doorway, that ship had sailed.

Zane jerked his attention to the front of the conference room as the door swung inward. Blinds clattered against glass as the door swung closed behind Agent Redker. For most people, any reference to a Cyber Crime specialist conjured to mind an image of a lanky man with wire-framed glasses, wrinkled clothes, and a constant smattering of patchy facial hair. In other words, a stereotypical geek.

However, Layton Redker didn't fit that stereotype at all. He stood an inch taller than Zane's six-three, and even with the fine material of his tailored suit, his muscular stature was obvious. The man's dark eyes were shrewd and observant, and his angular jawline might as well have been carved from stone. Despite the flecks of silver, his hair was styled with a youthful faux hawk that made his age hard to judge.

Zane had briefly worked with Redker during their search for a city police detective who'd aided Alton Dalessio's child exploitation ring. Though Joseph Larson and Amelia had done most of the groundwork, Zane almost wished he could see Layton Redker in the field. He was curious to learn if the man's imposing presence carried over to confrontations with murderers.

Lifting two fingers from the ceramic mug in his hands, Zane tipped his chin in the new arrival's direction. "Evening, Agent Redker. You got here quick."

"Agent Palmer, it's been a while." Layton slid the silver laptop out from beneath his arm and produced a flash drive from his pocket. "Storey's phone was cloned onto this. Forensics is keeping the device so they can search it for physical evidence."

Zane dared a sip of the dark liquid, but he winced as the scalding brew touched his tongue. Too damn hot. Break-room coffee at the Chicago Field Office existed in two forms: the temperature of the surface of the sun or lukewarm. With each cup Zane was forced to drink, he came closer to accepting the bizarre fact as certainty.

Shuffling a messy pile of photo printouts into a manila folder, Spencer shot Zane a questioning glance. "Where's Storm? She's been gone pretty much since we sat down in this room."

I was wondering the same thing.

Zane kept the thought to himself. "I don't know. Probably thawing out under one of the heated hand dryers in the bathroom. That's where I'd be if I were her."

"Yeah, fair enough." Spencer pushed aside the folder to clear a space for Layton's laptop.

With a couple of clicks and a bit of typing, Layton had the

laptop synced with the overhead projector. It came to life projecting Redker's desktop onto the blank whiteboard against the back wall.

Spencer flipped the switches, dimming the lights as a projector screen descended with a low mechanical whine.

Pulling his chair away from the now crowded table, Spencer lowered himself to the cushioned seat. "We can catch Agent Storm up when she gets here. Let's take a look and see if we can find anything in Storey's phone that might explain what the hell happened today."

As much as Zane wanted to excuse himself to go find Amelia and make sure she was okay, he reminded himself that Amelia Storm was a grown-up and that she was in the middle of the FBI office. Even if there was a killer after her, the would-be assassin wouldn't have been able to follow her through the front doors of the building.

She was safe. She just needed a minute, and he needed to stop fretting over her as if she was some wounded bird.

The image on the projection screen switched from the misty serene lake that was Layton's wallpaper to a photo of Ben Storey with his arms around two kids. Storey's wide grin revealed his straight, white teeth. A little red-haired girl stood at his side, scrunching her eyes shut in an effort to make her smile as wide as possible. Though the boy's expression was more muted than his sister and father's, the lines at the edge of his mouth told Zane that the kid was trying not to break out into laughter.

Time slowed to a crawl as Zane stared up at the happy faces of Ben and his two grade-school-aged kids. Two kids who would grow up without the father who'd so clearly adored them.

Zane didn't even know their names.

He'd been about the same age as the girl in the photo when his father had picked him and his youngest sister up from their aunt and uncle's house, smelling of booze. To this day, Zane wasn't sure how the smell of liquor on Wayne Johansen's breath had gone unnoticed by both of the other adults.

Then again, Wayne *was* Zane's aunt's younger brother, and as a successful businessman, Wayne threw enough money at his sister and her husband that they ignored the man's little indiscretions. Even if he'd walked through the door of that damn house with a bottle of vodka in one hand, neither of them would've had the mental fortitude to admonish him and risk losing their financial lifeline.

Wayne Johansen was what many circles referred to as a functional alcoholic. Even though he drank himself near to a stupor each night, he still managed to wake up and haul himself into work without fail every day. Zane didn't know why his father climbed into a bottle, and he didn't care to speculate on a reason.

Zane had let go of the malice he'd held for his Aunt Karie and Uncle Davis, but he wasn't sure he'd ever forgive his father for what happened that night.

Like they so often did, he and his little sister had piled into the back of their father's brand-new Mercedes. Tina, their other sister, had stayed home from school with a fever that day. Though the poor girl had spent most of that day puking, she'd been the lucky one.

Zane's youngest sister, Mallory, hadn't been a fan of seat belts and didn't understand why she couldn't move freely around the back seat.

But that night, a pit in the bottom of Zane's stomach had told him to make sure Mallory buckled up.

Twenty-five years later, he could still remember the smell of the car's interior as he'd climbed in to escape the biting cold of the New Jersey winter. Crisp leather and cedar—two staples of the so-called "new car" scent. Underneath it all, like a thin layer of frosting on a cake or a dusting of snow on a sidewalk, was the faint whiff of booze.

As they'd waited for Wayne to say goodbye to his sister and her husband, Zane had given his sister the stern instruction.

Use your damn seat belt.

He'd added the mild curse word to ensure Mallory caught onto the gravity of the situation. They were both strapped into their seats when their father took his place behind the wheel.

The man's cheery demeanor and his talk of their family's plans for Thanksgiving the next week chased away part of Zane's apprehension, but the sixth sense of dread never left him. He'd let Wayne and Mallory chat while he peered anxiously out the rear passenger window.

Hey, Robert, are you feeling okay? You've sure been quiet. How was school? I know you guys always have fun when your aunt and uncle pick you up. Sorry I'm so late. The office was crazy today. Holidays, you know?

Back then, Zane had still gone by his first name, Robert. He wouldn't make the switch to his middle name, Zane, until fifth grade.

Not that it mattered what he'd been called that night, Zane never got the chance to reply.

When Wayne had turned to look into the rearview mirror, they swerved into oncoming traffic. A pair of head-lights bore down on them like a couple laser beams, and in that split-second, Zane had been sure he was about to die.

The next few minutes were a blur, but he later learned that his father had overcorrected to steer them out of the other vehicle's path. He couldn't remember if the Mercedes had rolled twice or three times before the driver's side slammed into an old elm tree.

All he remembered was the blood. Hot tears had streaked

down his face as he'd tried to wake his little sister, and his hands were coated with crimson by the time the first shout echoed down to them.

Mallory had been airlifted to a children's hospital. Doctors put her into a medically induced coma as they hastened to mitigate the damage to her brain.

Despite the medical team's best effort, two days later, his mother had been forced to make an impossible choice. Mallory's brain function had been virtually nonexistent and the odds that she'd ever awaken from her unconscious state were slim to none. Even if she did by some remote miracle return to the land of the waking, her brain had been so badly damaged that the Mallory they'd known no longer existed.

Anne Johansen waited four more days—until the day after Thanksgiving—before she let her youngest child go.

A week after Mallory died, Anne filed for divorce and petitioned to change her, Zane, and Tina's surnames. Most in Anne's position would have had to wait months for all the legal requests to process, but the courts moved quickly for those whose bank accounts exceeded seven digits.

As Spencer Corsaw's voice cut through the reverie, Zane clamped his hands down around the ceramic mug to keep from jerking upright in his chair. He had no earthly idea how much time had passed while his mind replayed that terrible memory. Plenty had happened during his time with the CIA that he preferred not to think over, but if he could delete one recollection, he wouldn't hesitate to choose the night his little sister died.

But he wasn't in Russia, and he wasn't a nine-year-old kid anymore. Forcing his eyes to the projected image of Ben Storey's phone, he took in a long, silent breath and loosened his death grip on the navy-blue mug.

He was in the heart of the Chicago FBI Field Office, and

he was in the midst of an investigation to find out who had killed the loving father of the two kids on the screen.

"Go back to the second screen." Spencer hunched forward in his seat. "What's that messaging app? The one beside Chipotle."

Layton scooted the cursor to a purple icon in the bottom right-hand corner. "This one? It's a secure messaging service. With all the tracking and monitoring that companies like Facebook do, apps like this have been getting more popular. Their data is encrypted, so messages can't be intercepted. They're also notorious for fighting subpoenas and dragging out the process."

Tapping an index finger on the tabletop, Zane shook off the lingering despondency from his trip down memory lane.

Two kids had lost a parent, and he needed to keep himself grounded in the present, not the past. "I'm familiar with it. Most of the people who use it are just normal folks who're sick of having their privacy invaded. Considering Storey's position in the spotlight, I wouldn't be surprised if that's why he used it."

Without hesitance, Layton Redker opened the app. The interface was simple, with communication threads and contacts organized much like an average email provider.

Despite the ostensible normalcy, one glaring oddity stuck out to Zane. "There's only one message thread."

Spencer propped both elbows on his knees. "Open it up. Let's see what it says."

One click of the mouse was all it took to send Zane's heart thudding against his chest. "Oh, shit." Every beat sent ice water rushing through his veins. "That can't...that can't be right. Does that say *Amelia*?"

Layton expanded the message pane until the text bubbles took up the entire screen. "It's only a first name, but yeah. It says Amelia."

First name or not, Zane knew damn well there was only one Amelia who had come to mind for all three of them. "It's not a unique name. Could be anyone named Amelia."

"Scroll down. Go to the first one of these messages." Spencer's cool request belied none of the mental turmoil that had sunk into Zane's chest like a block of lead.

In the silence that followed, Zane could make out each minute tick of the mouse wheel as Layton took them to the beginning of the lengthy communication. The first text, dated all the way back to the third of August, had been sent by Ben.

How did they start talking before he'd even met with the FBI?

The answer smacked him in the back of the head like a wayward boomerang.

Vivian Kell. Did she introduce them? Why? When? Why didn't Amelia say anything?

Only years of practice in far deadlier situations gave Zane the ability to maintain an even expression as Redker scrolled through Amelia and Ben's message history. When Ben referred to her as *Ms. Storm* for the first time, Zane swore his heart dropped through the floor.

He didn't know why such a visceral reaction had taken hold of him, but he had to tap into every ounce of his self-control to keep the anxiety off his face. This had to be a setup. He just couldn't see Amelia doing this.

Four days after the initial contact, the conversation went from flirty to R-rated.

Hey, Ben, sorry it's the middle of the day, and you're probably at work. I just wanted to tell you that I had an amazing time last night, and I really hope we can do that again soon.

In case there was any uncertainty as to what they'd done, Ben's reply painfully clarified it. *You can message me any time, sweet thing. I was thinking the same thing...maybe we can meet up tonight? Those scratch marks you left on my back are still healing, but I think I'm up for the task again.*

The taste on Zane's tongue went bitter at the winking emoji that ended the sentence.

Tonight? That's perfect! I'll need it after today, even though I can barely walk straight.

Another emoji and another sting of bile.

The thread grew progressively heavier as the messages went from R to X-rated. In addition to the sexually charged banter, the two discussed their emotional desire for one another.

Zane was sure his stomach would have clenched if the text conversation hadn't already left him numb.

Mixed in among the professed feelings were musings from Ben about his terrible wife and about how he wished he could leave her to make a new life with Amelia. Amelia returned the sentiment, and she pleaded with Ben to follow his heart and make a change that would lessen the burden he carried.

Naturally, her directions for him to, "follow his heart," were thinly veiled efforts to reveal her intentions to be more than just his mistress.

According to the timestamps, Ben stopped replying to Amelia's messages two weeks earlier.

Zane made a mental note to circle back to the timestamps after he reviewed all the messages. If nothing else, comparing the time to Amelia's schedule might be a simple way to prove they were fake. Still, Zane couldn't pull his eyes from the screen as Redker scrolled to the next set of messages from the fraudulent Amelia.

She'd sent a slew of threats and promises alike, and she'd demanded and then begged to know why he'd ignored her.

I'm sorry, Amelia, but we have to stop this. I'm married. I've been with my wife since she and I were in college. We've got two kids. I can't break up my family for something that isn't even certain. I've got to do what's right. I need to try to keep my family together.

Amelia had responded within minutes. *Are you serious? After everything you've said to me, all the promises you've made, all the times we've laid in bed talking about what life would be like if we were together, and this is how you're going to leave? You like to talk about courage, and you say all this fluffy shit, but you don't even have the balls to divorce that nasty bitch? I'm not even the one who called her that—that was YOU.*

I'm so sorry, Amelia. This isn't how I wanted this to end. But this whole thing was a mistake. I know you know that too.

An hour later, Amelia came back with a hypothetical question about what Ben would do if she went to the media about their affair. *I've still got all the pictures. I can ruin your life, just like you've ruined mine.*

As he read through Ben's appeals for her to act rationally and for her to refrain from retaliation in the interest of whatever love she might have held for him, Zane clenched his hand into a tight fist. He didn't want to believe this was the Amelia he knew.

And there was something off about the way her replies were worded. After countless conversations with the real Amelia Storm, he had a good grasp of how she spoke. And this text exchange sounded all kinds of wrong in his head. Still, he couldn't help the part of him, his lizard brain, or whatever the scientists called it, that had him riled up at the slim possibility of it really being Amelia.

Was this why she still hadn't returned from the bathroom? Had she known they'd stumble upon the months-long string of personal messages, and she'd sought to save herself the embarrassment by hiding in the ladies' room?

Never mind that concealing a romantic entanglement with the victim of a murder they'd investigated was a textbook case of withholding evidence *and* obstruction. Not to mention the litany of FBI regulations she'd violated by failing to reveal the relationship back when Ben had acted as an informant.

The most recent exchange between Ben and Amelia had occurred a day ago. In the midst of Amelia's bitter assurances that she'd throw Ben's life into chaos by leaking a slew of dirty pictures to the media, Ben had managed to convince her to meet up with him to talk through the situation like a couple of adults.

He'd stipulated that they would meet at an out-of-the-way location for both of them, and Amelia had relented.

Though Ben claimed he'd provide her with the address the following day, he *had* listed a time.

Today.

At quarter to five.

7

Amelia had been crying for so long, she'd lost track of time. After hauling herself up from the tile floor, she stood and dried her tears with the only thing available... cheap, single-ply toilet paper.

She double-checked her appearance for evidence of her tears, glancing over her pastel blue button-down and slacks. No makeup splotches, no drying water marks that might have made her appear as if she'd pissed herself. Just the odd stray bit of cat hair, but that was to be expected.

With a steadying breath, she set off for the conference room her team had commandeered for their investigation.

Let's get this done.

If anyone asked, she'd just tell them she'd received an important phone call about a family member. Zane might catch on to the implication, but no one else would be the wiser.

Gingerly, she pressed down on the metal lever and opened the door just wide enough to slip into the dim room. Blinds clattered against the glass, announcing her arrival.

Amelia stopped dead in her tracks, cringing. The whole process was reminiscent of a teenager coming home after they'd snuck out to party with their friends.

And when she turned to the three men at the round conference table, she felt like she'd been caught with one leg out the window.

Their stares were a mixture of suspicion and disgust.

Even Zane's handsome face expressed a sense of disbelief.

Amelia's stomach lurched, and bile stung the back of her throat. She tried to force open her mouth to ask them what had happened, but her entire body froze as another sight stole her attention. Clenching both hands into fists to conceal the tremor, she skimmed the displayed series of text messages.

Ben Storey's phone. If they were reading through Ben's...

Then she saw it. Her name in bold at the top of three of the visible chat bubbles.

Heat crawled up her neck to her cheeks, and a sheen of sweat clammed up both of her clenched palms.

"Why is my name on Ben Storey's phone?"

Is that *why they're looking at me like I'm a human-sized cockroach?*

As she read the purple and lavender text blocks, the seconds crept by at the speed of molasses on a cold day. With each word she read, abject terror tightened its hold around her heart. "This is obviously fake. Who would do something like this?"

"Agent Storm."

She whipped her head around to meet Spencer's scrutinizing stare. "Please tell me this is some twisted joke. You can't honestly think this..." She whipped a finger toward the projection. "I don't even know what to call this. Gross impersonation."

Clasping the arms of the chair with both hands, he pushed himself to stand. "I think it's best if you come with me. We're going to need to get a statement from you about these messages. I think it goes without saying, but I'm pulling you off this case."

"What? You can't be serious…" Shock and anger warred for control of her voice as Amelia jabbed a finger toward the projector. "I didn't write those. I've never even talked to Ben outside of this office. I've never used that app in my life. I've…"

She turned her frantic gaze to Zane, her friend, her partner, hoping he would come to her aid. This was clearly some kind of setup. He, of all people, had to know that. Right?

"Zane, back me up here. You've been my partner for the last few months. Does that even sound like me?" She might have seemed insane pleading with him like that, with the rest of the team staring at her, but she didn't care. Amid a whirlwind of fear, sadness, and disbelief, she needed a lifeline.

She swore Zane's expression had a spark of determination. At any moment, he would speak up and tell her he'd figure out what the hell had happened. He'd always have her back. But Spencer's voice jerked her gaze away before she could be sure.

"Come on, Agent Storm." Fixing her with a stare that could have melted glass, Spencer wrenched open the door. "We're just following procedure. No one is pointing fingers."

Though every instinct told her to refuse, to ask for a lawyer, or to demand he obtain a warrant for her cooperation, she clenched her jaw and followed the Supervisory Special Agent into the harsh fluorescence of the hall. She wanted to turn around to catch one last glimpse of Zane, but the door swung shut at her back.

Spencer escorted Amelia down to the second floor.

Keeping herself from the verge of tears had become a Herculean task by the time she and Spencer reached the forensic lab.

The lead technician was kind enough to lead her to a bathroom so she could strip off her clothes for processing. Her hands trembled as she scrambled to change into gray sweatpants and a hoodie. In an effort to get ahold of herself, Amelia bit down on her tongue until she tasted blood. Pain often short-circuited the fear in her brain, a tactic she'd used to steady her nerves and maintain focus during her military career.

Her tremors were so severe that she had to pause to collect herself before she could unfasten the button of her slacks. Tears blurred her vision, but she refused to let them fall.

She could cry when this was over. When she was alone. When no one could see her.

With a quiet sniffle, Amelia jammed her blouse and pants into a plastic bag. If they wanted her bra and underwear, they could get a damn warrant.

After handing the garments over to the lab, Amelia followed Spencer to an interview room. A two-way mirror took up one beige wall and a table and chairs were placed in the center of the cramped space. Fortunately, the room was one of the more comfortable areas they reserved for witnesses and informants.

At least they didn't throw me in a real interrogation room.

Yet.

Based on the size of the scroll bar beside the message history displayed by the projector, she'd only witnessed the tip-top of the proverbial iceberg.

The cold truth was, Amelia had absolutely no idea what was in store for her. If the messages had blindsided her, then there was no telling what else might be stowed away on Storey's phone.

"The lab will test your clothes for gunshot residue." Spencer's announcement pierced through the haze that had settled in over her brain.

"They tested my hands at the crime scene." Amelia hardly recognized her voice as she croaked the words. "The test was negative."

Spencer slid one hand into the pocket of his black dress pants and shoved the other through his dark hair. All the while, his attention remained on the mirror, the wall, the floor. Anywhere but on Amelia. "I know, but they'll run the tests on your clothes in case…"

Icy barbed wire wrapped around her heart. "In case I wore gloves? Because you think that *I* killed Ben Storey? And if I did…where's the murder weapon?" She wanted to throw her arms in the air and shout obscenities until her voice gave out completely. If that didn't work, she could shake Spencer until he came to his senses. Maybe if she repeatedly screamed that she'd had nothing to do with Ben's death, someone would listen to her.

The SSA reached for the door handle, which Amelia knew locked from the *outside*. "Just…take it at face value, Storm. None of us are enjoying this, but we have to follow the leads that come up in front of us."

Even if it means turning on one of your own. She dug her nails into her palm to keep the bitter thought to herself.

"The Assistant U.S. Attorney is on her way here. Once we've briefed her on the standing of our investigation, she and I will be back here to take your official statement." Spencer hesitated for a beat, like he'd intended to add more to the comment, but decided to keep the remark to himself as he disappeared out into the hall.

As the latch clicked into place, she was left with naught but an oppressive silence.

Amelia was on her own. Alone in this damn room for god only knew how long.

And she still didn't have the first clue why.

Spencer Corsaw hadn't lied to Amelia. He took no amount of joy in escorting her to an interview room and locking the door closed on his way out. Amelia Storm was a valuable asset to the Organized Crime Division of the Chicago Field Office, and she'd proved herself at least ten times over since her transfer.

She was a hell of an investigator, and now...now she was a suspect, and he had a job to do.

To say he dreaded the return to acquire Amelia's statement was overkill, but as he walked down the hall beside Cassandra Halcott, he wished he was back in the conference room with Palmer and Redker. Any day of the week, he'd rather hunt for clues in a victim's phone than sit down across from one of his own and treat them like a criminal.

I go where the evidence leads. No more, no less. That's what I'm doing right now. Me and Cassandra both. This is part of the investigation, and we can't ignore it just because it's inconvenient or because it makes us uncomfortable.

As he approached a windowless wooden door at the end of the hall, he turned to the prosecutor. "We're just here to get her statement. Right now, Agent Storm hasn't been accused of anything, but if she gets obstinate or tries to leave..." He left the speculation unfinished.

Cassandra grasped the strap of her gray messenger bag. "What about a warrant?"

Spencer gritted his teeth. "We'll ask her first. If she refuses, then we'll go for a warrant. There's enough there for one, isn't there?"

The lawyer shifted her weight from one foot to the other, but she nodded. "Yes. The messages from Storey about meeting her today, plus the fact that she was the first to the scene, is…" She cleared her throat. "It's enough. Yeah."

"Okay. Let's do this." He didn't wait for Cassandra's confirmation before he pushed open the door and stepped into the dim space.

Huddled at the edge of the black cushioned bench in the right-hand corner, Amelia Storm had tucked both knees up to her chest and rested her head against the drywall. As Spencer stepped over the threshold, she straightened her back.

Spencer gestured to the prosecutor. "Agent Storm, you've met the Assistant U.S. Attorney, Cassandra Halcott. We're here to take down your statement." Metal screeched against tile as he pulled out one of two chairs that faced away from the mirror.

As Cassandra took her spot at Spencer's side, Amelia's puffy eyes shifted between the two of them as if they were predators ready to pounce. With little more than a whisper of sound, Amelia swung her legs over the side of the bench and trudged to the table. Though she didn't stare directly at him, her wary gaze was unfaltering.

The click of Cassandra's pen seemed to ring through the still air with the force of a gong. Smoothing a hand over the yellow legal pad, she straightened her back.

Spencer took his cue. "Agent Storm, could you please describe your relationship with Ben Storey?"

She folded her hands on the table, and he couldn't help but wonder if she was trying to hide a tremble. "He was an informant. If you want the details of *what* he was an informant for, you'll have to go through the proper channels. I'm not at liberty to go into detail without the express permission of SAC Keaton."

"Uh-huh." He didn't even attempt to hide his incredulity. "So, your relationship was professional? About how many times would you say you interacted with the councilman?"

"Once. A few weeks after Vivian Kell was killed. Agent Palmer and I were introduced to him by SAC Keaton. He had information relevant to a case we were working."

"And that's the only time you interacted with Mr. Storey?"

Amelia's jaw tightened. "Yes. Here." She pointed defiantly to the table. "In the FBI office. With both SAC Keaton and Agent Palmer present."

Spencer held out his hands, hoping to convey calm. He tried to place himself in her shoes, and if innocent, he might have acted with the same amount of anger. Still, he had to do his job. Get all the facts. "What about the messages we found on Storey's phone tonight?"

"What about them? You can't possibly believe that was me?" She blurted the words with a maniacal laugh and then ground her teeth as if regretting the outburst. A moment of silence passed, and Amelia took a breath before continuing. "I do not know anything about those messages. The ones that were on the screen, the most recent five or six texts, I guess, that's all I was able to see when I stepped into the room tonight. You, Agent Palmer, and Agent Redker were digging through Storey's phone. You could probably tell me about them, though, so I know what I'm being accused of. I sure as hell didn't *write* any of them."

Cassandra set her pen atop the notepad. "Then how do you think they got there." She held up a hand before Amelia could retort. "I mean that as an honest question, Agent Storm. I want to know what you think of those messages."

According to Agent Redker, the secure, encrypted nature of the application found on Storey's phone made tracing the origin of the messages next to impossible. Spencer didn't blame people for their desire to protect what little privacy they had left online, but at the same time, he'd be just as happy if the platform didn't exist. The ability to track down details about each message would end any debate about whether they were authentic.

"I don't know," Amelia finally said. Even in the lower light, Spencer noticed that her knuckles had turned white where she clasped her other hand. "Maybe someone was pretending to be me, or maybe the entire thing is fake. Maybe someone came up with an elaborate story so they could throw the suspicion of Storey's murder onto someone else. Me."

Spencer forced his expression to remain neutral. There had been rumors of an information leak in the Chicago Field Office for the last six months—since right around the time Amelia had transferred from her previous post in Boston.

His hands clammed up at the thought.

One mess at a time.

He cleared his throat. "Okay. If you don't mind, Agent Storm, could you walk us through your evening?"

Though the look was fleeting, Amelia's eyes narrowed. "I'd be able to remember it a little better if I had my damn phone."

"Your phone is being processed for evidence, just like your clothes and shoes." He straightened his suit jacket and crossed his arms as he pinned her with an expectant stare. "You'll have to do your best without it."

Rather than shrink away from the scrutiny, Amelia squared her shoulders. "Fine. I left here at a little after three and drove to Midway. I parked in the main garage, and there's still a ticket stub somewhere in my car. It should've recorded the time I got there and the time I left. And if that's not enough for you, you can verify it with the eight million security cameras they've got around that place."

She went on to detail the reason for her trip to Midway, as well as the email she'd received from Ben Storey with the Englewood address. Only after the request from Ben and the notification of her sister's flight delay did she decide to leave the airport. Supposedly, she'd driven straight to Englewood from Midway, and she'd stopped for fuel and a drink along the way.

All Amelia's claims should have been easy enough to verify. But even with the parking stub and the receipts from the gas station, there was enough variance in the potential time of Ben's death that the bits of evidence wouldn't be enough to clear her.

Spencer hated to admit it, but Amelia Storm's account of events did little to alleviate his suspicion. She was a competent agent and a smart woman. If she wanted to kill someone, she'd be well aware of the steps necessary to cover her tracks.

Spencer uncrossed his arms as Amelia finished. "We'll have to corroborate the times and locations from your statement."

She shot him a petulant glance. "What am I supposed to do in the meantime? And what the hell do you mean when you say you'll have to corroborate it? I told you exactly how to verify everything I said."

"You did, but it'll still take time." He scooted to the edge of his seat. Now came the real test. The search. "Agent Storm, I'm going to run this by you as a courtesy."

Her nostrils flared. "Run *what* by me as a courtesy?"

"We want to ask for permission to search your apartment before we go through the motions to get a warrant."

A storm cloud moved in to darken her face. "You want to

ask me for my permission so you don't have to go through the *trouble* of getting a warrant." Her glare never left him as she leaned forward. "No, SSA Corsaw. You don't have permission to search my apartment. Get the fucking warrant."

8

The shame from his momentary lapse of faith in Amelia weighed down on Zane's shoulders like a lead cape. He felt like an asshole for doubting her, especially after the hurt in her eyes just before Spencer had escorted her from the conference room.

Even if she *had* been sleeping with Ben Storey, he knew better than to suspect she'd ever be capable of killing the man.

Not that Zane even believed the affair was real. Hushed— the messaging app they'd found on Ben Storey's phone—was highly regarded for its privacy and security. Ironically, the two major selling points for consumers meant that the FBI would have no luck tracing a message or user.

Hushed was the perfect tool for a killer who wanted to throw blame onto another person.

Midway through Zane and Layton's second scan of Storey's camera roll, the glass and metal door swung inward with a light clatter. Zane hoped against all rational thought that Amelia would stroll into the room after Spencer, but the SSA was alone.

As Zane glanced over the man's shoulder to Cassandra, he rubbed below his nose to conceal a scowl he couldn't suppress.

"Where's Agent Storm?" To Zane's surprise, Layton was the first to pose the query.

Spencer's posture visibly stiffened, and Zane caught the faint motion at the man's side as he rubbed his thumb and index finger together. A tell. Spencer was uncomfortable, nervous, or both.

As if Spencer could read Zane's thoughts, he stuffed the hand into the pocket of his pants. "She's in an interview room. We've gotten her statement, but..." his Adam's apple bobbed, "she didn't sign off on a search of her apartment, so we have to get a warrant."

Cassandra set her messenger bag on the table. "I reached out to a judge a bit ago. I should hear back within the next hour."

Zane fixed her with a flat stare, fighting to keep his ass securely connected with his chair. "A search warrant? At eight on a Monday night?" He didn't bother to conceal the skepticism from his tone.

As Cassandra took the seat at Layton Redker's side, she shot Zane a matter-of-fact look. "A judge I know was working late."

Tilting his head to appear thoughtful, Zane shifted his attention to Spencer. "When's the last time we've executed a warrant at this time of night when we *didn't* think someone's life was in danger? Or when it *wasn't* urgent?" He held up his hands in feigned haplessness. "I mean, I'll be thirty-five in a few months, so maybe my memory's slipping."

"Look." Spencer brushed at his forehead like he was displacing an insect. "We're following a lead, Palmer. It's the only lead we've got right now, so we're going to chase it down until it either pans out or turns into a dead end."

Cassandra gestured to the picture displayed by the projector—a hearty breakfast Ben had ordered from a diner on the outskirts of downtown. He'd shared the image on his Instagram account with a caption about his interest in legislation that benefitted local businesses.

"Ben Storey was a popular man. He still *is* a popular man. He was preparing to go head-to-head with Stan Young in the primary, and there've been parts of his campaign that caught national coverage. We need to chase down each lead we find, even if it's something paltry. The sooner we can catch whoever did this, the sooner we can get ourselves out of the media's crosshairs."

"Everything in this case is being expedited," Spencer said. "Forensics has already retrieved the bullet for ballistics analysis. The clone of Storey's phone was moved ahead of all the other pending requests in the tech lab, and the medical examiner is performing an autopsy as we speak."

Zane lifted a hand. "But let's keep something in mind, Counselor. Like you said yourself, Ben Storey was a popular man. He was also a *complicated* man, and he was an FBI informant. There's no doubt that he had a hell of a lot of people out there who didn't like him, so I think we'd best not forget that. We're investigators. Let's not get tunnel vision just because we want to take the first easy route that pops up in front of us."

Not that any part of accusing a fellow FBI agent of murder was *easy*. Then again, Spencer and Cassandra could have fooled him into thinking such an event was commonplace.

As silence descended on the cramped conference room, Cassandra retrieved her phone from the messenger bag. Her blue eyes flicked to the screen, and a stony resolve took over her expression before she turned back to the three of them. "That's the judge I contacted. The request for a warrant to search Agent Storm's apartment was approved. All that's left is to stop to pick up the paperwork."

Zane forced himself to maintain his nonchalant demeanor even as his pulse rushed in his ears. He wasn't surprised to learn that Cassandra had managed to obtain a search warrant. Hell, he should have realized a search of Amelia's apartment was inevitable as soon as he saw the thread of messages on Storey's phone.

It doesn't matter. They won't find anything. She didn't do this.

He hated that he had to remind himself of her innocence, and he hated even more that there was a whispering voice in the back of his mind that asked him how he'd respond if she was guilty. The voice reminded him that Amelia was smart, and if she'd truly wanted to conceal an affair, he was sure she'd have found a way.

Then, of course, there was the tug of the stupid caveman instincts leftover from when humans had sheltered in caves and hunted woolly mammoths. He'd been struck by a pang of jealousy and possessiveness when he'd read the various dirty messages between Ben and "Amelia."

Whatever spark might have existed between the two of them didn't mean she was his, and their connection didn't mean she was forbidden from seeking a little fun of her own. Besides, he should have known better than to think Amelia would ever entertain the idea of an affair with a man who was married with two young children. And she *definitely* would never plead with that man to break up his family and ride off into the sunset with her.

I'm sorry, Amelia. I'm a terrible friend.

He reached for the mug of tepid coffee and took a long drink to keep himself from punching a wall.

"All right." Spencer pulled on a navy-blue FBI jacket and straightened his collar. "Counselor, we'll meet you out in the parking garage. Agent Redker, keep searching through

Storey's phone. Once you're finished, the clone of Agent Storm's phone should be ready."

Layton pressed a button on his laptop, and the projector went dark. The man looked from Spencer to Zane as he gathered his computer, but his face was unreadable. Not that he had much at stake right now.

Taking his cue to stand, Zane still wrestled with the sense of guilt worming through the back of his head. Amelia wasn't Layton's friend. Amelia wasn't Spencer or Cassandra's friend, either, and Zane wondered if either of them would even notice her absence.

The thought left a bitter taste in Zane's mouth, and he couldn't blame the subpar coffee.

Cassandra shrugged on her peacoat, shouldered her messenger bag, and paused at the door, but Spencer interjected before she could pose a question. "You two go ahead. I need a quick word with Agent Palmer."

As Cassandra and Layton shuffled out of the room, Zane shook out his own jacket. He'd known the one-on-one discussion was unavoidable, and he'd been prepared for the inquiry since Spencer had escorted Amelia to the forensic lab.

The latch clicked into place, and Spencer's full scrutiny fell on him. "I don't need to pull you off of this, do I? I know you and Storm have been working together since the Leila Jackson case. Will that impact your judgment here?"

Forcing himself from cursing, Zane rubbed his eyes. "My judgment? No. I want the truth as much as you do, but I just happen to have a little more faith in Amelia Storm than you or our prosecutor seem to."

Spencer threw both arms out to his sides. "Okay, then why in the hell did she tell me, and I quote: 'get the fucking warrant?' She could've cooperated just as easily."

Zane scoffed. "Right, you'd just let the FBI forensic team

into your house to rip the place apart when you hadn't done anything wrong? I get that we all understand the process of an investigation, and we all know that searches are important, but the Fourth Amendment extends to FBI agents, last I checked."

Spencer raised a hand. "Okay, this isn't a debate we need to have right now. We disagree about this, but that's fine. Keep your head level, all right, Palmer?"

Zane bit his tongue to keep a sarcastic remark at bay.

Maybe he was biased, but he wasn't so sure that *he* was the one who needed to heed Spencer's advice.

THOUGH ZANE HAD ONLY TRULY WORKED for the FBI for about three years, he'd been present for more search warrants than he could remember. However, aside from one incident at the start of his FBI career, he hadn't been tasked with wrangling animals at the site.

Brushing a few stray cat hairs off the sleeve of his jacket, he hurried down a set of carpeted stairs and out into the chilly night. After one of the forensic techs suggested involving animal control to deal with Amelia's cat, Zane offered to wrangle Hup himself. He'd met the longhaired calico a few times and was a familiar face to the frightened feline.

The search team hadn't even been in the apartment, but their impatience had been palpable while Zane used treats to lure Hup out of hiding. He'd been wracked with guilt when he'd scooped her up and gracelessly stuffed her into a carrier. Since he hadn't been permitted to carry out anything other than Hup and her pet taxi, and since he didn't want to leave the poor cat in his bathroom with nothing, he'd made a side trip to buy food and litter.

For the first time that night, he was finally satisfied that he'd done something to help Amelia. He doubted the sentiment would carry over when he returned to her apartment in the midst of an in-depth search warrant, but he'd take the small wins where he could find them.

As he opened the front door to Amelia's apartment building and headed to the stairwell, Zane braced himself for the worst.

His vision of the worst wasn't far off the mark. After flashing his badge to the uniformed city police officers who stood watch in the hallway, Zane let himself inside.

The foyer was mostly untouched, but all Amelia kept by the entrance was a shoe rack, a handful of wall-mounted coat hooks, and a square table beneath a row of key rings. Aside from messing up a neat pile of mail beside a three-wick candle, the search team had hardly touched the area.

Zane remembered how Amelia hated for guests to keep their shoes on past the tiled foyer, but he couldn't heed her stringent policy tonight.

Sorry, Amelia.

Clenching his jaw, he stalked down the short hall to the living room and kitchen. The upended couch cushions were expected, but his heart sank when he noticed the notebook-sized hole in the drywall next to a light switch. Two metal grates from the overhead air vents sat atop the dark, wooden coffee table, the drawers of which hung open, their contents splayed over the floor.

Before Zane could survey the damage to the kitchen, Spencer Corsaw's voice drew his attention to the hall at the other end of the room. "Palmer, good timing." From his post in the bathroom doorway, the SSA beckoned Zane forward with an outstretched hand.

Zane stormed past the sectional toward the bathroom. "For what?"

Spencer waited for Zane to reach the hall before he turned to the short woman at his side. "For this."

As she passed the SSA a red-taped evidence bag, Zane struggled to keep his shock hidden. "Is that?"

With one gloved hand, Spencer held up the item like a highly sought catch in a fishing competition. "A Colt M1911 forty and a sound suppressor. Found in the bathroom vent above the toilet." His expression darkened, and Zane took some solace in the fact that the discovery hadn't elicited any sense of joy or pride. "No serial number."

Before he even spoke, Zane sensed his words would fall on deaf ears but refused to go along with the apparent witch-hunt the team had set themselves on. "How do you suspect she managed to get it all the way in there when she was in Englewood, surrounded by police from the moment she got to the murder scene?"

"That's what we are going to find out because, as of fifteen minutes ago, we learned the weapon type that was used to murder Ben Storey." SSA Spencer held up the evidence bag.

"Ballistics sent over their preliminary analysis. They don't know the exact weapon, but they know that the bullet is forty-caliber and that the weapon's barrel had a left-hand twist. There's only one arms manufacturer that makes handguns with left-handed twists."

"Colt," Zane finished for him.

"Sorry, Palmer, but this doesn't look good." Spencer handed the bagged weapon to Zane. "We need to put a rush on ballistics for this, and we need to do the same for Agent Storm's laptop. I want you and Ms. Halcott to take the laptop and the weapon back to the field office."

Even as Zane's thoughts whipped through his head in a whirlwind and his pulse hammered in his ears, he kept his face carefully blank. "We're missing something. Even if this is the murder weapon, that doesn't seal the deal. How did it get here? Someone planted it, obviously. Just like those chat messages. Even you have to admit they didn't sound like our Agent Storm. We have to look deeper and stop this tunnel vision that has you ready to let a good FBI agent take the fall if it means closing this case quickly."

He didn't need a decade of CIA experience to realize that Spencer didn't share his adamancy. "No one is trying to blame Agent Storm out of convenience. We are following standard protocol. I'd do the same if it were your name attached to those filthy messages. Now, if you want to look deeper, get your ass back to the field office and process that laptop. We'll keep looking here, Palmer."

But you need to brace yourself if this doesn't pan out the way you want it to.

Spencer didn't have to speak the second part aloud. Zane read it plain and clear in the SSA's eyes.

"Okay." Zane looked down at the wood and steel finished handgun. "We'll get this to the lab. The sooner forensics finishes their analysis, the sooner we can start figuring this thing out."

With a snap, Cassandra removed her vinyl gloves. "I'll get the laptop, and we can head out."

Zane offered her a stiff nod in reply.

Amelia didn't do this. Someone's setting her up.

He kept the reminder in the front of his mind, the same way the main character in a horror film held a crucifix as they descended into the unknown.

His gut told him Amelia was innocent, but he wasn't sure how long his instincts would withstand the flimsy physical evidence they were hanging her with.

9

A s Amelia dropped her face into the crook of one arm, she was reminded of her high school years. Aside from art and history, she'd developed a habit of snoozing through almost all her classes. None of the material had ever been particularly challenging, nor had her coursework been interesting.

And with almost forty kids in the room to siphon their attention, none of the teachers had given Amelia's naps a second glance. Her grades never dipped below the A and B range, even if she was barely conscious for most of the lectures.

Whenever she'd tell her boyfriend at the time about her series of naps throughout the school day, he'd stare at her in awe.

Alex Passarelli's family was wealthier than Amelia's could ever hope to be, and his parents had sent him to a prestigious private school. If he'd been caught snoozing in his college-level calculus course, the instructor would have never let him hear the end of it.

Not that Alex *would* have slept through his classes if he'd been given the opportunity. Even when he was seventeen, Alex soaked up knowledge like a sponge.

High school boys had a propensity to seek danger and risky activities. Testosterone drove them to prove that they were no longer boys. Whether by dating the most attractive girl in their class, leading their football team to victory over a rival, or setting a record for the longest keg stand, they sought to carve out their place in the world.

However, Alex's spot had been carved out before he was born.

As the son of a D'Amato Family capo, he was automatically granted the sense of independence and masculinity that his peers so desperately sought.

Maybe his status was the reason he'd never taken an interest in the cliquey popularity spats of his peers. At seventeen, he'd commanded more respect than most of the boys in his grade would earn in a lifetime. Their parents might have been rich, but none of them were mafia royalty.

So, when he'd chosen to date a pretty girl from a poor neighborhood in Englewood—a massive faux pas for anyone else—the majority of his classmates and friends simply accepted his decision.

At one of the parties she and Alex had attended, not long after their relationship was official, a member of the football team had thought to make a jab at Amelia's less-than-affluent home life.

Alex dropped the six-foot-four musclebound jock with a single punch. Best of all, he'd done it in front of about thirty of his classmates. The guy's girlfriend had tried to catch him as he'd fallen, but her thin frame was no match for over two-hundred pounds of dead weight.

Later in the night, the same girl had approached Amelia

to apologize for her mouthy boyfriend, saying she'd already dumped his ass.

Faith Trostad was her name. She and Amelia became good friends in the months and years that followed. These days, Faith lived in California, where she was a practicing surgeon at a large metropolitan hospital.

Last time the two had spoken was right after Trevor's murder. Faith had injected some much-needed positivity into Amelia's life when she'd announced that she and her wife had been approved to adopt a little girl they'd fostered for close to a year. Amelia looked forward to the family's Christmas cards each season, and she hoped she'd receive one soon.

She also hoped she wouldn't have to give Faith the address of a Federal prison to send the card.

As if the universe had sensed Amelia's transition back to reality, the metallic click of a lock ripped her away from the memories.

Jerking to sit upright in the hard plastic chair, Amelia took in a sharp breath as the cobwebs fell away from her brain.

The door swung inward, and Cassandra Halcott zeroed in on Amelia. Wordlessly, the woman slid a manila folder out from under one arm. Amelia attempted to look into the hall as the door closed, but no one was there.

If the lawyer was alone, then Amelia wasn't being arrested. Not at that moment, anyway.

But if Cassandra was alone, the news couldn't be good, either. Amelia had been given a copy of the search warrant before the FBI had left for her apartment. Some warrants targeted items like computers or clothes, but to Amelia's chagrin, there had been no specific object or location mentioned.

She knew from experience that the lack of specificity

meant the Bureau had permission to search anywhere they pleased. They could rip open drywall, take apart furniture, and rifle through locked drawers and safes. Anywhere they suspected they might find a relevant piece of information, they could tear apart a barrier that stood in their way.

Her throat tightened as she thought of Hup. Hup was a sweet cat, but she was skittish to loud noises or boisterous people. When Amelia and Zane had first encountered her at the house of Leila Jackson's parents, the calico had walked right up to them for pets.

As Cassandra made her way to the other side of the laminate table, Amelia straightened. "Where's my cat?"

"Agent Palmer took the cat before anyone went in the apartment." Despite Cassandra's matter-of-fact tone, her rigid posture told Amelia that the prosecutor wasn't as confident as she sought to portray.

Amelia glanced reflexively at the two-way mirror. Was Zane standing in the adjacent room, watching as Cassandra took her seat to start this...whatever in the hell this was. An interview? Another statement? An interrogation?

The lawyer flipped open the folder and spun around a glossy photo of a handgun with a polished wooden grip and a stainless-steel frame. "Do you know what this is, Agent Storm?"

Biting the inside of her lip to withhold a sarcastic response, Amelia studied the picture. "An M1911. Can't tell the caliber, but it looks like it might be a Colt." She turned her scrutinizing stare to Cassandra. "Why? What is it? Is it...?"

The words died in her throat.

The murder weapon. They found the fucking murder weapon.

Cassandra folded her hands on the table, only inches away from the print. The woman's face was as expressive as a brick wall. "It is an M1911, and it is a Colt. Chambered in forty caliber, with the serial number filed off. It was found along with a silencer." She slid a photo of a silver sound suppressor across the table. "No identification on the silencer, either. Ballistics analysis is underway right now to determine if the striations on a bullet fired from this gun match the marks on the bullets that hit Ben Storey."

Amelia shoved away the pictures as if they'd bitten her. "No, this isn't mine. I don't know where the hell you found it, but it isn't mine. I own three firearms. Two handguns and a rifle, and they're all registered. None of them are even the same caliber as this. I don't even *own* a weapon made by Colt."

If Amelia's vehement reaction fazed Cassandra in the least, the woman didn't let the surprise show. Amelia suspected that the cool veneer was akin to what the prosecutor donned in a federal courtroom. "Ballistics determined that Ben Storey was killed by a forty-caliber handgun, and the marks on each bullet indicate that the weapon fired with a left-hand twist. This rules out all but one manufacturer, and that's Colt. We'll know for sure soon, but we believe this is the murder weapon."

This isn't happening. They couldn't have found this in my apartment. I've never seen this damn thing before in my life. How the hell was it found in my apartment? How did it get there?

Obviously, she couldn't have put it there. They had to realize that. She'd been surrounded by police from damn near the moment she got to that house. Maybe they did, and this took her off the suspect list, but they wanted to keep that information hush-hush because they suspected another FBI agent was involved. The rat.

As much as Amelia wanted to vocalize the rush of thoughts, her mouth was devoid of moisture, and she couldn't conjure up a single word.

Cassandra's voice dropped an octave. The first change in

her demeanor since she'd entered the room. "We found this weapon in the vent of your bathroom." Her eyes locked onto Amelia's. "Is this your weapon, Agent Storm? And did you kill Ben Storey?"

"No!" Her heart knocked against her chest as she looked to the two-way mirror and then back to Cassandra. "And no! This isn't mine! I keep a Beretta nine-millimeter in the drawer of my nightstand, and my other handgun and rifle in their cases in the back of my closet. Why would I keep a gun in a vent? In a *bathroom* vent? Who does that?"

The muscles in Cassandra's neck tensed as she shifted in her seat. "If this is the murder weapon, then it's likely that the vent was used to conceal its location."

Amelia didn't let her continue the half-assed explanation. "If that's the murder weapon, can you explain something to me? Using all your mental faculties, really take a moment here before you answer. We all know that I was at the house in Englewood, where the murder happened, and you've just told me that this gun was found in my apartment near Lincoln Park. Considering it's a good hour's drive in rush hour traffic, with a storm dumping buckets on the road, how the hell did it get there in the five minutes between my arrival on scene and CPD showing up? Please. Take all the time you need. I'm in no rush."

A crease formed between Cassandra's eyebrows. "It was in *your* apartment, Agent Storm."

Amelia had clearly been wrong in assuming the detective abilities of the other agents investigating this case. She shouldn't have had to spell it out for them, but if they needed Captain Obvious, she'd gladly take that role to clear her good name. Flattening both hands on the tabletop, Amelia forced every ounce of petulance she could manage into her stare. "I am so glad I have never had to rely on you to defend me in a court of law. Let's try this again, shall we? How did the gun get into my apartment?"

An accomplice?

Did they think someone was helping her cover up her dirty deed?

By hiding the murder weapon in her own apartment? Surely, they didn't think she was so stupid.

From the look that Cassandra was giving her, Amelia realized they may be thinking exactly that. If looks could kill, Amelia would have dropped on the spot. Cassandra looked at her as if she were a roach crawling up the wall. But that didn't matter.

Cassandra didn't have to fight ignorance and stupid assumptions to save her life. Amelia did. She knew what kind of fate awaited her if she was convicted of Ben's murder. She'd piss off every last person in the building if it meant someone would listen to sense.

When Cassandra failed to answer Amelia's question, she continued to bait her with the truth. "You know I was at Midway until four-fifty, and it took me almost an hour to get from there to Englewood. I hadn't even been in that house for more than five minutes when the CPD showed up. So, tell me, *Counselor*, when exactly did I have time to drive back to my apartment to stash the murder weapon in my fucking bathroom?"

As silence settled over the two of them, Amelia waited for a reply. A rationalization, another what-if, another hypothetical scenario to fit the narrative that she'd killed Ben Storey.

All she received were more excruciating seconds of oppressive quiet as Cassandra's knuckles turned white.

Cold threads of unease wound their way around Amelia's rapidly beating heart.

They hadn't stopped to ponder how the Colt had made its

way to her apartment. There was one lead in all their minds, and that was Amelia. Talk about tunnel vision.

What about Zane? Had he defended her at all? She'd placed her fragile trust in that man, like she'd given him a priceless Fabergé egg. He, of all the agents out there, should have kept it safe.

Had he dropped that delicate egg, or was he still fighting to keep it from harm? She hadn't seen him since Spencer had pulled her out of the conference room. For all she knew, the SSA might have taken him off the case altogether.

Amelia gritted her teeth and shoved the emotions down and out of reach. She'd have time to sort out her relationship with Zane Palmer when this mess was finished. Right now, her focus was getting *someone* to realize that she hadn't killed Ben Storey.

Cassandra's sigh cut through the still air like a machete through foliage. "That's not all we've found, Agent Storm. Your laptop is currently being processed, but so far, the tech team has located the same app on your computer that was used on Ben Storey's phone. The messages between the two of you are there as well."

Her computer? The murderer hadn't just stopped at shoving the Colt handgun in her bathroom vent, but they'd cracked open her computer to plant digital evidence too?

If they'd managed to get into her laptop, what else had they done? She'd only seen the most recent texts when she'd stumbled into the conference room earlier, but she suspected she didn't even *want* to see the rest. Just the thought of a fake affair with a married father of two was enough to make her stomach turn.

When Amelia spoke, her calm voice belied none of her inner turmoil. "I'm being set up. The sooner you verify what I'm telling you, the sooner you can find who *actually* killed Ben Storey. I don't know who did it, and I don't know why, but I do know that they're doing their damnedest to pin the blame on me."

And so far, their plan was working.

If the FBI didn't find the flaw in the killer's plan soon, Amelia wondered if they ever would.

10

Cassandra Halcott and Zane were long gone, but Spencer still lingered in the bathroom of Amelia Storm's apartment. Arms crossed over his chest, he peered up at the ceiling like he was waiting for the vent to talk to him. Like he was some twisted brand of *Alice in Wonderland*.

Following the discovery of the racy messages between Ben Storey and Amelia Storm, Spencer's primary goal had been to maintain a level head and a neutral outlook. He didn't want his review of the crime's evidence to be tainted by bias, either in favor of or against Special Agent Storm. As a Supervisory Special Agent, part of his responsibility was to act as a model for the behavior he expected from those in his department.

However, each time he reiterated the high potential for Amelia's guilt to Zane or Cassandra, he didn't *feel* like a leader. He felt like a dick.

His ex-wife's commentary about his propensity, or lack thereof, for leadership rang through his head like the echo of a bass line from a bad metal song.

Spencer, you're not what the FBI's looking for in a Supervisory

Special Agent. You're too nice. They're going to need you to play the office politics and make decisions you won't like. Do you really think you can do that?

When those words had fallen from Meghan Corsaw's lips, Spencer had thought at first that she'd been joking.

Him? Too nice? He wasn't overly nice.

Sure, he always gave a few bucks to the men and women who stood at intersections with cardboard signs, but life was hard. Downward spirals were relentless, and plenty of people were dealt a bad lot in life from the day they were born.

Yeah, he tipped well over the standard twenty percent, even if he received terrible service at a restaurant or bar. As far as he was concerned, servers' base wages were criminal. Ensuring they made enough money to survive, even just for one night, was the least he could do.

Maybe Spencer was still friends with a man who'd stolen sixty bucks from him a half-decade ago, but Brad Welsh had repaid him within days and apologized profusely. Life was hard, and Brad had been too embarrassed to ask for financial help. These days, Brad was a marketing VP, and his salary was easily double what Spencer made at the FBI. Brad wasn't the most money-wise person in Chicago, but he was generous.

Dealing with the worst of the worst in his career at the Bureau had given Spencer perspective. He wasn't *too nice*. His current dealings with Zane Palmer and Amelia Storm attested to Spencer's lack of niceness.

But at the same time, his emotionless presentation of a piece of physical evidence that could seal Amelia Storm's fate gnawed at the back of his mind like a termite in a wooden castle.

There was a reason he and Meghan were no longer married, but the woman *had* known him for the better part of his adult life. If anyone was qualified to make the observation that he was too nice, it was the woman with whom he'd shared more than a decade of his life.

A woman who'd cheated on him six years into that twelve-year marriage.

Shit. Maybe I am too nice.

Before he could slip any farther into the moment of introspection, a familiar voice jerked him from the reverie.

"SSA Corsaw." Norman Odgers, a seasoned crime scene technician who'd worked out of the Chicago Field Office for as long as Spencer, poked his head around the doorway to the master bedroom. "I've got something in here. A pair of shoes with a little blood spatter near the sole."

Curling one gloved hand into a fist, Spencer tried to ignore the sinking sensation in his stomach as he trudged down the hall. "All right, let's see it."

Norman waved him over to a dresser beside the walk-in closet. "I found the blood with a Luminol test. The stains only glow for about thirty seconds, but I took a few pictures. Here. Have a look." The tall man held out an unwieldy digital SLR camera.

Spencer rounded the edge of Amelia's disheveled bed to accept the Nikon from Norman.

The blue and white blankets had been neatly made when he'd arrived, but now the comforter and sheets rested in a heap beside pillows that had been stripped of their cases. Part of Spencer almost hoped Amelia had indeed killed Ben Storey so he wouldn't be assailed by guilt for helping the forensic crew rip apart her home.

Pushing aside the sullen thought, he clicked an arrow button beside the photo preview screen. In the first picture, two rubber-soled Mary Janes were tucked behind a pair of dark brown riding boots. The positioning of the shoes in such an obscure spot made Spencer wonder if Amelia had tried to hide them.

Or someone wanted him to think that Amelia was trying to hide them.

This case was becoming curiouser and curiouser by the minute, which didn't stop the phone calls from the powers that be demanding that he close this case up fast. It also didn't stop the media calls or the army of reporters who had already, almost magically, learned of Ben Storey's death before the body had even grown cold.

Curiouser and curiouser indeed.

But he couldn't let his internal doubts that his trusted agent would kill a man in cold blood stop him from investigating her until there was zero doubt of her guilt or innocence. His plan was to keep her trapped in that locked room until he knew one way or another.

If she was guilty, then that room was exactly where she needed to be.

If she was innocent, then something very strange was happening, and she was safer tucked away inside the FBI building.

Now, he just needed to bust ass and solve this damn case.

As he flipped over to the second image, Spencer blinked to adjust his vision to the lack of light on the screen. The Mary Janes had been moved to the carpet at the front of the closet, and their darker color was a scant difference from the shadowy background.

In the next few photos, a series of glowing blue specks near the toe of the left shoe stuck out like the explosion of a supernova in the black abyss of space.

Spencer's shoulders sagged with disappointment. He'd been secretly wishing the shoes would turn up squeaky clean. "Have you done a Kastle-Meyer test yet?"

Tilting his chin at the camera, Norman shook a small vial of clear liquid. "Yeah. It's after the pictures of the Luminol test. The results of that one are only reliable in the first ten seconds, so I documented it like I did with the Luminol."

Kastle-Meyer was another term for a swab analysis used in forensic science to make a preliminary determination about the presence of blood. The substance in question was first treated with the chemical phenolphthalein and then hydrogen peroxide. If the sample turned bright pink within a couple seconds, then there was a good chance it contained blood. However, since the chemical oxidized to that same pink shade naturally within a half-minute, the results could only truly be interpreted within ten seconds.

As he clicked to the next photo in line, Spencer reminded himself that the Kastle-Meyer test was a presumptive analysis for blood. The pink stain on the cotton swab displayed on the camera didn't tell them any specifics, only that the presence of blood was likely.

His first thought was to ask Norman to conduct the test again so he could see the results for himself, but he knew better than to doubt the seasoned crime scene analyst. Norman was likely capable of carrying out the straightforward analysis in his sleep.

Norman held up a plastic vial of liquid that was no larger than the cartridge of a nine-millimeter handgun. "I'm about to test to see if it's human or not. The sample is big enough that we still have plenty for DNA analysis."

Setting the camera beside Norman's makeshift workstation, Spencer managed an absent nod.

The CSU tech twisted open the plastic capsule and hunched over the dresser as he extracted a few drops with a miniature pipette. He squeezed the liquid into a circular depression on the left side of a small plastic tray. Spencer had seen the analysis in the field before, but its use wasn't as common as Kastle-Meyer.

Straightening to his full height, Norman discarded the

pipette and glanced to his watch. "This test looks for human glycophorin A, which is found in the membrane of red blood cells. It'll tell us whether the blood from the Kastle-Meyer test is human."

Spencer knew in his gut that the test would be positive. "How long does it take?"

"Ten minutes. The lines usually show up before then, but ten minutes is when we make the official call." He pointed to the right side of the rectangle. "It reads like a pregnancy test. Two lines mean human glycophorin A was present, one line means it wasn't."

As much as Spencer wanted to sigh or swear, he took in a deep breath to maintain his air of professionalism. "How old do you think the blood stains are?"

Norman pulled off one blue vinyl glove with a snap. "Not old. Best as I could tell, it hadn't even completely dried. Other than the blood, the shoes are spotless. We'll know more when we get them to the lab, but I think it's safe to say that no one wore them outside tonight. Not with all the rain we've had. If anyone's even worn them at all. They look brand new."

Why would Amelia buy a new pair of shoes to wear to a murder and then stash them in her closet? Along with the clothes she'd worn at the scene, the lab had taken her water-logged flats for examination. Had she stashed the Mary Janes in her apartment in case suspicion fell on her while she was still at the FBI office?

That made zero sense...unless she had an accomplice helping her out. But why, then, wouldn't she have the accomplice toss the weapon and other items into the river?

Was she playing them all?

Spencer clenched one hand into a fist and pushed aside the questions. He could try to make sense of the night's events once the forensic lab had a chance to pore over all the evidence.

When Spencer looked down to Norman's test, a rush of ice water surged through his veins. "There're two lines." The words came from between his clenched teeth.

"I see them." Norman's tone was even and cool…a reminder for Spencer to keep his composure. "Like I said, we read the results officially at ten minutes. The lines usually show up sooner, but ten minutes is standard protocol."

I don't think one of those lines is going to disappear.

Clearing his throat, Spencer kept the sentiment to himself.

"SSA Corsaw," a woman's voice called out from the doorway.

He couldn't remember the tech's name, but her golden blonde braid was familiar. She jerked a thumb over her shoulder toward the living room. "There's something out here you ought to see."

Great. What now?

He swallowed the irritable remark. "All right, I'm coming." Turning back to Norman, he waved at the dresser. "Let me know when the official results are here."

Norman pulled on a fresh pair of gloves. "Will do."

As Spencer followed the tech, she gestured to a broad-shouldered fellow with a full head of rust-brown hair. "I found this thing in the floor lamp, and Frankie helped me with it."

A growing sense of dread prickled Spencer's scalp. "What thing?"

The burly man—Rob Frankie, if Spencer's memory served him correctly—held out a sealed evidence bag that contained a device that was about half the size of a ballpoint pen. A cluster of thin wires sprouted from one end like dendrites on a neuron.

Spencer swore his heart stopped before he met the man's gray-green eyes. "Is this a camera?"

Balancing the device on his palm, Frankie prodded the rounded top with a gloved finger. "Yes. This is the lens."

The woman held out a second taped bag. "This is the battery. It was made to be easily disconnected so it could be replaced. We bagged it separately because…well…"

"Because you didn't want it to keep recording," Spencer finished for her.

"Exactly." She pointed to a pair of crime scene techs who hovered around the counter beside the stainless-steel refrigerator. "There's another camera in the kitchen, but it's attached to the outlet. Perez and Umberson are working on extracting it right now, but Frankie's the expert on these things."

Rob Frankie cleared his throat. "Well, I've worked a few scenes recently where we've found cameras like this one. These damn things are like roaches. Where there's one, there're usually plenty more that you can't see."

A surge of hope replaced Spencer's unease. "It was active when you found it? Was it recording tonight?"

Frankie rubbed his bearded chin. "It *was* functioning when Arnette found it. This model has a motion sensor, so it only captures footage when there's activity in the recording area. It's designed to minimize battery usage, but this one was wired directly into the floor lamp. The battery was just a backup in case the lamp lost power."

Spencer jabbed a finger at the spindly camera. "Where did the footage go? Do you know where it was stored?"

Turning the bag over in one hand, Frankie blew out a sigh. "It's hard to say. These things are designed to record and upload footage remotely, but I scanned the home Wi-Fi network for any recently active devices and didn't find anything other than the television, laptop, and Agent Storm's phone."

The series of cameras throughout Amelia's apartment might have been part of a security system, but if they were, why wouldn't the devices be connected to her wireless network? Moreover, why would they be hidden so thoroughly?

Spencer glanced to the mess that had *been* the floor lamp. The metal pole, all three bulbs and their shades as well as the base lay separated on the floor. "Could this have been a security system?"

When he turned back to Frankie, the man's expression had turned stony. "If you want my honest opinion, I don't think it was. I've seen plenty of home security systems in my career, and not a single one of them has been set up like this. Sometimes, parents will hook up something like this." He held up the bagged camera. "Because they want to plant the camera without their kid noticing it."

"Because they want to spy on their kid." Spencer dropped both hands to his hips. "But if someone lives alone and they want to set up a security system, why go through all the trouble of wiring a camera into the power source on your lamp?"

"Exactly." Frankie inclined his chin at the kitchen. "For the outlet camera in there, and for this one, there's no indication they've been touched in weeks, maybe months. It's all inconsistent with anything I've ever seen in terms of home security."

So much for Spencer's hope that the hidden cameras might have captured Amelia as she'd hidden the Colt in the bathroom or the shoes in her closet.

If she'd even handled the items in the first place.

With each second that passed in this damn apartment, the case took a new turn. Hidden cameras connected to a strange wireless network were less consistent with a security system and more consistent with a stalker. And if someone had been stalking Amelia, if someone had planted hidden cameras in her home, then they wouldn't have broken a sweat stashing a handgun in a vent and an unused pair of Mary Janes in the closet.

The biggest part of him was glad for the prospect of Amelia's innocence, but if she hadn't shot Ben Storey, then the murderer was still free.

A murderer who wanted to pin their crime on a federal agent.

11

With a fresh, steaming mug of coffee in one hand, Zane gave a gentle push to the glass and metal door with the other. While Zane and Cassandra had been at Amelia's apartment, Layton Redker had moved his operation back to the conference room where they'd initially gone through Ben Storey's phone. In addition to the laptop he'd used earlier, Layton had added a sleek tablet to his arsenal.

Redker was alone at the circular table, a handful of papers strewn beside his electronic devices. At the far end of the room, Cassandra had taken a seat at a cushioned leather bench beside the wall-spanning windows. One set of blinds was drawn down to the metal sill, but the lights of the city glinted through the narrow strip of glass beneath the second set.

Zane hadn't kept track of the time, but the darkness of the night sky told him that dinnertime had long since come and gone.

Not that he could conjure up much of an appetite when he knew Amelia was sitting on the precipice of a first-degree murder charge.

After watching Cassandra's interview with Amelia from behind the two-way mirror, the nagging voice of skepticism in the back of his mind had gone silent. The look on Amelia's face might not have been admissible in a court of law, but Zane knew his friend. She was as clueless about the identity of Storey's killer as the rest of them.

His certainty of her innocence may have wavered for a moment, but the more they tried to pin on Amelia, the more obvious it became that she had been set up.

The evidence they'd uncovered failed to hold up to even the slightest scrutiny. Receipts at the airport and gas station provided an accurate timeline of her arrival at the murder scene. The weapon being in Amelia's apartment proved she could not have transported it. She was with CPD until returning to the field office and hadn't left since.

Even the messages that had her name on them were too convenient to be real. What all their evidence did prove was that someone had it out for Amelia, and that brought Zane back to a topic he'd not considered.

Their first case had been hindered by a rat. One that had gone silent since. And Zane had yet to discover who that agent might be. It could stand to reason that one of the agents on this team was operating under orders from the Leóne family. And if that was true, Zane had to keep his thoughts to himself, at least until he uncovered proof.

Fortunately, Amelia had posed a game-changing question to Cassandra—a query that he had tried to articulate during the hasty search of Amelia's apartment.

How had the murder weapon wound up in her apartment?

As he stepped into the well-lit conference room, he eased the door closed behind himself. "I've got some more caffeine, and I'm ready to dive back in. Redker, did you find anything while we were gone?"

The stoic man leaned back to stretch before he brought the projector to life. "I looked through Agent Storm's phone, and now I'm just waiting for the clone of her computer's hard drive."

Zane took a seat in the open office chair at Redker's side. His pulse raced at the thought of what other damming information could have been placed on Amelia's phone. Had Ben's killer planted evidence on the mobile device like they had on her laptop? And what would the GPS monitoring tell them?

Before Zane was too tempted to lean over and shake the man, Layton pressed a key to display a map of Chicago. "The first thing I looked for on her phone was Hushed, or any sign that she'd ever installed that app. Nothing there, not even a record of the app's name in her search history. By the looks of it, she's probably never heard of it or had an interest in using their services."

Zane caught Cassandra's movement as she scooted to the edge of her seat. "The tech team says that they've already found the message thread with Storey on Agent Storm's laptop. That could be why there's no sign of it on her phone."

Redker's dark eyes flicked between the lawyer and his laptop. "Maybe. But it's an app that's supported across platforms, meaning it can be used on a PC or a smartphone. It seems odd to me that there'd be absolutely *no sign* of Hushed on her phone if she was a regular user on her computer."

"How about checking the install date for the app? Make sure it wasn't installed sometime recently."

"Yes, that is something we can check. You're thinking it was planted, right?" Redker nodded as he jotted the note down on his paper.

"We have to check out all the angles, right?" Zane watched to see if Redker's expression changed as he posed his next question. "Speaking of angles. Can we cross-reference the timestamps on Ben's phone messages with the ones on Amelia's laptop and her time logs at the office?"

A smile crossed Redker's face as he added to the list. "I like where you're going with this. We can see if any of those messages are during times of the day when Amelia would have obviously been in the office and not home on her computer, right?"

"Exactly. She can't be in two places at once, and that laptop is her personal one...for home use." Zane stared at Cassandra, watching her expression tighten as he and Redker volleyed real investigative ideas to each other.

She looked as if she were chewing on her tongue but remained quiet where she sat.

Why the hell was she so dead set on proving that Amelia had killed Ben? Over the past couple weeks, Zane had become certain that Cassandra Halcott was a cut above the average lawyer.

Many prosecutors sought easy wins to bolster their convictions. That made them more appealing to a future employer or, in some cases, the general electorate. Plenty of politicians started their careers in a courtroom.

However, rather than convictions, Cassandra sought justice. She didn't want a quick win so she could show off her resume to a high-paying law firm.

Or so Zane had thought.

Eventually, the system sank its hooks into those with even the highest sense of integrity. A swift conviction in a case as high-profile as Storey's murder could secure Cassandra's career, especially with such a sensational headline. "FBI Agent Murders Up-And-Coming Senatorial Hopeful" would undoubtedly capture the attention of mainstream media giants, thrusting Cassandra into the spotlight as a beacon of righteousness in a dark, twisted world.

Renewed determination rushed through Zane as surely as

the caffeine from his most recent cup of sludge. One way or another, he would uncover the truth. No lawyer was going to make her career on the broken back of his friend.

The light click of a mouse snapped Zane from his thoughts.

Layton Redker gestured to the screen. A red line now wove its way through part of the map. "Anyway." He zoomed in, and Zane noticed that the drawn path began at the FBI office. "I ran through the GPS of Agent Storm's phone, starting this morning at about seven."

"She lives in Lincoln Park." Zane set down his mug. "That first part of the line is her going from her apartment to the field office?"

Though the motion was slight, Redker dipped his chin. "Yes. At twelve-ten, she left the office to go to a coffee shop a few blocks away. She was gone for about twenty minutes, most of which was spent at the café. Then, she's back here until a few minutes past three when she leaves."

Zane followed the movement of the cursor as Redker followed Amelia's path northeast to Midway. He offered Redker an expectant glance. "She went to Midway to wait for her sister's flight. It was delayed because of those storms we had earlier."

"Which brings us to Agent Storm's trip to Englewood." Layton clicked on the map to highlight the newest line segment. "She left Midway at four-fifty, almost on the nose. GPS shows that the trip to the address where Storey's body was found took about forty minutes, and that included a stop at a gas station. Forensics found the receipts for fuel and a soda in Storm's car, along with a parking stub from Midway. All the timestamps match up with the statement she gave earlier. I put in a request for security camera footage from the airport and the convenience store. They've both replied already, and I ought to have the video in a few hours."

Rubbing his chin, Zane slumped back in his chair. "That corroborates everything she's told us so far."

As he held up a finger, Redker clicked over to a second map. "It does, and so does this." He waved at the screen. "This is the GPS tracking from her car. It has a built-in navigation system, and part of that is GPS to help with theft prevention."

The new path, marked in blue this time instead of red, was identical to the previous.

"See." Redker pointed to the projection. "Zero deviation. Wherever Storm and her phone went today, that's where she and her car went. Which brings me to a question that's been bothering me ever since I pulled up the location history of Agent Storm's phone."

A surge of hope rushed up to greet Zane, but he tamped the optimism down, not wanting to celebrate before victory had been achieved. "What's the question?"

Steepling his fingers, Redker tilted his head, shooting an inquisitive glance at Cassandra. "A Colt M1911 matching the suspected murder weapon was just found in Agent Storm's apartment, right?"

"Yes." Cassandra's response was a little too eager. "We brought the weapon and Agent Storm's laptop back for rush analysis."

"Okay." Redker moved the maps on the screen until they were side by side. "I don't see anywhere on either of these maps where she turned back to Lincoln Park. After Engle-wood, she went back to the FBI office, and that's where she's been ever since. Unless I'm missing something?"

The cautious optimism threatened to spill back over into Zane's otherwise grim thoughts. "No, you're not, Agent Redker. I was on video chat with her a few moments after she arrived at the house, and Chicago PD arrived at the Englewood address just a few minutes after Agent Storm.

There are plenty of officers who can account for her whereabouts in the time it took me and SSA Corsaw to get there."

"Then how in the hell did the murder weapon get back to her apartment?" A short silence followed the question as Redker's gaze shifted between Cassandra and Zane. "*She* didn't take it back there. And if you're operating under the assumption that she killed Storey and then tried to hide the Colt in her apartment, that theory falls apart here, doesn't it?"

A muscle twitched in Cassandra's jaw. "She could have had an accomplice."

"An accomplice?" Zane scoffed, not bothering to hide his annoyance at Cassandra's stubbornness. "Do we honestly think that someone as well-versed in murder investigations as Agent Storm would hand off a murder weapon to her accomplice and tell them to go hide it in her apartment?"

The prosecutor opened her mouth to respond, but Zane wasn't finished with his soapbox. He held a hand up for her to be silent as he finished.

"Look, the bathroom vent is a good hiding spot for a high school kid trying to keep their parents from finding their pot stash. But for an agent with the Federal Bureau of Investigation?" He shook his head. "Not even close. Any agent worth half their salt would have taken that Colt and chucked it into Lake Michigan."

Zane was on a roll, and if Spencer Corsaw hadn't opened the door, looking as if he had seen a ghost, Zane might have been inclined to continue.

But as the plastic blinds clattered against glass, all three of them turned their attention to the SSA.

Corsaw didn't speak until the latch had clicked into place behind him. "Agents, Counselor. We've got a new development." He fished his phone out of his pocket. "About a half hour ago, we found four of these in Agent Storm's apartment."

After a couple more taps, the SSA set his smartphone on the table and scooted the device over to Zane and Layton.

Beside an angled ruler rested a spindly device that Zane recognized right away.

A camera. Not as advanced as the tech he'd used in the CIA, but still top-of-the-line.

His tentative optimism gave way to the cold creep of dread. "Four of these?" he heard himself say.

"Yeah." Spencer hovered at the edge of the table, but Zane barely saw the man. "One in the bedroom, one in the kitchen, and two facing different angles in the living room."

Zane swallowed the bitter taste in his mouth and forced himself to turn away from the image. "Any idea how long they've been there?"

Spencer blew out a long breath. "The CSU noticed that there was a layer of dust on each of them, so they've been there for a while."

A fleeting expression of shock passed over Cassandra's face as she neared the table. "Hidden cameras? Were they part of a security system?"

Spencer crossed his arms. "We're not sure, but we don't think so. Most security systems can be traced, but so far, we haven't been able to track anything with these cameras. If they are part of a security system that Agent Storm set up, then she was the only one who monitored it."

Redker shoved the phone back across the table to Spencer. "Well, she didn't monitor it on her phone. There's nothing on the hard drive that's compatible with something like this."

As Cassandra knitted her brows together, Zane was struck with a pang of relief. Maybe the prosecutor didn't have tunnel vision after all.

She dropped both hands to her hips. "Who would set up a security system if they couldn't monitor it while away from home? What's the point of that?"

Zane clenched his jaw. He'd suppressed sarcastic remarks all night, and he figured he only had a matter of hours left before his head exploded from the effort. "Cameras like that aren't used in security systems. Those things have one purpose, spying on someone."

To Zane's continued surprise, Spencer nodded. "That's what I think. Someone's been stalking Agent Storm."

12

A melia had dozed off when she'd first been stuffed into the interview room, but after learning the suspected murder weapon had been pulled out of her bathroom vent, all hopes of sleep went right out the window.

Pacing wasn't Amelia's go-to when she was overwhelmed by anxiety, but she was surprised she hadn't worn a divot in the tile beside the table. She had no phone, no one to talk to, and no way to know when one of her colleagues might arrive to slap a pair of handcuffs on her wrists.

What was she supposed to do when there was nothing she *could* do? Sit idly by as her fate was decided?

Not like I have any other options.

She could shout at the pane of reflective glass until her voice was hoarse, but there was no guarantee she'd even be heard. Banging on it with her fists would only add "crazy" to the long list of adjectives her colleagues had most likely already assigned to her.

As she went to pick at her nail polish, she stopped herself. Save her undergarments, her clothes had all been taken by the forensic lab to test for gunshot residue and trace evidence. The burgundy lacquer was all she had from *before*.

Before any of this shit had happened.

Before an untraceable Colt M1911 had been found in her apartment before a series of text messages had made her out to be Ben Storey's mistress...

She groaned loudly in desperate frustration, listening as the sound echoed and faded as it bounced off the four gray walls. She barely knew the guy. He'd come across like a decent guy, but he certainly wasn't her type.

How could anyone think she'd go for him? For god's sake, he was a married man with two children. Of course she didn't know about the kids until they had told her. Still, though, she knew better than to deal with unavailable men. The fact that anyone in that conference room could believe otherwise was ridiculous. And it revealed so much more than she wished she had known about the people she worked with.

If she ever got out of this mess, how was she ever supposed to work with them again, let alone trust her life in their hands during dangerous missions? If they could turn on her so quickly now, who knew what they would do when the shit seriously hit the fan.

The rat she'd suspected all along had to be among them. That was the only explanation for their attempt to fast-track her to a prison cell.

Pausing at the end of her pacing path, she dragged a hand over her face and heaved an unsteady sigh. There had to be a way to prove that the messages were fake, that she hadn't actually interacted with Storey outside the FBI office.

She had no shortage of time, but anger seemed to be short-circuiting her brain. She was going insane...that was it. The walls were already closing in on her. It didn't matter what she said, anyway. If the rat wanted her blamed for

Storey's death, they could manipulate the evidence in any way they wanted to ensure she would be found guilty. Amelia wondered if she'd ever be able to leave this damn room. Maybe the FBI would imprison her here instead of at MCC Chicago.

There was no visible clock for her to agonize over the time, but she could only assume that, based on the size of her bladder, it surely must be closing in on midnight. Time passed at the same pace as a slow-motion sports replay, or a scene from *The Matrix*.

She'd never even seen those films until a couple weeks ago when Zane had brought up the franchise over their lunch break. According to him, the first movie was a sci-fi classic, and he'd been struck with disbelief when she told him she'd never seen any of the series. To make sure she wouldn't put off what he'd termed "necessary viewing," he'd penciled in a time for them to watch the film together.

Even if you don't like it, you have to watch it. You have to. It's like a piece of history at this point.

When the viewing night had rolled around, she'd been overcome with a brand of nervousness she hadn't experienced in years—the brand that came with clammy palms and a stomach full of butterflies.

For better or for worse, however, Hup had engaged her stealth mode and pawed a cup of fruit punch off the coffee table…directly onto Zane's stocking feet.

Before the bright red liquid had splashed onto the floor and her guest's legs, Amelia had been busy working up the courage to scoot closer to her handsome friend. Hup's antics had snapped her back to reality, and she'd spent the rest of the evening at a safely platonic distance from Zane.

In retrospect, Hup must have been watching out for Amelia's best interests. She could only imagine how much worse she'd feel right now if she'd given in to the stupid flutter in her stomach.

She paced to the door, did an about-face, and strode back to the mirror, being careful to avoid her own reflection. She didn't want to see if she looked as bad as she felt. She also didn't want to think about who was on the other side of the glass watching her every move.

As she did another about-face that would have made her bootcamp drill instructor proud, the handle on the door rattled. Amelia's stomach twisted as cold anticipation rushed through her veins.

Squaring her shoulders, she made her best effort to steel herself as Spencer Corsaw stepped into the room. When Zane appeared after the SSA, she almost faltered.

Almost.

"Agent Storm." Spencer's greeting was crisp and professional, but the twinge of dismay from earlier was gone. He waved at the table. "We've got a new development. Have a seat."

Great. What is it now? Did you find Storey's severed dick in my freezer?

She bit her tongue and took a few steps to sit in the rickety chair.

As the door latched, Zane took his spot beside Spencer on the other side of the table. Try as she might, Amelia couldn't discern a hint of anger or finality in his expression.

Were they about to charge her, and was Zane merely content to have an answer for Ben Storey's death?

Amelia set both hands on her lap so the men couldn't see her dig her nails into her palm. "Let's hear this new development."

Spencer tapped his phone a few times before sliding the device to Amelia. "Do you recognize this?"

The last time someone asked me that, they were showing me a picture of the murder weapon. She fixed Spencer with a glare before turning her focus to the screen.

She recognized the rich wooden background as the surface of her coffee table, but the small device beside an angled ruler was less familiar. Her pulse pounded in her ears as she leaned closer for a better look.

It was hard to judge at first, but she spotted a tiny camera lens.

She zoomed in on the image. "Is this a camera? Where did you find this? What kind of *development* is this, anyway?"

Spencer cocked an eyebrow as he reached for his phone. "You don't recognize it? It's not part of a security system you might have installed in your apartment?"

Every cell in Amelia's body went cold, and the edges of her vision turned gray as the enormity of the questions hit her like a blow. "What? No! A...a security system? What *is* this damn thing? You found it in my apartment?"

Palms flat, Zane rested his hands on the table. "They found it in your apartment, yes. One in the bedroom, two in the living room, and one in the kitchen. It's a video camera. It's tiny but captures high-quality footage. This model can connect to a wireless network to send the footage back to wherever it's stored. Usually on a cloud-based server, but it's also capable of uploading the feed to a physical storage device like a hard drive."

Any hope of maintaining an appearance of neutrality took a running leap from the nearest fourteenth-story window. "Someone's been *watching* me? They've been watching me sleep!"

The night of *The Matrix* flashed through Amelia's mind, and she now knew without a doubt that Hup had been watching out for her best interests. Whoever was behind the cameras would have had a front-row seat to...whatever she'd wanted to do with Zane. Or to her failed attempt to sidle up next to him. She wasn't sure which would have been worse.

Spencer took his phone back and tapped on the screen. "There's one more thing. Something else we found in your closet."

Probably the fortune that D.B. Cooper stole. Or maybe the Ark of the Covenant. At this point, who the hell knows?

As the SSA slid the device back to her, Amelia braced herself. Rather than a musty old stack of twenty-dollar bills from an age-old plane hijacking or a mythical religious artifact, she was face-to-face with a photo of a pair of shoes she'd never seen in her life.

Rubbing her temple, she shoved the phone back to Spencer. "A pair of Mary Janes? Do I even want to know?"

To her relief, Spencer pocketed his cell. With any luck, there were no more surprise items for her to identify. "Luminol revealed a smudge of blood near the toe of the left shoe, and a field test confirmed that it's human. We've expedited DNA analysis to determine if the blood belongs to Ben Storey. Other than the blood, the shoes looked new."

Amelia kept a slew of four-letter words to herself as she stared at the man who held her future in his hands. "They aren't mine." She turned to Zane. "Palmer, have you ever seen me wearing Mary Janes?"

"Nope." Zane's response was immediate. "Flats, Vans, and that one pair of heels you wear sometimes. That's about it."

"I don't wear Mary Janes, Corsaw." Amelia glowered at him. "I wear a size ten women's. Do you know how silly Mary Janes look when they're that damn big? Or how ridiculous they'd look on my giant feet?" She held her foot up as if that was all the evidence they would ever possibly need. Realizing how ridiculous she looked, she slammed it back down on the floor. "Run whatever tests you need to run on those shoes. I've never worn them. And something tells me that if a person broke into my apartment to plant four hidden cameras, they wouldn't have had much of a problem shoving a pair of shoes into the back of my closet."

Spencer lifted both hands in a placating gesture that made her want to scream. "I know. And they wouldn't have had any issues planting that Colt in your vent, either."

Amelia almost leapt out of her chair, and her heart clamored against her ribs. "Wait. Wait, are you...are you saying that...?" She paused to swallow before her voice could rise another octave. "You finally believe me? That I didn't kill Storey?"

Spencer dropped his hands. "What I think is irrelevant. Right now, the evidence indicates that someone's been stalking you. All tests for gunshot residue have been negative, and if ballistics confirm that the Colt is the murder weapon, then we have even more reason to believe someone's setting you up. Your phone and your car's GPS corroborate your route to Englewood, and Redker should have security camera verification soon."

'Bout freaking time!

They *had* listened to her. But as the weight of a murder charge lifted from her shoulders, another equally oppressive one came rushing right back down on them. She had a stalker. A stalker who'd been watching her most private moments.

"Storm?" Zane's voice pulled her back to reality before her anxiety ran away with her again. "Over the past few weeks, have you noticed anyone following you? Any strange vehicles that might've been around your apartment building, or any people lingering in the area who shouldn't be there?"

Tilting her head back to face the ceiling, Amelia let out a quiet sigh as she racked her memories. A new neighbor had moved in above her, but their arrival had been unremarkable. The young couple was far too busy with their infant daughter to take much interest in Amelia's existence.

Otherwise, who was there?

Joseph.

The man's pale eyes and self-assured smile lit up in her mind.

Joseph Larson, an FBI agent and a man who'd tried and failed to blackmail Amelia into sex. Had he killed Ben and then framed Amelia as some twisted method of revenge? Larson was prideful, almost to a fault, but to imagine him murdering a city councilman in cold blood just to get under Amelia's skin was as ridiculous as it was terrifying.

For all Amelia knew, Larson was standing on the other side of the two-way mirror right now. If she spilled her guts to Spencer and Zane in this damn room, and if Joseph caught wind of the confession, she didn't want to know what else he might have up his sleeve.

She bit her lower lip.

That's ridiculous. If Joseph was going to kill anyone, he'd kill me. If he wanted to get to me, he wouldn't do it by killing Ben Storey. Not someone that high profile. Joseph's not an idiot. He wouldn't target Ben. He'd target someone close to me. He'd target...

Her heart climbed into her throat.

Zane.

Resting a hand on her stomach, she shook her head. She didn't trust herself to vocalize a response.

Even before Amelia learned that Joseph was a scumbag, he and Zane had never gotten along. When she'd asked Zane about the unspoken spat between the two of them, he'd surmised that their mutual disdain was due to a lack of respect. Zane assumed Joseph thought less of him because he'd never been in the military, and at the time, the observation had made perfect sense. Now, however, Amelia wasn't so sure. Maybe Joseph viewed Zane as a rival. A roadblock to his ultimate goal of screwing her.

And if he was behind the cameras, then he'd seen how she and Agent Palmer behaved around one another outside of work.

Still, Joseph's involvement was a massive *if*. The man might not have a grasp on the concept of consent, but the leap to cold-blooded murderer was closer to a canyon than a jump.

Her suspicion was premature, and as frazzled as she was, she had the presence of mind to keep the paranoid thought to herself. Provided she wasn't charged and tossed in holding before the night's end, she'd delve into the possibility of Joseph's involvement in her own time.

"...received any threatening messages online? Any abnormalities on social media?" She'd missed the first part of Spencer's question, but she didn't have to ask for a repeat to be certain of the answer.

Amelia cleared her throat. "No. Nothing. Some new neighbors moved in upstairs, but there's nothing off about them."

But after tonight, they'll sure as hell think there's something off about me.

A twinge of concern softened Zane's crisp, professional expression as he fiddled with his tie. "We'll look into them. The tech lab is working on tracing whatever they can find from those cameras, but there isn't much for them to go on. Even if they find where the video feed was being stored or uploaded, there's no guarantee they'll be able to tie that to a suspect."

"Right." Amelia threaded her fingers together in her lap so she wouldn't be tempted to fidget with her hair or her gray sweatshirt. "So, what's next? Am I still a suspect, or am I free to go?"

Spencer scratched the side of his nose. "A suspect? Tentatively, no. Not anymore. There's enough evidence to suggest that you're being stalked and potentially set up. But..." he held up an index finger, "I need you to stay in this building until the lab is finished with a few more analyses. Those shoes, for instance. And the Colt. We need to get a better understanding of what we're dealing with."

Before she could stop herself, Amelia heaved a sigh and slumped down in her uncomfortable chair. She didn't always have a flair for the dramatic, but the moment of obvious irritability had been well-earned. "When can I leave this damn room? I don't have my phone. Don't have my purse. I don't even have a deck of cards or a Rubik's cube or a Sudoku puzzle." She made a show of looking around the room. "There isn't even a *clock* in here. I haven't eaten since I was at Midway. I'm hungry, I've got to pee, and I'm losing my mind in here."

"I know, Storm." Spencer almost looked sorrowful. "But the U.S. Attorney's office would rip me a new one if I let you leave right now. You're not a suspect, not to us, but you are still involved, and we need you here if anything else crops up. I can't let you leave, but we can feed you and set you up in a room that's a little more comfortable than this one."

She forced an agreeable smile to her lips. "Okay. That's fine. Somewhere with a seat that has a little cushion."

Zane let out a quiet snort. "That's no shit."

As the tension dissipated from Spencer's face, Amelia had to do a double take. Apparently, she wasn't the only person in the Chicago Field Office who was placated by Zane's commentary.

The SSA rapped his knuckles on the tabletop. "That's fair. Come on, Storm. We'll find somewhere a little more comfortable for you to wait while the lab finishes a few things."

Her stomach twisted at the thought of what the forensic team might still have left to analyze.

Spencer and Zane seemed amenable right now, but Amelia had already seen how quickly the atmosphere could change.

13

P rying open the glass door to the forensic lab, Spencer
stepped aside to make room for Agent Palmer. He'd
received a message only minutes earlier to advise that ballistics had been completed on the weapon found in Amelia's
apartment. Cassandra and Layton had stayed behind in the
conference room, and Zane had accompanied Spencer
downstairs.

Not that a confirmation that the Colt was the murder
weapon meant much. They'd all but ruled out the possibility
that Amelia had fired the forty-caliber handgun, much less
rushed home to stuff the damn thing in her bathroom vent.
The possibility of an accomplice hadn't been dismissed
completely, but based on what they'd learned so far, a helper
wasn't likely.

Once Spencer had found a suitably comfortable room for
Agent Storm, Redker and Palmer had caught him up on the
GPS tracking that had corroborated Amelia's path
throughout the day. The Bureau had received an update from
the office of the medical examiner, and Dr. Sabrina Ackerly

had confirmed her initial estimate of Ben Storey's time of death.

Ben had died between four-thirty and five-thirty, and the Chicago PD had arrived at the scene at 5:44. According to each of the officers and the sergeant, Ben's blood had already soaked into the carpet and coagulated.

Considering that the GPS from Storm's phone put her on the road from Midway to Englewood from 4:50 to 5:39—including a stop at a convenience store at exactly 5:22—there was no possible way she could have killed Ben *and* rushed home to hide the murder weapon.

The time of Ben's arrival in Englewood would have been easy enough to establish, but the man had gone through some trouble to disable GPS tracking on his car and his cell. Spencer couldn't say he blamed the guy. Storey's level of public recognition came with its fair share of pitfalls, especially in the digital age.

Obviously...considering how he ended up.

Spencer let out a quiet snort at his own thought. Refocusing himself on the task at hand, he stepped into the sleek ballistics lab behind Palmer.

A familiar woman with dark curls and a white lab coat rose to greet them. "Agent, SSA. Evening. That was fast." She picked up a manila folder from the table in the center of the room. "Here. This is everything in print, including the photos."

Spencer stepped forward to accept the file. "Thanks. We appreciate you prioritizing this case. I'm sure there are plenty of others that need your attention."

She tapped a keyboard at the end of the table. "I get it. Ben Storey's a big name in this city." Her tone told him that, though she might have understood the reason for the expedited review, she wasn't convinced that a big name ought to take precedence over less famous victims.

Though Spencer was tempted to pointedly advise her that a federal agent's livelihood was also on the line, he bit his tongue. "The bullets recovered from the scene were a match?"

"They were." With a couple mouse clicks, she turned one of the two monitors to face them. "The magnified image of the bullet from the scene is on the left. Then a test round fired from the Colt M1911 on the right." She hovered one finger over the markings on each side-by-side image. "The striations are identical. It's not my business to know where that Colt came from, but I can tell you that it's definitely your murder weapon."

As Spencer's pulse rushed in his ears, his desire to leave the room morphed into an all-consuming need. "All right. Thanks again." He turned to Zane Palmer and tilted his head at the door.

Zane looked decidedly confused by the interaction as he followed Spencer back into the hall without another word.

Neither of them spoke until the silver doors of the elevator were closed.

Leaning against the stainless-steel rail, Palmer crossed both arms over his pricey suit jacket. "What was that about? You in some kind of spat with the ballistics lab?"

Spencer would much rather not have to divulge any of his personal stories, but there was no escaping the conversation, trapped as they were in the small elevator cab. "No, but I know her." He let out a loud sigh. "I've worked with her before, and she's my ex-wife's sister-in-law. She's been married to Meghan's brother for sixteen years."

Palmer's brows quirked up. "Oh, really? Guess that explains why she was so happy to see us."

"That's what happens when you meet your spouse through your workplace." Spencer shot Palmer a knowing look.

Though Spencer had intended to tell Palmer he'd noticed the close friendship Zane had developed with Amelia, he thought better of it. Zane often rubbed him the wrong way with his overbearing Boy-Scout-like personality, but nothing seemed to escape that man's shrewd attention.

Palmer scratched the side of his face. "Speaking of workplace...partnerships. You know our prosecutor is dating Joseph Larson, right?"

"What?" Spencer choked on the word. "Why...would you tell me that?"

Amusement flashed across Palmer's face. "Just making conversation."

He hated being right sometimes. *Nothing* got past Zane. Not even the slight interest Spencer had taken in Cassandra.

During one of the lawyer's frequent visits to the FBI office over the past few weeks, she and Spencer had engaged in lengthy conversations that had nothing to do with work. They'd recently spent forty-five minutes discussing the merits of classic horror over the more modern jump-scare style movies.

Cassandra had struck Spencer as a friendly, albeit introverted, woman with a host of geeky interests. She *hadn't* struck him as the type of girl who'd entertain the likes of Joseph Larson.

Not that Spencer had an issue with Larson, but they *had* worked together at the same office for close to a decade. Considering that the majority of their tenure had been spent in the same department, it was no small wonder that Spencer had become at least somewhat familiar with Larson's personal life.

There was a reason the man had two ex-wives, and Spencer doubted it had anything to do with the women.

Tapping the manila folder against his leg, Spencer made a valiant effort to steer his thoughts to a different subject. To barometric pressure, the vastness of space, or that physics exam he'd flunked in college.

No matter how hard he tried, his mind kept looping back to Zane's offhand comment.

A few seconds passed before Spencer asked with hushed disbelief, "Larson? She's dating Larson?"

Zane held up both hands as if he was showing Spencer that he was unarmed. "Hey, I didn't introduce them. Don't look at me like that. I'm just reporting what I've seen."

Spencer let his head loll backward. "I thought Larson had a thing for Storm. What the hell happened to that?"

From the corner of his eye, Spencer didn't miss the way Zane's posture stiffened. "Is there any attractive woman Larson hasn't had a thing for? I don't like to shame people for stuff like that, but Larson doesn't exactly keep his relationships with women on the straight and narrow, you know? If he hasn't cheated on any of his girlfriends in the last three years, I'd eat my badge."

"As much as I'd like to see you try that, I know a sucker's bet when I hear one."

Zane shrugged.

The noncommittal gesture almost convinced Spencer he'd imagined the moment of tension.

Almost.

There was more to the story than Palmer's casual dismissal, but the inquiry would have to wait for another day. As the elevator car stopped, Spencer pulled his wandering mind back to the present.

He had a job to do, and that job had become markedly more complicated in the last couple hours. Dealing with the fact that Amelia Storm was a murderer wouldn't have been easy, and he was relieved that they'd established a solid basis to argue her innocence.

Now, however, they had to find whoever had actually

shot Ben Storey before they killed again. Not to mention the murderer's attempt to frame one of the FBI's own.

As Spencer stepped into the conference room after Zane, he made a point to avoid Cassandra's curious gaze.

Raising the manila folder for the group to see, Spencer pulled out the chair next to Layton Redker and dropped to sit. "Ballistics results. Analysis of the bullets found at the crime scene match test shots fired from the Colt M1911 found in Agent Storm's apartment."

Cassandra scooted closer to the table. "It's the murder weapon? And what about the shoes found in Agent Storm's closet?"

Layton Redker flipped open the folder to reveal a glossy print of the handgun and accompanying silencer. "If someone planted the murder weapon in her apartment, it's not a stretch to imagine they planted a pair of shoes, Counselor."

Before Cassandra could offer a rebuttal, Spencer interjected. "Agent Redker is right. We have a parking stub and security camera footage that put Agent Storm at Midway until she left at 4:51. There's also a receipt and footage that places her at a convenience store at 5:22. According to her own account, which is corroborated by the GPS from her car and phone, she got to the scene right around five-forty."

"And the Chicago Police Department got there a couple minutes later." The matter-of-fact twinge in Zane Palmer's voice made Spencer glad he was no longer playing devil's advocate. "They were responding to a call they got at about five-thirty. Someone reported..." Palmer frowned and reached for the photo of the Colt.

A muscle beneath Spencer's eye twitched. This case was going to kill him. "Reported what?"

Palmer held up the picture like he was a kid at show-and-tell. "The reporting officer, Cynthia McAdam, stated that she was responding to a call of shots fired." He tapped the silencer in the photo. "That seem weird to anyone else?"

"Shit." Despite Spencer's effort to maintain professionalism, the word slipped out all the same. "The suppressor. The killer used a damn silencer, and someone still reported gunshots."

"The sergeant said it was an anonymous call." Palmer waved the print for emphasis. "Unless the caller was sitting in the next room when Storey was shot, there's no way they heard anything."

"We'll get the call from the CPD and see what we can learn from it." Leaning back in his chair, Spencer rubbed his chin. He was confident in the decision he was about to make, but his confidence did little to allay his concern about the shit fest that might follow. "Agent Storm didn't have anything to do with this."

He was prepared for a protest from the Assistant U.S. Attorney, but she seemed lost in thought.

"I agree." Layton Redker shuffled through a few more pages in the ballistics report. "I've been through her phone, and there's no sign of the Hushed app. No sign of any interaction with Storey, either. Not even a Google search in her browser history. Just lots of text messages about…food. Lots of cat pictures. Not much else."

Pressing her lips together, Cassandra looked from Layton to Spencer.

"Counselor." Nervousness clawed at Spencer's thoughts, but he refused to let the anxiety take hold. "We're cutting Amelia Storm loose. As far as the Bureau is concerned, she's no longer a suspect. Speak now or forever hold your peace."

The room descended into silence for a beat before Cassandra replied. "Okay. Make sure she stays in the city. She might not be a suspect, but she's still considered a witness."

In spite of the weight that lifted from Spencer's shoulders at the lawyer's concession, he couldn't shake the feeling that he'd completed one rat race just to stumble into another.

If Amelia Storm had been in the killer's sights before, Spencer doubted their interest would wane just because the Bureau eliminated her as a suspect.

They had to find Storey's killer before they could do any more damage.

14

The creak of a door jerked Amelia from the edge of sleep. At least this go-around, she'd been moved to a room reserved for witnesses and their families. A room with a cushioned loveseat and no two-way mirror. Though she was still freezing her ass off, the new nap location was a vast improvement.

As the windowless door swung inward, Amelia blinked to focus her vision on the visitor.

"Hey." Zane's face was devoid of the grim finality she'd seen earlier in the night. Now, he just looked...tired. Like he was the one desperate for sleep.

Amelia rubbed her eyes as she propped herself to sit upright. "Hey. What's the news?"

He reached into his tailored suit jacket to retrieve a familiar smartphone. "It's good this time. Your phone was cloned, and forensics gave the green light to return it to you. Should be nice and squeaky clean after they went over it."

"It wasn't dirty." Amelia's tone was flat as she accepted the device. "But thank you. Does this mean I can leave now?"

Stuffing one hand into the pocket of his slacks, he rubbed his forehead with the other. "Yes, but…"

Amelia pinned Zane with an expectant stare. "But?"

Blowing out a heavy sigh, he plopped down beside her on the loveseat. "But forensics has your car. You're not a suspect anymore, but they're sweeping it for any other piece of evidence the killer might have planted. And there are still a few techs at your apartment. I think they're trying to make sure there aren't any more hidden cameras."

Amelia's stomach clenched. She'd almost forgotten about the damn cameras. "Great. That's just great. Maybe one of them can tuck me in."

With a snort of laughter, Zane squeezed her shoulder. "I'm sure they would if you asked nicely, but since your cat is already at my place, and I have a spare bedroom." He made a show of weighing his hands. "You can stay with me if you want to. Unless you're really set on having one of the techs tuck you in tonight. Which I can understand."

Amelia gave him a playful shove. She avoided physical contact with almost every other human on the planet, but she'd become accustomed to the closeness around Zane. In fact, she enjoyed it. "I think I can do without it. I'll take that spare bedroom."

Maybe you can tuck me in instead.

She bit her tongue to keep from laughing aloud at the silly thought. Apparently, the overwhelming relief of being eliminated as a murder suspect had come with a wave of giddiness.

Clapping both hands, Zane angled his head toward the door. "Okay. Let's get the hell out of here. It's," he checked his watch, "almost quarter after midnight. Wow, that explains why I've been yawning so much."

Amelia rose to her feet and stretched both arms above her head until she felt a light pop in her lower back. "I guess that explains why I was about to fall asleep again. Either that or I've got hypothermia."

He flashed her a contemplative glance and opened the door. "That's possible. The temperature in here *is* about the same as a meat locker."

Amelia plucked at the gray, hooded sweatshirt she'd been given when her clothes were taken by the lab. "This thing isn't anywhere near as warm as it looks, either. I miss my jacket."

At the mention of her wardrobe trouble, Zane's shoulders seemed to sag for a split-second. Wordlessly, he turned off the light and followed her into the hall. "We can stop by on our way out. They should be done with most of your stuff by now. Corsaw put a rush on anything he could."

As they walked to the nearest elevator, Amelia noticed for the first time that an air of guilt hung over Zane like a shroud. The elevator doors slid closed, and though she wanted to ask what was on his mind, she clenched and unclenched one hand to stave off the burning curiosity.

Why would he feel guilty? She knew damn well he hadn't planted the Colt M1911 in her bathroom vent.

Their conversation was limited to small talk as they made the side trip to the forensic lab to collect Amelia's personal effects. The majority of the items from her handbag had been processed, as well as her clothes and shoes. After Amelia unceremoniously crammed the slacks and dress shirt into her purse, she and Zane set off for the parking garage.

Her apartment was their first stop. Fortunately, at the late hour, the roads were mostly clear, and the trip went quickly.

The short drive was especially fortunate, considering the entire journey was made in silence. For seventeen minutes, they merely listened to a collection of songs that featured frantic guitar riffs and thunderous bass lines. Amelia didn't mind the music, but her anxiety mounted as each note rang out over the Acura's speakers.

By the time Zane shifted the car into park, Amelia's jaw ached from how tightly she'd clamped her teeth together.

Maybe Zane would renege on his offer to let her sleep in the spare room, leaving her to spend the rest of the damn night obsessing over what had led him to the decision. Tomorrow, perhaps, she'd wake up in the shambles of her apartment to a text message advising that he'd commandeered her cat.

Hup, you traitor.

Her heart ached at even the imagined betrayal. She had no earthly idea how she'd handle a bona fide stab in the back like that.

Shaking herself from the unsettling thoughts, Amelia shoved open the passenger's side door. She was prepared to march up to the second floor by herself, but to her surprise— and relief—Zane stepped out of the car and straightened his suit jacket.

He followed her through the damp courtyard, past the glass double doors, and up a flight of carpeted stairs. As they neared her apartment, he spoke for the first time in what felt like a lifetime. "Um, before you go in there," he waved to the door, "they took a lot of shit apart, and there may or may not be a few holes in the drywall that weren't there before."

Amelia groaned. "You know, I can't really say I'm surprised. I've been on the other end of enough warrants to know that most of the places look like a damn war zone when we're through with them." She'd had ample time alone to craft a mental visual of the damage that had been done to her home, but she left off the glum sentiment.

There was a distinct possibility that Zane's bizarre, downtrodden demeanor was linked to Amelia's remarks about her predicament. All she wanted was to make light of the situation so she could laugh instead of burst into tears, but she reminded herself that she wasn't the only one who felt some kind of way about what had happened so far that night.

A twinge of Zane's usual good humor brightened his otherwise stoic face. "If it makes you feel any better, a lot of it was done after they found the first camera. They wanted to make sure they got all of them."

Right. The fucking cameras.

Perhaps her mind was making an effort to block out the knowledge that she had a stalker, and that was why she kept forgetting about the damn things.

Swallowing the bile that threatened to crawl up the back of her throat, Amelia shoved open the heavy door.

As her gaze fell on the mostly undisturbed foyer, she came close to convincing herself that Zane had exaggerated. The pile of mail on the table beneath the hooks for her keys was a mess, but at least the letters and bills hadn't been put through a shredder.

But when she emerged at the end of the short hall, the illusion shattered like a pane of glass in a cheesy action flick.

"Agent Palmer." A familiar man with neatly combed hair and piercing blue eyes stepped out from behind the granite bar. "Agent Storm. What can I do for you?"

Zane scratched his temple. "Just a quick stop for Agent Storm to grab some of her things. We'll be out of your hair in a couple minutes."

Though she managed an absent nod of agreement, Amelia barely heard the men.

Amelia had always prided herself on maintaining cleanliness and organization wherever she lived, even in a military barracks overseas. The trait had been passed down from her mother, though tidiness wasn't a strong suit for either of her siblings.

Now, as she surveyed the chaotic disarray that had over-taken her living room and kitchen, she wondered why she'd ever bothered cleaning in the first place.

The FBI had pulled all the books from the two shelves to either side of the entertainment stand, and they'd discon-nected the gaming console she'd taken to calling her "Netflix machine." All the cables rested lengthwise beside the base of the television. The few decorative items, including a twenty-year-old wooden Maneki-Neko her father had bought for her while he was stationed in Japan, were lined up behind the cords.

Any semblance of organization ended there. The rest of the room was, as Zane had said, a war zone. In fact, Amelia was sure she'd seen tidier combat zones.

A plentiful assortment of tools—most of which belonged to Amelia—were scattered over the breakfast bar. Canisters of flour and sugar had been emptied into the trash, and dust from ruined drywall coated the granite countertop beside the kitchen sink.

As if she'd been struck by lightning, her entire body went hot. Had they thought that she kept another murder weapon hidden in a plastic container of dry oatmeal?

When she went to replace all the pantry items that had been ruined, she fully intended to send the FBI an invoice for the cost.

At least they hadn't felt the need to break anything.

Well, nothing aside from the damn walls. And, by proxy, Amelia's security deposit.

The pounding of her pulse coupled with the churning sensation in her stomach. This was her apartment, but at that moment, she wanted to be far away from the cursed place. Far away from where *someone* had watched her sleep. From where they'd studied her while she'd cooked or while she'd lounged on the couch to binge a television show.

"Are you okay?" Zane's quiet voice cut through the spiral of paranoia like the glow of a lighthouse to a wayward ship.

With a steadying breath, she turned to him. "Honestly? I've been better."

"I can tell. You look like you just stumbled out of a North Vietnamese jungle after the Tet Offensive in 1968."

Amelia blinked a few times. "That was...really specific. But not inaccurate. Thanks, I guess?"

He grinned. "I don't know where that came from. I'm getting tired, and you know I say weird shit when I'm tired." He waved a dismissive hand. "Anyway, Norman gave the all clear to get whatever you need. He and Rob Frankie are just wrapping things up."

Amelia had been so engrossed with the disheveled state of her home that she hadn't even heard the back-and-forth between Zane and the lead forensic technician.

After ten years in the military, an invasion of privacy wasn't a foreign concept to Amelia. As far as she was concerned, there were no parts of her day-to-day life that warranted secrecy, anyway. She had her fair share of secrets about her past relationship with the D'Amato family—not to mention her *brother's* dealings with Alex Passarelli or whoever in the hell had hired Trevor to search for Alex's little sister, Gianna.

Midway down the hall, she almost froze as a new wave of disquiet rose up to smack her in the face.

Did Alex plant the cameras?

No, she couldn't picture him stooping to the level of a common creeper. His father, Luca Passarelli, was a different story.

If she learned tomorrow that Luca had been spying on her, she wouldn't be at all surprised.

When did I get on so many people's bad sides? I've only been back in this city for less than eight months.

She could contemplate the unsettling number of possibilities after she escaped the apartment. For the time being, she'd focus on getting to a warm shower and a soft bed.

One thing at a time, Amelia. One foot in front of the other. Luca Passarelli and Joseph Larson and any other pervy men you know will still be here for you to worry about tomorrow.

Before her overactive imagination could conjure up another nightmare to ruminate over, she fished a backpack out of her closet and set about prepping for her stay with Zane.

Hopefully, no one would plant hidden cameras to record her while she was at his place.

Unless someone already has.

Gritting her teeth, she stuffed three pairs of socks into the bag. Her sense of organization long since destroyed, she didn't make note of what she grabbed. As long as she had at least one of each article of clothing, she'd be fine. If her stay lasted longer than her supplies, she'd come back to restock.

Though she was by herself in the bedroom, the unsettling sensation of eyes on the back of her head was relentless. She could have sworn a stalker lurked in the shadows, following each of her movements as she fought to keep her head level.

Stop it!

She was driving herself crazy.

With her military and FBI training, Amelia considered herself to be a strong person, and she hated how spooked she was right then.

Her gaze fell onto the clothes she'd worn the night she'd gone to Larson's home. She turned away from them, deciding to toss them in the trash later. She didn't want to remember anything about that night.

She'd intended to keep the incident with Joseph to herself. Even in her own head, she hated to admit that she'd fallen for Joseph's ploy. That she'd come closer than she'd like to admit to—even to herself—to screwing him. In fact, she'd almost allowed him to blackmail her into climbing into his bed.

Almost? The tactic *had* worked, just not in the way Joseph had wanted. Instead of taking what many people would have called the easy way out of his clutches, Amelia had been fully prepared to go to prison.

Her secret hope had been that the bastard would quit his job and drop off the face of the planet, but now she wasn't quite so keen on the idea. At least if he was at the Chicago Field Office, she could keep tabs on him.

However, her ability to monitor him was a two-way street. If he was close, then *he* could stalk *her* too.

By the time she'd closed the zipper of the overstuffed backpack, she knew what she had to do.

RUNNING the fingers of one hand through his still-damp hair, Zane slumped down in his cushioned seat at the end of the couch. He usually showered in the morning before he left for work, but after such an eventful night, warm water and fresh soap to cleanse away the stress of the day was exactly what he'd needed. As Zane glanced to the closed door across from the second bedroom, he caught the faint scent of fruity shampoo.

Guilt over doubting Amelia when he'd first seen the messages on Ben Storey's phone still nibbled at the back of Zane's mind. On the trip to her apartment, the sense of remorse had been so thorough that he'd spent the duration searching for a suitable apology.

Hey, I know you're pretty much my only friend in this city. Sorry I thought you were a secret scumbag who had an affair with a father of two. Sorry my stupid caveman brain had me convinced we were a thing just because we had a moment *that one time. We good?*

He snorted and rubbed his forehead. There were times, however infrequent, when honesty was *not* the best policy. Zane wasn't one to rush to judgment often, but he'd let his emotions get the better of him. In a normal case, he'd be disappointed in himself. However, this went beyond the norm, and his so-called "decision" had cast his friend in a truly negative light. Ashamed couldn't accurately describe how low he felt.

He couldn't be sure how long his thoughts wandered down the bizarre road of introspection and guilt. When he returned to the present, golden light from the bathroom doorway fell along the dark hardwood floor.

As a familiar longhaired calico trotted into the hall, he almost had to do a double take. Zane hadn't lived with a pet since high school, and the sight of a cat in his place was as foreign as a woman showering in his spare bathroom. Any woman, other than a relative, who showered in his apartment was also sleeping in his bed.

"Dammit, Hup." Amelia emerged just after her cat.

Zane pushed himself to sit straight as she came into view. Her dark, caramel-tipped hair hung in long, ropy strands, and damp splotches darkened the back of her blue t-shirt. A pair of black running shorts revealed more of her shapely legs than he'd seen since their undercover venture to a nightclub called Evoked.

Before his eyes could linger, he forced himself to look at Hup.

Flattening her orange and black ears, Hup increased her pace until she was at the edge of the coffee table. At the lessened distance, Zane noticed the elastic hair tie in the cat's mouth.

"Your cat steals your stuff?" With a quick glance to

Amelia, he hunched forward and extended a hand toward Hup. "C'mere, kitty. Give me that."

Tail swishing back and forth, Hup darted back to Amelia.

Amelia blew a raspberry as the calico disappeared into the gloom of the bedroom. "She can be a real dick."

The deadpan way Amelia had delivered the insult sent Zane into a fit of laughter. All cats were dicks in their own special way, and Hup made sure they all remembered it. "Oh, I know. I've got a pair of pink socks from the fruit punch she spilled all over me when we were watching *The Matrix*."

What he hadn't told Amelia—and never intended to reveal—was that he'd had an ulterior motive that night. Sure, he wanted to see if she'd actually sit down and watch the sci-fi classic, but he'd finally worked up the gumption to give himself the green light to make a move.

Nervousness wasn't a hurdle he often had to overcome when interacting with women who'd caught his interest, but Amelia was a different story. She'd already been subjected to the unwanted advance of one male coworker, and as her friend, the last thing he'd wanted was to be the second man from the FBI office to make her uncomfortable.

A whiff of strawberry-coconut shampoo drifted over to him as Amelia dropped onto the center cushion of the sectional couch. "You know, it was weird. She'd never really knocked over *full* cups before. She loved to knock them over when they were empty, but she'd leave them alone if they were full."

Zane let himself slide back down into the corner where the sofa met the chaise. "Maybe she just hates fruit punch. Or maybe she hates me."

Amelia rested a hand over her heart as if the suggestion had offended her. "She does *not* hate you. It was my drink. She was being a jackass. Just cat stuff, you know. Probably because we weren't paying enough attention to her."

Or because she knew what I was trying to do.

The thought made Zane feel like he needed another shower. He'd never so much as entertained the idea of doing anything—*anything*—with a woman unless he had her enthusiastic consent, but the knowledge did little to put him at ease when he considered that night.

Maybe Amelia was right, and Hup didn't hate him. The cat was merely ensuring *he* didn't make an ass out of himself.

He bit his tongue to keep from groaning aloud.

Tucking one leg beneath herself, Amelia cleared her throat, breaking the peculiar blanket of silence that had fallen over them. "I…I have something I need to tell you."

Though Zane didn't recall initiating the movement, he sat up stick straight. Those few words never heralded good news, no matter who spoke them. "Something to tell me?" He pronounced each word as if he was reading them off for contestants at a spelling bee.

Eyes widening, Amelia waved off his concern. "Oh, shit. No, not that. No, I'm sorry." She pinched the bridge of her nose and let out a long breath. "Sorry, that's not how I meant for that to sound. That came across all wrong. I *do* want to tell you something, but it has nothing to do with…that. With Ben Storey, or that whole…*situation.*"

His breath came a little easier. "Okay. That's all right. It happens to the best of us."

Only a split-second passed before Amelia spoke again, but in that sliver of time, Zane's mind raced through every conclusion.

Was she sick? Had she been diagnosed with a terminal illness or a debilitating autoimmune disorder? The thought made his heart sink, but he kept his face carefully blank.

Had she decided to transfer to a different field office to get away from Joseph Larson and the Leóne family? He couldn't find it within himself to fault her if she had, and he'd prefer the sudden move to cancer or lupus.

They lived in the digital age, and he was sure they'd keep in touch. Hell, depending on where she went, maybe he'd follow her someday. He'd miss her being so close, but if leaving Chicago would help her mental health, far be it from him to stop her.

A slew of other ridiculous scenarios played out, but he didn't bother to entertain any of them.

Taking in a deep breath, Amelia hung her head. "It's about Joseph Larson. About something that happened with him. And me."

The combination of anticipation and anger burned like acid in Zane's veins. As he scooted closer to her, he kept his movements diligent and measured. If *something* had happened between Amelia and Joseph, there was no part of Zane that thought for even a half-second that the event had been positive. Though the effort was monumental, he kept the simmering ire out of his voice. "What happened?"

Her shoulders sagged. "It's…it's a long story, but I'll try to make it fast."

"You don't have to do that."

She turned until her glassy eyes met his. "What do you mean?"

He channeled as much compassion and empathy into his expression as he could manage. "Take your time. Or don't. Don't worry about making it fast for my sake. I'll be here for as long as you need."

Brushing at the corner of her eye, she sniffled and averted her gaze. "Thank you. You're so…*good* with this type of thing."

"You make me want to be good at it."

"What?" When Amelia's attention jerked back to him, he realized he'd spoken the words out loud.

He wished he could shrink down and crawl into the gap between couch cushions. His cool, collected persona didn't falter often, but there was something about this woman that caused his brain to malfunction.

"That was cheesy. I just meant...you know." If he tried to salvage his misstep, he'd only dig himself into a deeper hole. Better to steer into the skid than lose control. "Sorry," he said instead.

A faint smile touched her face. "Maybe it was a little cheesy, but it was still sweet."

"I'm glad to hear that." The reply was a grave understatement. He was beyond relieved that he hadn't added "creepy friend" to Amelia's list of stressors.

In the newest spell of quiet, she wrung her hands in her lap before she heaved a sigh. "Okay. Well, like I said, it's a long story. You remember what happened at the Leónes' farm in Kankakee County? What happened with Alton Dalessio and...and me?"

"Yeah. I remember." He beat back all his questions before they formed.

"I told you I wasn't sure if I should have pulled the trigger? I thought maybe I saw some kind of movement just because I was jumpy, or because I was trigger happy, or... something." She spat the last word. "Larson was the only one who saw it happen. Well, him and the girl who was in the room, but the U.S. Attorney's Office thought she'd be too traumatized to remember everything correctly."

"Yeah. You thought Larson might have been backing you up just to back you up." The taste on his tongue turned sour. He didn't like the direction Amelia's story was headed.

"I was right." She ran a fingertip over the burgundy lacquer of her nails. "He lied to the Bureau in the hearing. About Dalessio. He told them he saw me shoot Alton and that I'd only done so after Alton looked like he was about to raise his weapon."

Zane was surprised Amelia couldn't hear the thud of his pulse. "He *didn't* see it?"

"No. He didn't see anything." Her words were laden with venom, but he was certain the ill intent was directed at Joseph. "But he claimed he did, and the Bureau thought he did. He made that pretty clear to me when we were on our way to MCC Chicago after Carlo Enrico was killed."

All Zane could do was blink.

"I can't remember his exact words, but he said something to the effect of 'it's good I was there to corroborate your story, or the FBI wouldn't have bought it.' I thought I was imagining things, but he kept standing closer to me for the rest of the night. Like he was...*testing*. Like he was trying to see if his plan was working. We were at a crime scene, and he was playing with me."

Stretching one arm along the back of the couch, Zane balled his hand into a fist as he braced himself for what Amelia would say next. He suspected he knew the direction her recollection was headed, and the familiar embers of rage burned low in his gut.

"That's how it was for the entire investigation. Every time we were together, he'd do that sort of shit. At one point, he came across like an actual human being, and I thought I was imagining everything. He told me about his brother, about how the two of them used to buy giant bags of gummy worms and pig out." She swallowed hard and folded her hands. "But that didn't last long. Next thing I knew, we were in a parking lot after getting something to eat, and he just..."

Mentally, Zane crossed his fingers that the story would end there. That the extent of Joseph Larson's sleaze would end at a second uncomfortable advance outside a restaurant.

But he knew better. He was kidding himself.

Amelia's shoulders rose and fell as she let out another sigh. "He tried to kiss me, but I turned my head. He had me up against a car, and I tried to be nice and let him down easy. Explain that I wasn't interested, even though he should have picked up on that a few months ago when he tried this shit for the first time. But he cut me off and went on some spiel about how he knew I was under a lot of stress after lying to the Bureau about Dalessio."

Zane glanced at the bottle of pricey bourbon he kept on the granite counter beside the fridge. If he already wanted a drink, he could only imagine where Amelia's mind was at or how she must have felt while she was stuck with Joseph in that damned parking lot.

She rubbed her burgundy thumbnail and swallowed. "I...I don't know how it got out of control so fast. I don't know why I couldn't just tell him to go to hell." She wrinkled her nose. "Okay, maybe I do know why. I thought he was going to rat me out, and I'd go to prison if I didn't do what he wanted. Maybe I could have come up with a plan if I'd had a little more time, but he asked me about it the next day. After we got back from arresting Cliff Allworth."

The acid was back in Zane's veins. "Asked you what?"

"Asked me to come over to his place. He said it was a stressful day, and we ought to celebrate by," she air quoted, "relieving that stress."

Zane's stomach clenched as he remembered that night and how Amelia looked when she'd stepped into the elevator with him.

He'd been preoccupied with Stan Young's security clearance and what that man could unearth about his past that he hadn't possessed the mental bandwidth to deal with anything else. Still, he'd recognized her distress and should have tried to offer support. Could he be a shittier friend?

"At first, I talked myself into it." She licked her lips. "I thought I could treat it like a transaction like working girls have to do every damn day, you know? When I got there, I barely had a second to think before he was...kissing me. Groping me."

Though Zane had never cared for Joseph Larson, he didn't have the faintest clue that the man was this twisted. From what Amelia had said so far, Larson's actions were calculated. The guy had planned three steps ahead of every move he'd made.

Men like Joseph weren't unfamiliar to Zane. He'd seen plenty of them, had *arrested* plenty of them. He just hadn't imagined that there was one so close by or that one would prey on his friend. One who was supposed to be one of the good guys. The thought sickened him.

Amelia's gaze was back on her hands when she spoke again. "When he shoved his hand down my pants, that's when I realized I couldn't do it. But..."

Zane's heart was in his throat, and he could barely keep his ass on the couch.

She swallowed again, but this time it wasn't sadness or guilt he saw in her expression. It was rage. "I told him no and tried to push him away. We struggled a bit before I got him off me. And you know what he did after that?"

Zane was afraid to answer, so he simply shook his head.

"He tried turning it around on me. He said that I'd gone over there to bang him so he'd keep my secret about Dalessio."

"I'm sorry." Zane wanted to remain quiet until Amelia was finished, but the apology forced its way out into the open.

Amelia blinked a few times. "Sorry for what?"

"That night. I was...worried about something else. The meeting Glenn and I had with Stan Young. I knew you seemed off, and I should have..." He trailed off and rubbed his eyes.

Should have been all-knowing and used my X-Men powers to throw Larson into the Marianas Trench.

The warmth of her hand on his forearm yanked him back to reality. "Don't be sorry. You did nothing wrong. You're not a psychic, and even if you were," with a half-smile, she lifted a shoulder, "there wasn't anything you could have done."

I could have killed him.

No, he couldn't have killed Joseph Larson. He was on American soil now, and the tactics he'd employed in Russia wouldn't fly.

Zane rubbed at the site of a faded tattoo at the end of his collarbone. "Yeah, you're right. But I'm still sorry that happened. Sorry there wasn't more I could do."

She gave his arm a reassuring squeeze. "It's okay. After that all happened, I told him I'd just go to SAC Keaton myself. And I did, the next morning. It turns out Yanira Flores had a good memory of what happened and testified that Joseph Larson wasn't even in the room when I shot Dalessio. She saved me."

"She's a good kid." Zane's nails scraped his scalp as he ran a hand through his hair. "My god, Amelia. I had no idea Joseph Larson was such a piece of shit. I thought he was an asshole, but I didn't think he'd try to *rape* you."

Every emotion every human could ever feel flitted across Amelia's features. "It's weird. I'd thought about what he'd done as just about everything but rape, but that was what he very nearly did."

Though Zane wanted to let loose a collection of four-letter descriptors that suited Joseph Larson, he kept the expletives to himself and reached for Amelia's hand. He doubted she wanted to hear him swear at their fellow agent. Chances were, she'd already done plenty of that herself.

Glancing down at her painted nails, he brushed a thumb over her knuckles. Rage burned in the back of his mind, but this wasn't about him. "You probably already know this, but it wasn't your fault. Guys like that...like Larson...they're predators. I can guarantee this isn't the first time he's done this."

She nodded. "And I also now understand better why so few women report sexual assault. Here I am, a big bad FBI agent and I haven't said a word about it until now."

Zane remembered his mother ranting about the same thing, about how unfair the system was to victims.

"This...probably sounds crazy, but do you," Amelia blinked repeatedly as she pushed a few strands of hair from her face, "do you think that he...might have had something to do with Ben? That he might have done that too. And the cameras?" When her voice cracked, he tightened his grasp on her hand.

"You don't sound crazy. Honestly, after what you just told me, I wouldn't put it past him, but..." He let out an unsteady breath. He'd love nothing more than to slap a pair of handcuffs on Joseph Larson's wrists and watch the sick son of a bitch rot in a prison cell for the rest of his life, but not at the expense of allowing Ben Storey's murderer to go free. "I passed Larson when Spencer and I were heading out to Englewood. I don't think he could've killed Storey."

"I guess that's...good? Right?" Her shoulders slumped as the words left her lips.

Though Zane could tell that the threat of tears had passed, Amelia's despondency was no less palpable.

Zane still wasn't convinced that Larson was incapable of killing an innocent person in cold blood, but that line of discussion could wait for another day. He made his best effort at a reassuring smile, though he didn't *feel* reassuring.

"Yeah. For what it's worth, Joseph not being Ben's killer is a good thing."

With a gentle squeeze to his hand, Amelia rubbed her forehead. "Well, that's a relief, I suppose. But I'm wiped out. That comfortable bed in your spare room is calling my name."

Straightening his back, Zane looked to the clock. "Shit, yeah, I guess it's almost two-thirty in the morning."

"Thank you again for letting me and my jackass cat stay here." Amelia swung her legs over the side of the couch and stretched.

A pang of guilt struck his heart. "It's no problem. I know you'd do the same for me."

Amelia snorted out a quiet laugh. "If someone tried to frame you for killing a city councilman and the FBI ripped apart your place for a search warrant, yeah, I would."

"I'm sorry." He felt like a parrot, and he wished he could come up with an original, genuine apology instead of the platitudes he'd squawked out so far.

"It's not your fault. I know *you* didn't kill Ben Storey either." A hint of her usual sarcastic humor had returned as Amelia stood. "And the forensic people *did* find four hidden cameras that had been spying on me. So, honestly, that warrant might have been for the best."

"I just wish they'd done it without making all those holes in your drywall." Zane followed her lead, ready for a little shut-eye.

Amelia waved a finger at him. "That's a good point, but I'll have to just take what I can get. Hopefully, the lab can find something from them that'll help track down Storey's killer."

Hopefully was the operative word.

Neither Layton Redker nor the FBI's tech specialists had located an identifying marker on the cameras so far, and

Zane wasn't optimistic that the standing would change any time soon.

However, there was one aspect of the debacle so far that told him they were on the right track. The killer clearly hadn't wanted them to find the cameras in Amelia's apartment.

Whoever they were, their plan hadn't been executed to perfection.

He just had to hope their finds wouldn't lead the killer to retaliate against the person they'd intended to frame in the first place.

15

The pinks and blues of the sunrise glittered along the water's surface as ripples extended toward the shore of the pond. Even with the quacks and occasional splashes of the resident waterfowl, the park was serene. I'd been a night owl in my younger years, but these days, I was glad for the peaceful hours of the early morning.

I took in a breath of crisp morning air as I fished in my pocket for another handful of oats. Years earlier, I'd learned that the typical bread most people loved to feed to ducks was detrimental to the birds' health. Plain, white bread provided no nutritional value, and the leftover scraps were a breeding ground for algae.

As I hunched over to toss the oats to the mallard closest to the water's edge, I caught the shadow of an approaching man in the corner of my vision.

The events of my previous day came rushing back to mind, and I gritted my teeth to steel myself for the impromptu meeting with my newest boss.

I'd never truly wanted to kill Ben Storey, but he'd betrayed me, ruining my damn life.

Ben might not have remembered what he'd done, but I wouldn't forget. I'd thought that my boss's order to kill the man would give me a sense of closure, but the sense of relief was nowhere to be found. Maybe I had to let more time pass, or maybe I'd be forever trapped in this veritable purgatory of regret and anger.

My visitor neared, but I didn't bother to acknowledge him. I kept my focus on the smaller gray duck that had joined the mallard.

As the man moved beyond my periphery, I waited for the sound of his footsteps to cease. Not far behind me, a pair of benches were set back-to-back. Any passersby wouldn't have the first clue that my boss and I were here together.

Not that there *were* any other people at the park this early. There was no walking trail for joggers, no open field of grass for dogs. The only real attractions were the paddleboats at the other end of the lake and the handful of picnic areas that rested beneath the pines and oaks that dotted the area. Of course, when autumn's chill arrived, neither casual boating nor outdoor dining were popular in the Midwest.

If the seclusion meant I didn't have to drive to the city limits to avoid being seen, I'd take it. I wasn't a lifelong Chicago resident, and though I'd been in the city for a while, I still hadn't become accustomed to the atrocious traffic.

"Good morning." The man's voice cut through my thoughts with the precision of a razor blade.

Blinking, I bent forward to toss the remaining oats to the ducks. As I brushed off both hands on the front of my peacoat, I tossed a piece of blonde hair over my shoulder. A wig, though the relative isolation made me wonder why I'd gone through the trouble.

I turned to the benches. His back faced me, but I recognized the familiar chestnut brown shade of his neatly styled hair. Apparently, *he* didn't feel the need to disguise himself. I cleared my throat to keep from scoffing. "Good morning, Senator."

National and local politics had never captured much of my interest over the years, but Benjamin Storey had become Stanley Young's arch-political rival over the past six months.

Ben's betrayal was why I'd chosen to work with Stan Young. Not because I gave two shits about Young's standing in the U.S. Senate.

I didn't.

I answered to Stan Young for one reason and one reason alone: power.

As a multi-billionaire and an influential member of the U.S. Senate's Intelligence Committee, Stan Young commanded authority on a national scale.

For most of my life, I'd been screwed over and looked past thanks to my gender's kindness and sense of...of what? Morality? Honor? I wasn't even sure anymore. I'd always thought hard work and dedication were the best methods to move up in life, but I'd learned recently how wrong that assumption had been.

Money and connections. *Those* were the only real ways to advance my standing in a world that had viewed me as dispensable for so long.

I climbed the slight incline and took a seat beside my handbag. At least on this side of the bench, I could watch the lake.

"Good work." From the edge of my vision, I watched as Stan pulled out his smartphone. "Storey's the big headline so far this morning, and I'm sure the press will expect me to say something about it before too long."

A third duck joined the pair that had waddled over to the oats. I tucked both hands in my pockets. "Nothing about Amelia Storm?"

"No mention of her in any of the articles I saw."

Shit.

I bit my tongue to keep my face impassive. We'd known the evidence wouldn't stick, but I'd hoped her being questioned would make a significant media splash. "I planted the murder weapon in her apartment and the messages on her computer and his phone. Just like we discussed."

Young dipped his chin. "I know, and as we suspected, it wasn't enough to make the charges stick. You can't predict every variable in something like this. 'Expect the unexpected,' as they say. We have to derail the Feds by throwing as many monkey wrenches into the works to keep them on their toes."

His point was valid. I wasn't keen on the fact that he hadn't shared additional backup schemes with me, but I'd learned enough about Stan Young to understand that the man kept his cards close to the vest.

"She should already be dead, and this wouldn't be a problem."

The muscle moving in his jaw was the only sign of his agitation. "As I said, we can't predict every variable."

I smiled as two ducks got into a fight over a piece of food and decided that the past was the past. I needed to look forward. "What's the next move?"

As Stan tilted his head, I could swear I heard the gears grinding in his brain. "This is unfortunate, but it was never really out of the realm of possibility. We continue to plant confusing clues to keep the spotlight off ourselves, but as far as Agent Storm is concerned, she's become…" He twirled a finger in the air.

"A loose end?" I finished for him.

"Exactly." He returned his grasp to the smartphone. "Come to think of it. Her very public and tragic end could be a blessing in disguise."

A muscle at the corner of my eye twitched. I hated that damn saying.

My mother had uttered those words countless times when I was younger. If my father got drunk and trashed the living room, she'd wake me up to help her clean. As we swept up pieces of broken glass—we never vacuumed for fear we'd wake him—she'd tell me about all the new items we could buy for the entertainment stand and the bookshelves.

It's a blessing in disguise, she'd say. *I didn't really like those picture frames, anyway. We can go buy some new ones today while your dad sleeps this off.*

I'd thought that my father's drunken rage only extended to inanimate objects. One night when I'd been sick with the flu and couldn't sleep, I'd wandered down to my parents' bedroom to ask my mom for some more Tylenol.

I'd thought my father had gone out on one of his benders. I hadn't bothered to knock before I pushed open the door.

The image of my mother's pleading eyes as my father had held her down to force himself on her burned itself into my psyche.

Like a naïve eleven-year-old girl, I'd tried to reason with the prick instead of sneaking away like I should have. My mother had begged me to leave, but I'd been as stubborn as I was naïve back then.

Buck naked, my father strode over and clocked me in the side of the head with a right hook that knocked me unconscious. I was sure he'd given me a concussion, but of course, we hadn't dared go to a hospital.

I should have learned my lesson and slid into subservience like all the other women in my family. Unfortunately for my father, his brutality inspired the opposite response.

Five years later, he was the unfortunate victim of a hunting accident.

My male relatives had been prone to carrying flasks of hard liquor with them when they'd gone out to the woods for deer season. No one had asked questions when my father had tripped and fallen down a fifty-foot incline to his death. Hell, the county hadn't even ordered an autopsy. They'd tested for intoxicants, determined his blood alcohol content was more than triple the legal limit to drive, and ruled the death an accident.

Everyone had seen me as the poor sixteen-year-old girl who'd just lost her father. As far as they were all concerned, I'd been in my room sleeping off a particularly painful round of menstrual cramps.

I'd taken a risk by slinking through the trees in the middle of deer season, but I knew the area like the back of my hand. Including the potentially treacherous route my father and uncles had intended to take. Father dearest had excused himself to piss, and I'd seen my opening.

There were no tracks to show another person had been present. No witnesses, either. Just a tragic, preventable death.

Crossing my legs, I turned my attention back to the lake and the ducks. "A blessing in disguise? How so?"

Stan blew out a long breath. "I won't go into too much detail, but Amelia Storm's become something of a...distraction to one of my guys. He's been my go-to for years, and he's damn near obsessed with that woman. It's affecting his work. I'd had great hopes that our scheme would have worked last night. It would have been good to have her out of the way."

I was glad that Stan couldn't see me roll my eyes. Some men could be so pathetic. They'd let their entire professional lives derail just for a chance with a woman who didn't want them. "She's an FBI agent. Since we missed our chance, another attempt won't be easy."

"I know." I caught the flicker of movement as Stan made a show of scrolling through his phone. "But you'll be compensated handsomely. Once we get this whole Ben Storey situation out of the way, we'll be on to bigger and better things. That is, if you're up to the task."

In terms of skill, a hit on Amelia Storm—an FBI special agent with ten years of military experience—would be markedly more difficult than the execution of Ben Storey. However, in terms of emotional fallout, killing Amelia would be easy.

I wasn't a psychopath, but I knew how to compartmentalize. Though I didn't have a personal vendetta with Amelia like I had with Ben, she was a means to an end.

"I'm up for it." I ignored the small voice that reminded me I'd just agreed to murder an FBI agent. A woman who'd arguably done me no wrong, and who'd only been caught up in this mess because Stan Young's "guy" was prone to using his dick to make decisions rather than his brain.

I was familiar with that small voice, and I knew how to silence it.

Amelia Storm was collateral damage. No more, and no less.

16

As Joseph Larson stepped onto the plush bathmat in front of his frosted glass shower stall, he held his breath and stood as still as a statue. Water still dripped behind him, but other than the droplets and the more distant sound of the refrigerator humming to life, his loft-style apartment was silent. Even with the wall-spanning windows of the living room, the place was well-insulated, and little of the city's hustle and bustle permeated all the way back to the master bathroom.

Rubbing his tired eyes, Joseph plucked a forest green towel from the edge of the marble vanity. The polished white of the counter stood out in stark contrast to the sleek, wooden cabinetry while the glass tile matched the dark ash almost exactly.

Joseph had always liked the sleek fixtures, but at that moment, he wanted nothing more than to escape the little room.

Ever since Cassandra had given him the news of Ben Storey's murder, Joseph had been on high alert. That news, coupled with eight years in the military, had left him with a particular dislike for confined spaces with only one exit.

Not that he was often worried about the capability to make a hasty escape, but the past fourteen hours were an exception.

Joseph had no idea who'd killed Ben, but he was sure he knew who had ordered the assassination.

Initially, Senator Stan Young had hired *Joseph* to off Storey. Hell, Joseph had even outlined the entire plan to his employer of more than ten years. He'd explained to Stan how he intended to shift the blame for the crime onto another FBI agent—Amelia Storm. As far as Joseph had known, he had a green light to carry out the execution once all his pieces were in place.

But now, Ben Storey was dead, and Joseph didn't have the first clue who'd pulled the trigger.

He'd been at the FBI office when he'd first learned of the senatorial hopeful's death, but even there, he'd caught himself looking over his shoulder for any signs of a stalker. On his trip home, he'd taken a zigzagging route, adding an extra thirty minutes to his commute. As soon as he'd stepped through the front door, he'd swept the entire apartment for bugs.

When he'd discovered none, his surprise had been genuine. He'd checked again, then a third time, and a fourth.

Nothing.

No hidden audio recording devices, no cameras, just *nothing*. The hardware he used for the sweep was state-of-the-art, and he made a point to keep himself updated regarding the latest spy-related technology. But for the majority of the evening, he'd convinced himself that his imagined stalker had access to equipment more advanced than his own.

Which wasn't a stretch of the imagination.

Stan Young was a member of the U.S. Senate's Intelligence Committee, after all. If anyone could get ahold of such sophisticated hardware, it was Stan.

Halfway through Joseph's manual search for hidden bugs, he'd been alerted to activity on the motion-sensor cameras he'd installed in Amelia Storm's apartment. His first assumption had been that Amelia was finally home from work, but when he'd securely signed in to monitor the video feed, he'd seen the FBI forensic team rifling through Amelia's belongings.

In Joseph's decade-long tenure with the FBI, he couldn't recall the last incident that had scraped his nerves so raw.

The only solace he could find was the knowledge that, if Stan wanted Joseph dead, he wouldn't have lasted long enough to witness the Bureau's search.

Shaking off the lingering paranoia, Joseph pulled on a pair of tailored slacks, black socks, and a plain, white t-shirt. He unlocked his cell to check for a reply to the messages he'd sent Brian Kolthoff the night before, but there were no new notifications. Kolthoff was a busy man, but he'd always had time to send a quick reply, and his current radio silence was adding fuel to the raging inferno in Joseph's mind.

He pocketed the phone and set about his typical morning routine. First a shower, then coffee, and a bite to eat.

His brain might have been fried from a night of constant hyperawareness, but he fully intended to show up for work as he did every weekday. Rattled or not, he needed to maintain appearances.

With a fresh cup of coffee in hand, Joseph dropped onto the center cushion of his overstuffed couch that overlooked a bustling intersection. He pulled a laptop from the lower level of the matte black coffee table, pushed open the screen, and tapped the power button.

After one last gander through the footage of Amelia's

apartment and the information he'd intended to frame her with, he'd stash the computer in a more secure location. Part of him wanted to wipe the hard drive and trash the damn thing entirely, but the digital trail could still prove useful.

Online storage was a double-edged sword. On one hand, there was always the possibility that the data could be accessed by an unauthorized third party. No matter how many firewalls protected the servers, somewhere in the world was a hacker proficient enough to bypass the litany of security measures. Joseph knew his way around the dark web, but he was far from a coding expert.

But on the other hand, the online nature of virtual storage was convenient in more than a few ways. As long as Joseph treaded carefully, he could sever his connection to the data with little more than a click. None of the recordings from Amelia's place would be traced back to him, not even with the vast resources of the Federal Bureau of Investigation. And if he could determine the assassin who'd pulled the trigger on Ben, he could leverage what he had as evidence to bring them in, ensuring no suspicion ever landed on him.

Joseph hadn't gleaned many specifics about Storey's case before the first tech located the camera he'd wired to Amelia's floor lamp. Three of the others had fallen in rapid succession after the first, but the tiny lens in the showerhead of the master bath still hadn't been discovered.

Maybe that was why he was loath to wash his hands of the footage. Amelia's apartment had been ripped apart, but eventually, she'd return to that shower. And, as he'd had for the past three months, Joseph would have a front-row seat.

Unless she moves.

He uttered a low growl at the thought and reached for the mug of coffee before slumping back into the cushions. "This is going to be a long day."

Six days. He'd been six days away from carrying out his

hit on Storey, and now the task had been jerked out from under his feet like a cheap piece of carpet. Sure, Ben Storey might have pissed off another powerful person who'd wanted him dead as well, but that didn't explain why Amelia Storm was involved.

Framing Amelia had been *Joseph's* idea. No one knew about the plan aside from him and Stan.

With a grunt, Joseph replaced the coffee and leaned toward his laptop. Amelia's shower was empty. The night before, he'd watched as she'd collected the bottles of soap and other bath essentials, but he wasn't sure where she'd gone from there. It *wasn't* prison, that much was certain.

If he'd been the one to frame her, she'd already be planted under the jail.

Joseph closed the video feed and navigated to a new page in his web browser. As he pulled up the first in a lengthy series of photos, he rubbed his chin. A couple weeks earlier, he'd paid a pretty penny for an expert photo editor to craft him a slew of explicit pictures featuring Amelia Storm and Ben Storey.

The images were about as real as the Loch Ness Monster, but they *looked* like they could have been pulled straight from Ben or Amelia's phone. Joseph had provided plenty of stills from the recording of Amelia's shower, but ensuring the accuracy of Ben Storey's likeness had proved more challenging.

In the end, social media had given him the tools he needed. Photos of Storey and his wife on a tropical vacation and a more recent album that included pictures of Ben at the beach with his family. The references weren't as...*thorough* as Amelia's nudes, but Joseph's chosen photo editor had come through.

He wasn't stupid. Even as he'd commissioned the images, he'd known that the Bureau's advanced algorithms would make quick work of the photoshopped pictures. Part of him had known all along that the fakes wouldn't hold up, but in a strange way, the process had been cathartic.

Amelia might have pushed him away before he could physically take her, but seeing such a realistic depiction of her so exposed served as a reminder. A reminder that she wasn't out of reach yet.

With a long sip of scalding coffee to keep the blood in his brain from rushing to a different part of his body, Joseph pieced together the first inklings of a plan. He still wasn't entirely sure why Stan had apparently hired a different hitman for Storey or what the senator's change of heart meant for him, but for the time being, he'd operate under the assumption that his relationship with Young had deteriorated.

If Stan intended to exclude him from his inner circle, Joseph would make the task as treacherous as possible. Joseph had helped the good senator's operation succeed for the better part of a decade, and he'd be damned if he went down without a fight.

Joseph's fingers flew over the keyboard as he opened the website of a less-than-reputable news site that had become well-known across Chicago in the past couple years. Personally, Joseph hated the tabloid, but the owners showed a clear bias in favor of Stan Young.

If they received compromising pictures of Stan's rival, Ben Storey, they wouldn't think twice. They'd just publish.

Once the FBI's analysis proved that the photos were altered, Stan's hired gun would trip over himself to keep the blame pinned on Amelia. All the while, Amelia's naked body would be plastered across the internet for the entire world to see.

The situation was a win-win.

Joseph chuckled to himself as he opened up his Tor

browser and set his VPN to the highest security setting, ensuring his IP would be masked through multiple bounces across the world. Secure that he would remain anonymous, he navigated back to the tabloid website and clicked their *Anonymous Tip* contact link. A few clicks later, the images were uploaded.

If he couldn't put her sexy ass in jail, Joseph Larson would see to Amelia Storm's ruin in a much more explicit way.

17

A melia flopped an arm over her face to block out the rays of sunshine piercing through the picture window. For the first time in weeks, she'd enjoyed a deep, dreamless slumber. Not quite ready to crawl out of bed and rejoin the waking world, Amelia knew she couldn't hide under the covers forever. The sun's warm glow told her she'd already slept well into the morning.

Though she doubted anyone expected her to come to work the day after she'd been falsely accused of murder, Amelia wasn't the type to play hooky. She'd used personal time, but the unplanned absence left her with a bizarre, nagging guilt in the back of her head.

As the mattress to her side sank under the weight of a small animal, she moved her arm and pried open her eyes.

Hup stared curiously before letting out a loud *meow*.

Feeding time. No matter the time of day, Hup never missed an opportunity to beg for more kibble. Amelia wasn't falling for it. "I know Zane fed you." She pointed to a neon green sticky note he'd placed on the alarm clock. Big sloppy letters read, *Don't believe the cat, she's been fed*.

Behind the note, glowing red numbers of the alarm clock drew her attention. "Twelve-thirty, oh my god." Even as she racked her memory, she couldn't recall the last morning she'd slept later than ten.

With another meow, Hup arched her back and stretched both white paws, sending her tiny claws into the comforter.

Before Amelia could give the calico another reminder that she'd indeed been fed that morning, her phone vibrated against the nightstand. At least the caller had been kind enough to wait until she'd woken up.

Propping herself to sit upright, Amelia reached for the phone. Zane's name flashed across the screen. Gentleman that he was, Amelia assumed he was calling to check on her during his lunch break.

She coughed to clear her throat of any signs of sleep and answered brightly. "Hey. How's work?"

"Hey. Yeah. Work is...work." Zane's tone sounded unusually strained, as if he were trying to keep his voice low enough not to be overheard.

That doesn't sound good.

Goose bumps prickled the back of Amelia's neck. "What is it? Has something happened?"

"Yes, something has. Hold on." A car door thudded in the background, and the line went quiet. "Sorry, I just finished getting a coffee so I could drink my lunch."

Amelia's hands had become clammy as she swallowed a lump of anticipation in her throat. "It's okay. What happened?" The last thing she needed was more bad news.

"There's been a...development. You've heard of Real Chicago News dot com, right?"

Slumping back against the pillows, Amelia rubbed her temple. "Yeah, I've heard of it. Back when I still had a Facebook account, some of my conspiracy theorist friends would share articles from that site. They're not exactly…reputable, from what I remember. Why?"

Zane let out a cross between a groan and a sigh. "Well, they posted an article a couple hours ago."

"About Ben Storey?" Amelia expected as much. A dead senatorial candidate would be hot stuff on a slow news day.

"Yeah. And…and you."

She choked on her breath, coughing as she jerked bolt upright in bed. "What? How? How would anyone outside the Bureau even know that I was a suspect? How would…"

She trailed off as the unsettling realization dawned on her, sending her heart racing to punch a hole straight through her chest.

"It had to have been the same person who tried to frame you." Zane's tone darkened as the words came out. "That's our working theory right now. Whoever sent those pictures to Real—"

"Pictures?" Amelia clapped a hand over her mouth to stop the string of obscenities she wanted to shout.

"Sorry," Zane muttered. "Yeah. I probably should have led with that. There were about ten…um…uncensored pictures included in the article."

"Un…*what?*" She grasped the green and white comforter with a death grip. She'd *thought* that Zane was referring to fake images of her killing Ben Storey or her milling about the crime scene when she'd claimed to be elsewhere. Then she remembered the messaging app. Hushed. The damn affair— all the dirty texts she'd never sent about the sex she'd never had with a man she'd barely known. "Oh my god. You mean?"

"Explicit pictures."

"One moment, please," she spoke the words with a restraint usually reserved for customer service reps and dropped the phone onto the bed.

Grabbing the nearest pillow, Amelia unleashed a stress-filled and explicit tirade into it. Venomous words, in both Russian and English, spewed from her mouth with such speed it was as if she had invented her own language. She emptied her stores of angry vocabulary into the standard-size pillow, stuffing it with every last syllable of profanity she could utter before tossing it aside.

Breathless, Amelia gave herself a moment to regain composure before retrieving the phone to continue her conversation with Zane. No doubt he had heard her. Hell, the neighbors probably did too.

The pillow may have been soft, but little could muffle the rage burning through her at that moment. She considered crawling under the blankets to hide from the world, but short of witness protection, nothing would save her from the shame. Whatever damage had been done, it was already out there. She'd have to face it eventually.

Biting her bottom lip to keep any additional expletives from escaping, she tugged the comforter up to her stomach as a half-assed compromise with herself. Glancing to where Hup rested at her side, she spotted her matte silver work laptop.

"Hold on." She stabbed the speaker button with her finger before reaching for the computer that was half-buried under her rage pillow.

"Amelia...don't do it." Zane's pleading tone wouldn't distract her from the truth, no matter how well-intentioned he was trying to be in stopping her. "Seriously. Just take my word on this one."

"I have to. If this shit is all over the internet, I should at least know what I'm dealing with. Wouldn't you want to know if it was you?" She prayed she'd find some horribly doctored images. Obvious fakes. Those she could stomach. But in the back of her mind, she knew they wouldn't be. Not with those cameras that had been found in her apartment.

At any moment, someone could have taken still images of her while getting dressed. Or maybe they had caught her quickly streaking through the living room as she sprinted to the kitchen to grab a bottle of wine before taking a bubble bath. At any given moment, whoever had been watching her could have caught an image, which could easily have been turned explicit.

"Yeah. I guess I would. But just a warning…they didn't censor anything. And I mean *any*thing."

Amelia furiously typed in her login credentials. "Is that even legal?"

He snorted. "According to our Assistant U.S. Attorney, the answer to that is, and I quote, 'Hell no! Those stupid bastards are just asking for a lawsuit.' End quote."

As much as Amelia wanted to laugh, she was in the midst of mentally cursing the laptop's load time. Though the computer was a newer model, the boot up felt like she was waiting for a dial-up connection circa the late nineties. "Why would they post an article like that if they knew they could get slapped with a lawsuit?"

"Views, revenue, infamy. Fifteen seconds of fame. Take your pick. It's a pissant operation that's run out of a rented office space on the edge of downtown. My guess is that they figure if they're sued by Storey's estate, or even by you, that they can turn it into a big production about freedom of speech. Maybe reach a wider audience."

Amelia pulled up a search engine and typed in the tabloid's web address. Her pulse rushed in her ears as she clicked on the first result.

The home page was all simple, sleek font and a straight-forward design. She might have been impressed by the layout if she hadn't been in the midst of searching for an article that included photoshopped pictures of *her* naked body.

Not that she had to search for long. There it was, just below the standard headers printed in bold, block letters.

BREAKING: New, Unseen Photos of Chicago City Councilman Ben Storey and His Long-Term Mistress Emerge Shortly After His Death.

Amelia's hands trembled as she clicked the hyperlink. Gritting her teeth, she steeled herself and scrolled past the first couple paragraphs. When her gaze settled on a grayscale image of a woman on her knees in front of a familiar man, she took in a sharp breath.

Part of the woman's face was obscured by hair. *Amelia's* hair. The woman was *her*.

To her chagrin, the second picture sported a full-on frontal of her naked body. Even the little crescent moon tattooed on her right hip and the Japanese-style panther on her thigh.

Those damn spy cameras!

"Amelia, are you okay?" Zane's worried voice was like a lifeline in the chaos and panic that threatened to swallow her whole.

"I'm...I'm not sure." She swallowed the invisible cotton balls that had been jammed into her mouth. "These pictures, they're not real. This isn't me. I didn't do this! I didn't sleep with Ben, and I sure as hell didn't kill him! Oh my...for the love of God, the guy was married. He had two kids! Even if I *had* seen him outside the office...which, to be clear, I *didn't*. But if I had, if we'd run into one another, I wouldn't have. If he'd made a move..."

Shit. She was rambling. She clamped her lips together before any more nonsense could slip out into the open.

"I know. I know, Amelia. I believe you. So does Spencer, and so does Cassandra. We're going to head over to the Real Chicago News office soon. Spencer had me call you so you'd hear about it from us and not them. Plus, I'm pretty sure we all wanted an opportunity to down some more caffeine before we left. Even though I'm starting to think I should've asked the barista to spike this latte with whiskey."

Sometimes, Amelia wondered if Zane moonlighted as a hostage negotiator. The Bureau employed agents who specialized in talking down armed men and women in tense situations. Covering her face with one hand, Amelia took in a long, steadying breath. "Sorry. I, um, lost it a little there."

"It's okay. Don't sweat it. You're under a lot of stress right now. There's some good news that comes with this, though. It's a lead, which we didn't have before. We're going to head to their office and figure out where the hell they got these pictures. The tech department needs the original images to analyze them, not the cropped, pixelated shit on this website."

Amelia blinked to clear her vision. "Right. Yeah, that makes sense." Whether they'd glean any real, usable information from the stupid pictures remained to be seen. Amelia had dealt with digital photo evidence in a case she'd worked in Boston, and they'd used the source code to tie the photos to a suspect. But their success was the exception and not the rule.

After Zane assured her that he'd provide her with an update, they said their goodbyes, though Amelia was reluctant to end the call. Part of her wanted him to come back to the apartment so she wouldn't be alone, but the other half of her wanted to crawl into the corner of the nearby walk-in closet and lock the door so no one would ever see her again.

She knew that neither her father nor her sister-in-law, Joanna, bought into the tabloid-style reporting of websites like Real Chicago News, but she couldn't say the same for their circles of friends.

What if one of the stylists who worked with Joanna pulled up the article for her to see?

Oh my god, isn't that your sister-in-law? She was screwing Ben Storey? They'd flash Jo a look of sheer horror and speculate that Amelia had been involved in the man's murder.

Or her father. What if Jim Storm was sipping his break-time coffee, only to stumble across a link shared on one of the social media outlets he used? A link that displayed photos of his daughter screwing a married father of two?

What about Hailey and Nolan. As much as Amelia doubted that grade-school-aged kids cared in the slightest about the news, what about their parents or their older siblings? What if someone showed her niece or nephew that damned article?

"I'm never leaving this apartment." Amelia let her muscles go slack, melting back into the soft mattress.

Hup took the cue, scooted closer, and buried her face in Amelia's upper arm.

Amelia had always preferred taking action to sulking, but what could she do? Spencer had already pulled her off the Storey investigation, and rightfully so. There was no part of the FBI's standard operating procedure that allowed for an agent who had been framed to investigate their own case.

Not to mention, the situation would be a nightmare in court. Any defense lawyer worth the change in their pocket would rip the prosecution to shreds.

No. Amelia was stuck in this veritable purgatory, filled with anxious thoughts and an overactive imagination.

Something had to give because she wasn't sure how much more she could take.

18

Angrier than he'd been in his entire life, Zane shifted the car into park and killed the ignition. To his side, Cassandra unfastened her seat belt and reached for her handbag. So far, the prosecutor had been more agreeable than she had the day before. Maybe all she'd needed was a little shut-eye.

By Zane's best estimate, he'd managed a total of three hours of sleep. The previous evening's conversation with Amelia had left him lying awake for hours, considering whether he still had the connections to ship Joseph Larson off to a CIA black site in the middle of an African jungle.

Zane hadn't been a frequent flyer at the CIA's more remote bases, but he knew of their existence, and he knew damn well that none were pleasant.

None of the secretive detention centers officially existed, of course. Their remoteness varied, but each black site operated as a sovereign entity, only accountable to the rules of the men and women in charge of that location.

There, Larson could bunk with war criminals who'd mysteriously disappeared. Maybe one of those sick bastards would smother Joseph in his sleep, or maybe Larson would kill them first. The world would be all the better for either loss.

Throwing back the last of his latte, he opened the driver's side door and stepped out into the parking garage. Normally, he'd have brought another federal agent to the office of Real Chicago News. Spencer, however, had strongly recommended that Cassandra accompany him to throw around the weight of the U.S. Attorney's office, considering they were dealing with a business that operated in murky legal territory.

A receptionist greeted them as they strode through the set of double doors that opened into the seven-story building's sleek lobby. Zane flashed his badge, introduced Cassandra, and requested the floor and suite number that belonged to Real Chicago News. The office building housed a number of smaller businesses, each renting their own suite. Most of the companies were startups, but some, like Real Chicago News, had called the place home for a few years.

Since Real Chicago News was located on the second floor, he and Cassandra opted to take the stairs.

Badge in hand, Zane opened the door to allow Cassandra in first. The pair walked past a handful of chairs situated in the front half of the room, where a receptionist's desk blocked further access into the business suite.

"I'm Agent Palmer, and this is the Assistant U.S. Attorney, Cassandra Halcott. We're here to speak to the owner of this business."

He couldn't bring himself to say the name Real Chicago News out loud. There was nothing real about the sexually explicit photos he'd spent the better part of the day analyzing alongside two of his colleagues.

Never mind that they'd been staring at Amelia Storm's naked body.

The receptionist looked up from her computer, and her expression darkened as she spotted Zane's identification. "I'm sorry, Agent, but do you have a warrant?"

Zane's eyes narrowed as the fires of anger crept through his veins. "I'm sorry, Miss…" He paused to make note of the gold name plaque. "Deidra Decker. Do I need to come back here with a warrant? Because if I do, it sure as hell won't be limited to talking to the owner."

She blinked a couple times. "I'm…um…"

He pinned the younger woman with a withering stare. "If you make me get a warrant, I'll come back here with a whole team of FBI personnel, and we'll spend the next twelve hours ripping this place apart piece by piece."

A flush crept to her cheeks as she pushed to her feet. "No, Agent. That won't be necessary. Give me a second. I'll call Ms. Bakkal and ask her to come out here to greet you."

"Thank you," he responded tersely, hoping she'd give him a reason to carry out the threat he'd described. Even though he doubted they'd find any useful information, he'd enjoy the opportunity to rip this office down to the studs in the walls. It wouldn't heal the damage they had done to Amelia, but it would certainly work out a little of the aggression they'd incited.

Zane and Cassandra stood by the door, waiting to pounce when the owner of the so-called news came out.

Ms. Bakkal emerged from the hall beside the receptionist's desk. Her dark eyes instantly spotted Zane and Cassandra, and for the briefest of moments, the owner's jaw clenched. Tension was obvious, but Ms. Bakkal kept her head held high. Raven black hair framed her face in an asymmetrical bob, and her turquoise eyeshadow stood out in stark contrast to her tan complexion.

Clearing her throat, she stepped forward and extended a

hand. "Agent. Counselor. I'm Farida Bakkal, the owner of RCN. What can I help you with?"

Though Zane wanted to smack her hand away, he accepted the greeting. By appearances, she didn't seem the type to have founded such a ridiculous news outlet. "Thank you, Ms. Bakkal. I'm Special Agent Palmer, and this is the Assistant U.S. Attorney, Cassandra Halcott. We're here about an article your site published this morning. It's probably best that we discuss this in private."

Farida's cool smile and casual demeanor told him this wasn't the first time her company had received a visit from law enforcement. "Of course. Follow me. We can talk in my office."

They passed by a wall of glass. Just beyond it, a series of cubicles had been arranged diagonally. By Zane's best estimate, there were about ten desks and six occupants. On the other side of the hall, the breakroom was unoccupied, though Zane caught a whiff of freshly brewed coffee.

Probably better than what they give us at the Bureau.

He almost snorted aloud. The idea that a news website with all the validity of a counterfeit handbag provided its employees with higher quality drinks than the Federal Bureau of Investigation was ridiculous at first blush but far from improbable. Zane wished he knew who decided on the brand of coffee that was brewed in the Chicago Field Office, because he had a few choice words for them.

Pulling open a glass door, Farida waved Zane and Cassandra into the room first and allowed the door to close behind them as she circled around to her desk. Sunlight streamed in through an expansive window with an unhindered view of the parking garage.

I guess tabloid money doesn't pay for the nice corner office, does it, Ms. Bakkal?

Farida gestured to a pair of chairs facing the black Ushaped desk. "Have a seat. Now, what can I help you with?"

As the woman posed the question, Zane realized he and Cassandra hadn't come up with a plan or even a general tactic. Cassandra had been on the phone the entire trip over, plus he was so used to having Amelia by his side that the thought of preparation hadn't crossed his mind.

Great. They were about to fly by the seat of their pants. He hoped the prosecutor was good at improvisation.

Zane took the offered seat. "We're following up on an article that your...website published a few hours ago. At around ten this morning."

Folding her hands atop the unusually sparse desk, Farida tilted her head. "We publish a number of articles every day, Agent. I'm afraid you'll have to be more specific."

He smiled with all the condescension he could muster. "Well, based on the fact that the FBI showed up at your door and not a group of anti-vaccine conspiracy theorists, I'd say our visit probably has something to do with the story your writers published about the city councilman who was murdered last night, and not the so-called 'long-term effects' of the flu shot."

Farida's poker face was impressive. "You're referring to the article about Ben Storey, yes?"

"Unless you and your people know of another councilman who was killed last night." Zane matched her lack of expression with his own monotone. "Maybe you ought to just call in the author. Archer Eburn, if memory serves. Seems like he might be a little more familiar."

Reaching for a white mouse, Farida opened a file on her computer that appeared to contain employee records.

Her fingers flew over the keys, and her attention was back on Zane and Cassandra in short order. "Archer should be here soon. In the meantime, could I ask what exactly you're looking for?"

Zane fought against an exasperated quip. "Ms. Bakkal, you seem like a smart person, so I won't insult your intelligence by explaining what the FBI does. Your website posted an article about a man whose murder has made national headlines. Included in that article were ten different pictures of the deceased and a…woman who your writer claimed was his mistress."

One of Farida's sculpted eyebrows quirked up. "Oh? Does the FBI not have those photos? I'd assumed they were leaked from Mr. Storey's phone."

Cassandra crossed her legs as an unmistakable flicker of indignation passed over her features. "You came into possession of images, which you just alleged were leaked from Ben Storey's phone, and the thought did not cross your mind to alert the authorities? Obviously, you were aware of the murder, and given the recent nature of it, would undoubtedly know it was actively being investigated."

Palms up, Farida rested both hands beside the keyboard. "Ms. Halcott, RCN is a news outlet. We seek to provide the people of this city and this country with the stories that the mainstream media is too afraid to bring into the spotlight. There's no story too controversial for us to cover. We're here for the truth, and that's why we have such a high reader retention rate."

The federal prosecutor made a show of studying her ruby fingernails. "We're not potential investors, so do me a favor and save the sales pitch. Like Agent Palmer said, you seem like a smart woman, so let's not pretend that half the subject matter published on your site isn't blatantly untrue. Your motive is the same as any other business owner." Cassandra leaned forward, blue fire alight in her eyes. "Money, Ms. Bakkal. Your motive is *money*."

If Amelia and Cassandra's voices hadn't been so distinct from one another, and if Cassandra had interspersed her dialogue with a couple more four-letter words, Zane could have tricked himself into thinking he was in the company of Agent Storm.

Farida didn't get a chance to reply before a quiet knock rattled against the doorframe. "Come in, Archer. It's unlocked."

Brushing both palms along his dark wash jeans, a bald man with a neat goatee stepped into the room. Though Zane expected the newcomer to take a seat, he merely closed the door and stood in place. "Far…" he cleared his throat, "Ms. Bakkal, you and your, um, guests wanted to see me?"

"Yes." She pointed to a spare office chair in the corner. "Please, sit. This is Agent Palmer with the FBI, and the Assistant U.S. Attorney, Ms. Cassandra Halcott."

Archer's movements were jerky and uneven as he took his seat. Though the man might have simply been nervous in the presence of federal law enforcement officials, Zane made a mental note of his anxiety.

"Well, we're all here now." Farida's beaded bracelet clinked as she folded her hands. "I don't see any more need to beat around the bush. Ask your questions so we can get back to work. We have quite the task list today, and it's already close to three."

Zane and Cassandra exchanged unimpressed looks before he shifted in his seat to face Archer. "Mr. Eburn, we're here about an article you published this morning. The article relating to the late city councilman Ben Storey and his alleged mistress."

"What about it?" As Archer crossed his arms, Zane suspected the man was trying to avoid a nervous tic that would give away his unease.

That ship's already sailed, buddy. "Where did you get the pictures that you included in the article?"

Eburn tapped his foot as if *he* was the one who'd grown

impatient. Again, he was masking anxiety. "I'm a reporter, Agent. I don't have to reveal my sources."

Cassandra barked out a mirthless laugh. "Okay, let's back up for a moment, Mr. Eburn. You're a reporter, so I can assume you abide by a reporter's code of ethics."

A flush crept to the man's cheeks. "I don't know what that has to do—"

Cassandra's voice cut through Archer's protest like a blowtorch through ice cream. "It is the responsibility of every journalist to verify the accuracy of their work before releasing it into the public domain. I'd like to think you vetted whatever source sent you those photos, not just for the parties involved but also for your own reputation and career in journalism. God forbid you get yourself caught up in the dissemination of falsified information that pertains to such a high-profile case. We wouldn't want you to get smacked with a libel or defamation case on top of all that. The court cost to you alone would be astronomical. You do carry media liability insurance, I hope." Her words were laden with enough mocking derision to knock even the most confident and composed person on their ass.

"I...no, I don't, um..." The journalist seemed to have trouble finding the right words. "I—"

"Perfect," Cassandra cut him off before he could utter a coherent sentence. "Then we have no need to worry about the credibility of the information you have already released to the public. Glad we have that on the record. Now, I'll ask you again, Mr. Eburn. Where did you get those photos?"

"I don't have to give my sources—"

Zane snapped up a hand. "Let me explain something to you before you finish that thought. You're currently in possession of evidence that's relevant to a federal murder investigation. Now, I'm not sure how much of your conscience is even left, but there's a real possibility that you're sitting on evidence that could point us in the direction of a murderer."

Archer turned pale as a ghost and looked to his boss for guidance.

Propping her elbows on the desk, Farida steepled her fingers. "They're just trying to scare you, Archer. We are under no obligation to reveal anything to them until compelled to do so by the courts. We *are* talking about compromising pictures of one of their own, so I can see why they'd use smoke and mirrors to intimidate us into giving up confidential information."

"Ms. Bakkal." Cassandra uncrossed her legs and squared her shoulders. "Agent Palmer isn't using 'smoke and mirrors' to trick you out of your valuable source of fake photographs."

Farida swatted at an invisible insect. "Please. If I gave up my sources to every cop who wandered in here asking for them, I'd have been out of business years ago. No one trusts a reporter who's a rat. Just because one of your people at the FBI got caught screwing Ben Storey doesn't mean you're an exception to the rule."

Cassandra scooted to the edge of her chair, her glare fixed unerringly on Farida Bakkal. "Are you familiar with Illinois law regarding the nonconsensual dissemination of private sexual images? Also known as 'revenge porn' laws?"

Finally, exasperation was plain on Farida's unlined face. Truthfully, she'd held her composure for longer than Zane would have guessed. "Don't patronize me, Counselor. Of course, I'm—"

"No, I doubt you are. If you were, as the editor in chief of this," Cassandra wrinkled her nose, "agency, you wouldn't have posted that article or those photos. Distributing 'revenge porn' is a Class 4 felony in our great state."

Zane whistled, pretending this was news to him. "Felony, huh? How many years would these two get for that?"

Cassandra played along, not missing a beat. "We have every reason to believe those photos were altered. But, hypothetically, even if they were real, sharing them on your so-called news website is a felony, which carries a sentence of one to three years in prison, up to a twenty-five thousand dollar fine, and let's not forget the devastating effect it will have on your reputation. Unless, of course, you had the express permission of both people. Did you, by chance, obtain express permission of all parties depicted in those images?"

Farida's mouth was a hard line, but she didn't respond.

"I didn't think so." With an aloof sigh, Cassandra leaned back in her chair. "As we are well beyond the threshold relevance standard for reporter's privilege under shield laws, here's what we're going to do. Either your nervous writer over there can give us the name, email address, and submitted photos, or I can have the U.S. Attorney's office subpoena you for every teeny-tiny *crumb* of information you have relating to Councilman Storey. Every communication between this source and Mr. Eburn, every rough draft, every single copy of those pictures, we'll want all of it. Or you can cooperate, and we'll make this all as seamless as possible. The choice is yours."

Zane had never seen Cassandra in a courtroom, but now he suspected he knew why she'd advanced so far in her career. The woman was a shark.

"Oh." Cassandra raised a finger. "And if you refuse to cooperate, and we prove that those images are fake, you can fully expect a defamation lawsuit. Unlike the previous suits you've dealt with, this one *will* see trial. I will personally make sure of it."

Settling civil cases with sums of cash was standard practice for almost every business industry in the country and even around the world. The payouts varied in size based on the severity of the infraction, but rare were the instances where such legal action was dragged into a courtroom.

For an operation the size of Real Chicago News, Zane figured any trial that lasted longer than a couple weeks would be a far more severe financial impairment than a fifty-grand settlement.

Though the movement was slight, Farida leaned forward. "Go ahead and get the subpoena, Counselor. We'll be waiting."

Zane was stunned silent by Farida's response. Her entire news brand might have been complete bullshit, but she had heart. He'd give her that much.

Brushing off her black slacks, Cassandra's face contorted into the wickedest smile Zane had ever seen. She rose to her feet and slowly reached for her handbag. "Expect the subpoena by the end of the day."

Zane rose and buttoned his suit jacket. "Well, I'd thank you two for your cooperation, but…" He left the sentiment unfinished with a chuckle.

Without waiting for Archer or Farida to grunt out a grudging farewell, he yanked open the door and followed Cassandra out into the hall. He didn't offer so much as a sideways glance to the receptionist as they made their way back to the main corridor.

As the heavy door latched and they set off for the stairs, Cassandra raked a hand through her feathery hair. "Wow. I've never had to deal with RCN before, but those people are about as helpful as I'd expected."

Zane snorted. "If that's your way of saying they're the worst, I agree."

Since the young man on the ground floor was employed by the organization that owned the building and *not* the woman who ran Real Chicago News, Zane gave him a polite smile and a nod.

The pushback by Farida and her writer was predictable, but the burning question in the back of Zane's mind had more to do with Cassandra's sudden change of heart about Amelia. She'd been ready to drag Amelia into a witness box the night before, but today, she'd gone straight for Farida and Archer's throats in *defense of* his partner.

"I'm surprised." He reminded himself to choose his words carefully. Just because Cassandra had shown little mercy on Farida didn't mean she'd truly changed her tune.

Drawing her brows together, the lawyer flashed him a curious look as they reached the parking garage. "Surprised about what?"

"I thought you were hell-bent on Agent Storm being guilty." Well, so much for tact. He was too damn tired for finesse.

Cassandra blew out a sigh. "I guess it seemed that way, didn't it?"

"You could say that." Zane's voice was cooler than he'd intended, and he hurried to finish his thought before Cassandra could glare at him. "I get if you were playing devil's advocate. It's important to have someone challenge the consensus, or else you just wind up with an echo chamber. But it seemed like it was more than that."

She moved her bag from one shoulder to the other. "Yeah. I can see that. Honestly, I was under a lot of pressure from the U.S. Attorney. She told me that there were media outlets breathing down her neck and some of them were trying to hint that Storey's death might have been an inside job by the FBI."

"Wow," Zane fished in his pocket for the key fob, "I sometimes forget how fast news travels in a city this size."

"Me too, but the U.S. Attorney is *always* there to remind me. Fortunately, when SSA Corsaw ruled Agent Storm out as a suspect, that was good enough to get the reporters to back down. I think Simone Julliard and SAC Keaton teamed up for a press conference earlier today, didn't they?"

Pulling open the driver's side door, Zane was tempted to pull his phone from his pocket, eager to see if the U.S. Attorney for the Northern District of Illinois and his special agent in charge had done just that. It would have to wait, though. He needed to get back to the office.

"Spencer mentioned it, but I haven't watched it yet. I'm sure the media circus is coming, though."

Cassandra's expression darkened. "I hope we can do something about those pictures before anything gets to the national headlines. Otherwise, Agent Storm is going to wind up being tried in the court of public opinion even though we've ruled her out."

Shit.

Cassandra was right.

If a major news network like CNN or Fox picked up the story, they might censor the pictures, but they wouldn't blur Amelia's face. For reasons Zane didn't completely grasp, the public loved to grab their pitchforks and torches when a woman's naked pictures were leaked online. Never mind the creep that stole the images in the first place…all the blame was shifted onto the woman's shoulders.

"Shit." This time, he muttered the word aloud. Settling in behind the wheel, he turned the key over in the ignition as Cassandra fastened her seat belt. "All right. Let's get back to the office so you can send those assholes a subpoena."

"As soon as we get there, I'll get it started."

For the first time in the investigation, Cassandra's spark of determination reassured Zane that she would be a fierce ally.

Whether her allegiance was too-little-too-late remained to be seen.

19

Dropping to her knees, Amelia peered at the hole in the drywall that surrounded an unadorned outlet. The plastic plate—one of four hidden cameras from Amelia's apartment—had been shipped off to the FBI's forensic lab the day before, but according to the most recent update she'd received, nothing remotely useful had been recovered from the device.

Despondent, Amelia fell back to sit on the carpet.

Zane's earlier phone call, coupled with a message from forensics to advise that her car had been processed, had given her the motivation she'd needed to leave the comfort of the soft cotton sheets in which she'd been enveloped for most of the day.

To say Amelia had been shocked was an understatement. Zane had described Cassandra verbally sparring with the owner of the conspiracy-driven "news" site as a popcorn-worthy battle. Amelia had thought for sure that the lawyer had it out for her, even after being eliminated as the prime suspect in Ben's murder case.

Cassandra's vehemence and willingness to go for the

article author's throat had inspired Amelia to escape the pity party she'd thrown for most of the day. That and she would lose her mind if she didn't find something useful to occupy it.

Her tech skills ended at tracing an IP address, so searching for clues by researching the Real Chicago News was out of the question. And if anyone at the FBI caught wind of Amelia using federal databases to research Ben Storey or another aspect of the case, her job would be at risk.

With the Leóne RICO case in the toilet, she didn't even have the tedium of sifting through old investigations to keep her company. So, she'd turned to a different avenue to make herself useful.

Zane's refrigerator had been even sparser than she'd expected, so earlier Amelia opted for grocery shopping to replenish his food supply. In stealth mode, she'd slipped on an oversized hoodie, a baseball cap, and an oversized pair of sunglasses to disguise herself from both the media and anyone more nefarious who might be following her.

She'd exited at the rear of the building and had doubled back a few times to make sure she didn't have a tail. Both her car and service weapon had been returned to her earlier that day, and she was happy to have the gun on her. She almost wished her stalker would make himself known. She was ready to get this battle over.

The store hadn't been crowded, but any time a patron's gaze lingered in Amelia's direction for longer than a millisecond, she'd convinced herself that they recognized her from that damn article. She might have looked ridiculous wearing the shades indoors, but the alternative was much worse than fifteen minutes of misguided fashion.

On her way to load the bags into her trunk, she could have sworn she'd spotted a figure watching her from the edge of the parking lot. She hadn't been able to make out any details, not even whether the person was male or female. By the time she'd gingerly placed the eggs atop the rest of the food, they were gone.

They were probably never even there at all. She was probably just cracking up.

That had been an hour ago. After the grocery, she'd only had one more stop to make...her apartment. She hadn't meant to stay this long. All she'd come for was more clothes and toiletries.

Zane hadn't given an expiration date for his generosity but based on the pitiable state of her apartment, plus the knowledge that a stalker had planted cleverly hidden spy cameras, Amelia didn't plan on returning home any time soon. Even if Zane requested she leave by the end of the week, she could go stay with Joanna or fork over the cash for a hotel.

The latter, more than likely. Amelia loved her family, but she also valued her personal space. Zane's apartment was large enough to provide her with a sense of isolation, but the same couldn't be said for Joanna's house. Her small ranch was barely enough for one adult, two kids, and a corgi. Amelia didn't want to jeopardize her *and* Joanna's sanity by imposing on them.

Her father lived alone with his two cats, Cheese and George, but he'd recently moved to cut down on costs, and his new apartment sported only one bedroom. Unless Amelia wanted to spend the foreseeable future hunched over from back pain, she'd avoid couch surfing with Jim Storm.

Tilting her head back to stare at the ceiling, Amelia blew a raspberry. The temperature outside was cool enough that she didn't have to worry about the food in the trunk spoiling, but she'd prefer to make it back to Zane's apartment before he finished his workday. Surprise groceries wouldn't come across quite the same if Amelia had to ask him to help her haul the bags inside.

She tightened her ponytail and studied the gloom that had come with the sunset. Just one sunset ago, her life had been very different. In the space of twenty-four hours, she no longer recognized anything about her life.

Including this place.

The cameras might have been gone, but as she walked through the hall, she couldn't shake the nagging sensation of eyes on the back of her head.

Aside from the person she'd noticed at the grocery store —who likely didn't exist—Amelia had no concrete reason to believe she'd been followed. And even if she'd been tailed, the man or woman could be just a nosy reporter for the same website that had posted the initial article about Ben Storey's alleged infidelity.

Sure, a conspiracy theorist news author with a poor understanding of personal boundaries wasn't appealing, but they were a damn sight better than the alternative.

It could still be Joseph.

Amelia clenched her teeth and shook her head at the thought. No. If Zane saw Joseph when he left for Englewood the night before, then Joseph's involvement in Storey's death was a physical impossibility. Unless the man owned a private helicopter that he flew to work each day, he couldn't have made it to Englewood and back to the FBI office in time. That was assuming he'd left in the first place.

Technically, Joseph could have hired a hitman, but contract killers worth half a shit were far more difficult to find than Hollywood made them seem. Joseph would have had to shell out a small fortune for the murder of a man as prominent as Ben Storey, and the money trail would be easy to follow.

She smacked a hand on the side of her head. There her

mind went again, wandering off to parts unknown as the sun fell behind the horizon.

"Toothpaste, a phone charger, some spices, and clothes." She rubbed her forehead. "I should have made a list."

Though Zane had assured her on more than one occasion that he was a passable chef, when Amelia perused his spice collection, she'd wondered who in the hell had taught him to season food. All she'd found was basil, thyme, salt, oregano, and more basil.

There, focus on what you need to get. Stop thinking about Joseph or stalkers. Get the stuff you need and get the hell out of here. The sooner you're back in Zane's apartment, the sooner you can stop worrying about all this shit.

She flicked on the kitchen's overhead track lighting, and the sudden brightness stung her eyes. How long had she spent wandering around in the dark, anyway?

"Who knows," she muttered to herself.

Before the words even left her lips, time moved into... slow...motion.

The clatter of breaking glass jerked her attention to the living room's picture window. The gray and orange curtains swayed as if a gust of wind had blown them out of place, and golden light glittered off shards of glass that exploded onto the beige carpet.

Amelia's brain hadn't even processed what had happened as the cabinet to her side splintered into countless slivers of ruined wood with little more than a *crack*.

Other than the melodic breaking of glass and the bizarre rip and crack of the wood, there was no sound to accompany the disturbance. But Amelia didn't need the report of a gunshot to tell her what had happened.

Vibrations that carried sound traveled at approximately eleven-hundred feet per second, whereas the bullet from a

Barrett fifty-caliber sniper rifle traveled at more than double that speed.

At long distances, the damage caused by a shot often noticeably preceded the sound of the weapon firing.

On more than one occasion, Amelia had watched a wayward bullet rip a chunk out of a concrete barricade before the telltale crack split the desert air.

Before her brain had even registered these thoughts, Amelia let the muscles in her legs go slack. Her hands smacked the ceramic tile before the shooter could pull the trigger again. Though there was no more glass to break, another thud sounded out as a second shot slammed into the drywall below the first, followed by a third.

Time sped up as if to compensate for the slow motion that had come with the initial impact.

Using her knees and elbows, Amelia crawled toward the hallway with her body as low to the floor as she could manage. She saw the sectional couch and the coffee table clearly, but she swore she could smell dusty sand and sulfur as a different scene played out in her mind.

In the distance, the concussive force of a mortar reverberated along her stomach as she hurried to reach her post to return fire. A light breeze swirled dust and sand along the concrete walkway in front of Amelia. Was it the wind or had the debris been knocked loose by an explosion?

"We need a medic over here!" The call was distant and tinny, like a song heard through a battered old boom box.

Though she registered the cry, she couldn't divert precious cognitive resources to the other soldier's plight. They were on the lower level, anyway. She couldn't save them.

Without relinquishing her forward momentum, Amelia squeezed her eyes closed to rid herself of the onslaught of memories.

She'd been shot at—there was no alternative explanation

—but she wasn't crawling toward a sniper's post or a Barrett fifty-cal. She was crawling to the windowless hallway, and she was in her apartment in the middle of Chicago.

The *who, why, where,* and *how* would have to wait.

Right now, she had one goal. Get out of the line of fire.

Her elbows ached with the first hint of bruising, and the fabric of her jeans rubbed her knees raw as she crossed the lengthy stretch of carpet.

She ignored the discomfort, increasing her gait as she neared the hall.

Only when her feet were behind the relative cover of the drywall did she realize she'd held her breath for the last half of the crawl.

Gulping in a lungful of air, she flopped over to her back. On instinct, she pulled out her phone and service weapon. She might have been out of sight, but she didn't dare sit upright.

Aside from a slight tremble, her grasp was steady as she unlocked the screen of her phone.

Popular media liked to portray adrenaline as a helpful tool in a life-or-death situation. Though there was some truth to the cliché Hollywood spin, the body's fight-or-flight response worked against finesse. The rush of the sympathetic nervous system was useful for a burst of speed or strength, but fine motor movements such as aiming a rifle or dialing a damn phone number became almost impossible.

More often than not, adrenaline was an obstacle to be overcome, and Amelia had plenty of practice doing just that.

First, she dialed 911 and reported the incident, rattling off both her credentials and address. She answered the approximate six thousand questions the dispatch operator asked before managing to get off the line.

Zane was next.

"Hey." His voice was tired but alert. "What's up?"

"I'm at my apartment. Someone just shot at me. They missed, but I don't know where they are." Amelia surprised herself with how calm and level she kept her voice.

"What?" His deep timber jumped a couple of octaves. "Someone *shot* at you? Just now?"

"Yeah. I was, um, I was in the kitchen. At my apartment. The curtains were closed, so I don't know." She gulped another steadying breath. "Maybe they were trying to aim at my shadow. You were right. I should've gotten darker curtains for the living room."

"You sound *really* calm right now. Did you get hit?" Zane's tone sharpened. "Don't go into shock on me, Storm."

"This isn't the first time I've been shot at." Laughter erupted from her mouth. She was in shock, but not from a bullet wound. "I used to live in a combat zone, remember?"

"Where are you now? Exact location."

"On the floor. I have my service weapon. I got it and my car back earlier." She licked her dry lips as she craned her neck to catch a glimpse of the bedroom. "I don't know if they're going to try to come in here or not. There's no fire escape, so if they do, they'll have to come through the front. The door is locked, and I'm not in a direct line of it. Besides, if they try to force their way in or shoot through the door, they'll make a lot of noise. Not exactly a contract killer's best friend." She laughed again, more to ease her mounting tension than amusement at the poor excuse of a joke. "I should be fine if I stay here, but I can't risk leaving alone. Whoever is out there, if they're smart, they'll be watching my car."

"Right." The word was almost a growl. "I'll send CPD over. I'm grabbing Spencer too, so we can back them up."

"I've already called it in. I'm just hanging out, waiting for the cavalry to arrive."

"I'm on my way." It was the same thing he'd said twenty-four hours ago. "Call me if anything changes, okay?"

"You want me to put the killer on the phone before they off me?" She'd meant it as a joke but realized a second too late that her dark sarcasm sounded a lot more like defeatism. "Sorry. Yes. I'll keep you updated. Just get here quick."

"On my way!"

Clasping the phone in one hand and the Glock in the other, Amelia crossed both arms over her chest as if she was an ancient Egyptian queen preparing for her eternal slumber as she listened for any sound.

At the rate the past two days had gone, Amelia wondered if she ought to prepare for her final rest.

Lowering the semi-automatic rifle, I spat out a slew of four-letter words that would have made my mother faint if she'd still been alive.

I'd missed.

I never missed, but I'd missed three times.

My breath came out in a gauzy cloud as I went to work unscrewing the sound suppressor and folding the weapon's stock. I popped out the magazine, released the chambered round, and scooped up the spent shell casing. Without another glance to the faint glow of Amelia Storm's window, I replaced the Heckler and Koch rifle in a scuffed, leather guitar case. There were better ways to disguise firearms, but none were quite as convenient.

I took stock of the shadowy area one last time, hunched over—a precaution in case Amelia was ballsy enough to try and catch a glimpse of me—and hurried to the roof access door.

Earlier in the day, I couldn't believe my luck when I'd

spotted her leaving Zane Palmer's place. I'd been casing the building, moving from the front to the back to watch both exits. If I'd been a minute later, she would have slipped out and driven away without me knowing any better.

Luck had been on my side.

Just as luck had gifted me with a three stories high repurposed grocery store that was the perfect perch for an unobstructed view of Amelia's window when I followed her to her apartment. Since the building had been built for commercial use, the flat rooftop was much easier to navigate than the sharply pitched residential designs.

That was when my luck had run out.

Three damn shots. I was disgusted with myself.

Aside from the creak of hinges, the metal door was silent as I eased it closed. I'd only passed one person on my way into the building, but I'd made a point to keep my eyes on the ground. Not that I was recognizable with the blonde wig and hooded sweatshirt.

I might have been disguised, but I didn't need to take any stupid chances tonight. One was plenty.

To my relief, I didn't encounter any residents on my way down the three flights of steps. As I emerged behind the building, I kept my focus on the path ahead. The Chicago Police Department *and* the FBI were no doubt en route, and I needed to make myself scarce.

I struggled for breath, panting by the time I reached my rental car. For good measure, I stashed the guitar case in the trunk. Without a scanner, I couldn't be sure how soon law enforcement would surround the neighborhood, nor could I be sure if any barricades had been erected.

Three shots!

Growling to myself, I realized my mistake.

I'd tried to take a shot at the shape of Amelia Storm's shadow after she'd turned on the light in her apartment.

Until I'd spotted the woman's silhouette, I hadn't even been sure I'd catch a glimpse of her inside. I should have waited until she stepped out into the open.

Shooting her in the courtyard would have been a risk, sure, but I was familiar with the psychological phenomenon referred to as diffusion of responsibility. Also known as the bystander effect.

In short, the more people who were present to witness an emergency situation, the less likely each individual was to either help or report the incident. Most assumed that another onlooker would take on the responsibility, and there were plenty of well-documented incidents of the bystander effect at work.

The entire scenario seemed counterintuitive, but I knew better. It was a calculated risk, but I'd gotten ahead of myself. I'd pulled the trigger even though I wasn't sure I should have.

I'd just wanted the entire thing over with.

As I sped away from the cluster of apartment buildings, I clamped my hands around the steering wheel until my knuckles were white.

I might not have been a trained sniper like Amelia, and I suspected my informal lessons had just bit me in the ass. I doubted that a person who'd completed military sniper school would have taken aim at a damn shadow.

Gritting my teeth, I thumped the heel of one hand against the wheel. "Shit!"

I could have sworn I heard my father's mocking laughter as I went over the series of events one more time. The light had come on. I saw her. I knew *that* silhouette belonged to Amelia. I'd watched her enter the apartment building twenty minutes before my botched assassination attempt.

That's what I get for trying to beat a damn sniper at her own game.

Back when my miserable father had been alive, he and my

uncles made a tradition of going out for a twelve-hour hunting expedition on the first official day of deer season. Armed with bolt-action Remington and Winchester rifles, flasks filled with whiskey, and bags of beef jerky, they'd depart at dawn and return not long after the sun went down.

Of course, I'd been expected to remain at home with my mother, all the other female relatives, and the boys who were too young to wield a rifle.

At age thirteen, two years after I'd seen my father for what he really was, I'd piped up for the first time to ask if I could join them someday. My father and uncles hadn't given me the same attentive shooting lessons they'd provided to my male relatives, so I'd been sure to add the caveat to my request. None of my cousins had shown half the aptitude with a firearm that I had, but my natural inclination didn't seem to matter more than my two X chromosomes.

I'd kept the hypothetical question short and sweet. "If I learn to shoot, can I go with you guys?"

My father had given me a look like I'd sprouted a third arm before he laughed. He'd taken the moment to remind me, for the hundredth time, that my place was at home with my mother and my aunt.

I'd been schooled in sexism from a young age and expected his condescending response. Still, disappointment slammed into my chest like a blow from Mike Tyson in his prime.

After sulking for a couple of days, I picked myself up. Our family's values were sexist as hell, but everyone could agree on a love of firearms. I'd learned gun safety and handling from the moment I'd been physically capable of firing one. With self-defense in mind, I'd asked my mother to let me take her low-caliber rifle to our makeshift shooting range, intending to become a better shot.

She, of course, granted me permission without a second thought.

For an entire year, any time I had the opportunity, I headed out to the range, but only if I could be alone. I didn't need my domineering uncle or my half-drunk father breathing down my neck to ask me questions about what, exactly, I was doing.

The following deer season, I again asked my father if I could join the hunt.

He had responded with snorting laughter and waved me away with a hand as if I was a gnat he wanted to swat. To this day, his words haunted me.

"We've been over this. You're a girl, so stay here and learn to be a half-decent cook so a man will actually want to marry your ass someday. But watch what you eat. You're getting a little chubby, and you know how guys feel about fat women."

His words had hurt, but I held to my plan, determined to see it through.

My Uncle Doug had been regarded as the best shot of the entire miserable family. That in mind, I'd proposed to dear ole dad that, if I could best him in a shooting contest, my father would have to let me join the hunting trip. Before my father could hurl any four-letter words at me, my uncle asked what he would get if he won. The sinister way he'd looked at me while posing the question still sent a chill down my spine.

Despite the pressure, I still proved myself to both my father and Uncle Doug. And for maybe the first time in my life, I'd earned something none of the other women in my family had. As my father mocked his brother, laughing so hard he had to wipe tears from his cheeks, he'd looked at me with pride.

The bright red flash of taillights yanked me out of the reverie like the deployment of a parachute. With a sharp intake of breath, I slammed on the brake pedal as I tightened my hands into a death grip on the steering wheel.

Tires squealed, and my heart leapt into my throat. *No, not like this. No one can know I was here tonight.*

Just before the fender of my rental could smash into the rear bumper of the SUV in front of me, my sedan ground to a stop.

The driver had pulled to a lazy stop well ahead of the traffic lights. If I'd hit their damn Jeep, there was a good chance that a passing Chicago police officer would take note and stop to ensure the accident was being handled properly. I was still too close to Amelia Storm's apartment to risk being seen.

"Shit!" I sagged against the seat. "What is *wrong* with you?" Despite the irritability that thrummed alongside my moment of panic, I was relieved. The close call was a sign for me to focus. My task wasn't finished yet. I had to get home, out of this ridiculous blonde wig, and form a *real* plan.

Now that Amelia knew someone was trying to kill her, she'd be more difficult to reach.

Because an ex-military FBI agent wasn't hard enough to get to before.

I snorted at the thought. Stan Young had offered a handsome sum of cash for the hit on Amelia Storm—even more than he'd paid for Ben Storey. There was a reason for the high price.

My goal had been to take Amelia out with a single shot and deal with the fallout later. As confident as I was in my physical prowess, I had no desire to engage in a hand-to-hand brawl with a woman who'd spent ten years in the military.

I needed to come up with a better tactic than an anonymous bullet to the head.

As the red glow of the traffic light gave way to green, I

inched along behind the Jeep, keeping my focus on the road. I wouldn't make the same mistake twice.

The same went for Amelia Storm.

I'd missed yet another opportunity, but I wouldn't miss another.

20

Zane's heart thundered in his chest as he plucked his black coat off the mesh-backed office chair and set off toward the conference room. It was their base of operation for the Storey case, and he'd put money on Spencer being there.

When he reached the end of the row of desks, Zane spotted a familiar head of red hair through the open door of the break area. Cassandra Halcott held a navy-blue mug in both hands, and she leaned against the laminate counter as she blew on the steaming beverage.

Maybe she knows where Spencer is.

Zane could have sworn that the SSA had avoided Cassandra ever since he'd told him about her and Joseph Larson's relationship. Then again, Spencer *had* been busy over the last twenty-four hours.

Fastening the buttons of his coat, Zane strode up to the doorway and spotted another familiar face.

Speak of the devil.

Joseph Larson's scrutinizing stare fell on Zane. He paused mid-sentence to sip his cup of coffee.

The first pinpricks of anger stabbed at Zane's heart, but he ignored the sensation. Amelia had almost been killed, and he didn't have time for Larson's shit.

"Hey, Palmer." Cassandra straightened to her full height. "You headed out for the day? I thought you and SSA Corsaw planned to talk to Iris Storey."

"We were." Zane kept his focus on the prosecutor and away from Larson. "But someone just shot at Agent Storm when she went back to her apartment."

"Oh my god." The pang of worry in Cassandra's voice was, as best as Zane could tell, genuine. "Is she okay? When did this happen?"

"Storm's fine." Zane was already backing out into the hallway. "It just happened. I was hoping I'd find Corsaw here so we could—"

"I'll go with you." Larson's announcement turned the pinpricks of ire in Zane's chest into daggers.

Son of a bitch.

Zane swallowed the retort and held up a hand. "It's fine, Larson. CPD is probably there. I'll just go by myself and get ahold of Corsaw once I have more information."

Though Larson appeared steady and collected, there was a twinge of unfettered anxiety in his expression.

Larson's reaction was curious, and it caused Zane to stop in his tracks. He studied the man closely. Zane didn't have the time to question his instincts because he needed to get to Amelia as soon as possible.

Damn. Damn. Damn.

Following his gut, Zane made a decision he might regret. "All right. Let's go."

"Right behind you." Larson set his coffee beside the sink.

Zane didn't stick around for the agent's departing words to Cassandra. Larson caught up to him as he waited for the elevator. The more he thought about it, the more he liked this decision.

When he'd worked as a CIA operative, Zane had received a piece of advice that helped keep him alive during his decade of covert operations. *Never reveal your allegiance to the enemy. Let them think you're their friend. Keep them close.*

Joseph Larson had tried to rape Amelia. At some point, he'd have to address that, even if there was nothing he could legally do about it.

With all his CIA connections and his tenure in covert operations, how could he sit idly by and watch him go about his life unpunished? Especially when, with a single phone call, he could have Larson carried off to a secret CIA prison or have the bastard meet with an unfortunate accident.

No. I can't. That was Russia, and that was the CIA. This is the U.S., and Larson's an FBI agent, not an insurgent.

The desire was tempting, but if Zane abused that power, he'd be no different than the mobsters he and Amelia helped to put away. As he slid behind the wheel, he repeated the mantra to himself a few times for good measure. Justice would eventually be served. He'd find a way, but he'd stay within the boundaries of the law.

Mostly.

To say that the drive to Amelia's apartment was the longest twenty minutes of Zane's life wasn't much of an exaggeration. A butter knife wouldn't have been adequate to slice through the tension in the air. He'd need a machete.

Screw that.

"Let's get something clear right now."

Larson gave him a sidelong look. "What's that?"

Zane waited until he stopped completely at a traffic light before turning in his seat. "Amelia told me what happened between the two of you, and I'm going to say this just once..."

He waited until Larson met his gaze. "You hurt her again, I'll fucking kill you."

When Larson opened his mouth to speak, Zane turned the radio station all the way up. There was no conversation to be had. He wasn't going to listen to excuses. He'd said what he wanted to say, and that was going to be it.

Larson now knew he would be watching him. And he would.

The dial was set to NPR to avoid any snarky comments about his music preference, but at the same time, he lamented the days when Larson's taste in music was the worst aspect of his personality.

Back then, he hadn't known Larson was a scumbag rapist who had to blackmail women to sleep with him. All he'd known was that Larson listened to far too many songs about blue jeans and trucks and that he'd almost driven Amelia insane with his playlists.

As he pulled into a parking spot on Amelia's street, Zane counted four black and white squad cars. The police presence was lighter than he'd expected, but the CPD was almost always spread thin.

He showed his badge to a burly officer outside the apartment building, opened the double doors, and took the stairs two at a time. Larson was close on his heels, though he'd rather have left the man in the car. Preferably the trunk.

But having him here was good, Zane reminded himself. He could watch Larson like a damn hawk, and he could also support Amelia whenever she was forced to be in the man's presence. He wished he could save her from ever having to lay eyes on the man again, but since that wasn't possible, playing referee was something he could do.

He was greeted by the squawk of a police radio the moment he stepped into Amelia's living room. The space was still disheveled from the night before, and now it boasted three new holes in the drywall.

A uniformed officer stood in front of the granite breakfast bar, Amelia at her side. Zane recognized the woman from the scene of Ben Storey's murder. Officer McAdam, if memory served.

What the hell?

Chicago was a major U.S. city populated by millions of inhabitants. Zane wasn't sure of the odds, but he figured the likelihood of the same cop responding to two related crime scenes within twenty-four hours was slim.

Is it, or am I just jumping at shadows now?

Turning to Larson, he stepped into the agent's space. "How about you step back outside for about ten minutes and see what they've learned about the sniper's hide?"

Larson's jaw tightened, but he nodded. "Sure thing."

When he was gone, Zane cleared his throat to announce his presence and approached the two women.

Amelia turned to face him, a weary looking smile on her face. "About time."

He grinned. "I'll be faster when the Bureau issues us flying cars." He kept the smile in place when he acknowledged the officer. "Officer McAdam, right?"

"Evening, Agent Palmer." McAdam gestured to Amelia. "I was just giving Agent Storm an update. We've secured the area, and there are a couple cruisers at each end of the block to monitor traffic coming and going."

Zane dipped his chin. "Thank you for getting here so quickly. You responded to the scene of Ben Storey's murder too, didn't you?"

Clicking her pen closed, the officer returned a small notepad to her pocket. "That's right. My partner and I both did."

"You're from the Seventh Precinct, right?" He'd maintained an amicable tone, but Officer McAdam's posture stiffened as Zane asked the question.

She squared her shoulders, clearly catching his intent. "I am. But tonight, my partner and I were at the Eighteenth to help with a training exercise. He ought to be back here soon if you want to verify that with him."

Well, at least her alibi would be easy to confirm. Zane pushed past the moment of suspicion. Sometimes a coincidence was simply a coincidence. Sometimes.

"We appreciate you backing Agent Storm up these last couple days. Thank you."

Some of her borderline hostility dissipated. "Of course. Like Sergeant Karasek says, we're all on the same team."

Zane tilted his head in the direction of the hall. "Agent Storm, a word?"

Amelia gave her thanks to Officer McAdam before following him to the shadowy doorway of her room.

As the door latched closed, he and Amelia were enveloped in darkness. Based on the shots that had been taken at Amelia through her closed curtains a half hour earlier, Zane wasn't inclined to reach for the light switch.

He reached out to touch her shoulder. "Are you doing okay?" A stupid question, but necessary.

She gave his hand a light squeeze. "Physically? I'm fine. Mentally? Well, I've definitely had better days, but I've had worse too."

"I'm afraid I'm about to make it worse." Before she could question him or worry too long, he ripped the bandage off. "Larson's here. Sorry I couldn't give you a heads-up." He watched her for any sign of agitation, but the professional that she was, she kept a straight face. "I was looking for Corsaw, but I ran into Larson in the breakroom with Cassandra. Don't ask me what the hell he was still doing at work past five-thirty. On the plus side, it means he wasn't the one who shot at you."

Amelia did the very thing he'd hoped she'd do...she snorted. "It's okay. Compared to a sniper, Joseph seems like a pussycat right about now. Besides, when he is doing his job, he doesn't have time to be a creeper."

"You know what they say. Can't take the creep out of the creeper."

Even in the low light, he noted the obvious confusion on Amelia's face. "What? Who says that?"

Zane held up his hands in feigned surrender. "Okay, you got me. No one says that. I'm running on two hours of sleep, and caffeine is the only reason I'm even coherent."

She wiggled her fingers for air quotes. "'Coherent,' he says."

"Can you see this?" He flipped her off. "It's dark, but I hope you can see that."

Their shared laughter helped to ease some of the tension of the past twenty-four hours. "Okay, we can duke this out later. Come on, our resident creeper will be up here in a few minutes. Corsaw and the CSU should be here soon too."

Sure as shit, the SSA was in the living room. Zane half-expected Larson to be at the man's side, but he was nowhere to be found.

Zane checked over his shoulder before he addressed the SSA. "Did you see Larson?"

"Across the street. He and a couple officers are going to canvass the apartment building since that's where we suspect the shots were fired from." He gestured to a familiar man who was busy in the kitchen. "That's our ballistics expert. He should be able to tell us for sure where the shooter was. Speaking of, it's nice to see you in one piece, Agent Storm."

Amelia shoved both hands in the pockets of her hooded sweatshirt. "Thanks. The apartment building across the street has a flat roof. It used to be a store, but it was remodeled into apartments in the seventies."

"Noted." His expression darkened. "Agent Storm, it's looking like there's someone out there who views you as a loose end. Now, I don't say this lightly, but I think you should consider a safe house until we figure out who's behind this."

Amelia's face twisted into confusion, followed by defiance.

Before the suggestion—which he suspected was closer to an order than a recommendation—could devolve into an argument, Zane raised a hand. "She's already staying in my spare bedroom."

A muscle in Spencer's jaw tightened. "No disrespect, Palmer. I know you're competent, but your apartment isn't anywhere near as secure as a safe house."

"Maybe," Zane wasn't going to back down easily, "but safe houses are usually reserved for civilian witnesses, right? *Agent* Storm isn't a civilian. And considering that either a U.S. Marshal or an FBI agent are in charge of security for witnesses staying in our safe houses, and since Storm's staying with an FBI agent…" He left the observation unfinished and lifted his shoulders.

Spencer pressed his lips together, but the moment of indignation seemed to have passed. "You've got a point, Palmer. I'll give you that this time, but if anything like this happens again. *Anything*…Agent Storm's going to a damn safe house."

As Amelia opened her mouth to reply, Zane shot her a warning glance. Though Spencer could hardly be described as an upbeat person, the SSA was reasonable, and he tended to keep an open mind.

Unless he was pushed. If that happened, he'd hold his ground out of sheer stubbornness. Zane did *not* want to deal with the obstinate part of Spencer Corsaw. Not when he was fully rested, and sure as hell not on little to no sleep.

Amelia cleared her throat. "Okay. That's fair."

In his gut, Zane knew that Amelia's living situation was only temporary. If they didn't find a lead, and if the attempts on her life continued, the Bureau would be obligated to consider Witness Security until they caught Storey's killer.

He'd mentally ruled out Joseph Larson, but otherwise, Zane was no closer to the would-be assassin's identity. The motive might have been selfish, but he realized that if he didn't find the failed hitman, he'd lose Amelia for good.

One way or another, she'd be gone.

The clock was ticking.

21

The metallic click of the front door's deadbolt jerked Amelia away from the edge of unconsciousness. Though her rational mind knew who was behind the disturbance, a jolt of panic still rushed up her spine as she blinked to clear the film from her eyes.

Spencer had sent her back to Zane's place with another stern reminder that she wasn't permitted to work on the Storey investigation. As much as she wanted to find the person who'd almost killed her, she was grateful to be away from that damn apartment. In the span of twenty-four hours, her home had gone from comfortable to anxiety inducing.

From her perch atop the arm of the sectional, Hup flattened her ears and swished her tail.

"It's just Zane." Amelia stifled a yawn as she pushed herself to sit upright. "Not that you're even a good guard cat. Someone could break in, but as long as they gave you some treats, you'd help them carry the stuff out, wouldn't you?"

The calico meowed.

"You're right. Cats don't move. They supervise." Amelia

stretched both arms above her head and shook the remaining cobwebs from her brain.

Since there wasn't much she could do to help the FBI identify who'd shot at her, she had spent the past couple hours in curiosity-satisfying research.

She'd started with Farida Bakkal, the owner of Real Chicago News. Zane and Spencer had no doubt looked through the woman's history, but Amelia wasn't privy to any of their findings.

To her surprise, Farida sported a collection of impressive credentials. Both her parents were retired surgeons, and her two brothers had followed in their footsteps.

Farida, on the other hand, had attended an Ivy League school where she initially majored in business and marketing but later switched to journalism. She'd worked for a couple major news networks, including a stint as a field reporter for a local Chicago news station.

What had driven the woman to switch from supporting legitimate sources of news to funding her own conspiracy-ridden website was a mystery to Amelia. Maybe she was playing the entire city for chumps, or maybe she'd just lost touch with reality.

Neither Farida nor the article's author, Archer Eburn, had a criminal background. Both had graduated from college near the top of their class, and for reasons Amelia would never understand, they'd gravitated toward the veritable sludge at the bottom of the internet.

Once Amelia had finished her research on Farida and Archer, she moved on to another name that had been burning a hole in the back of her mind.

Luca Passarelli.

Tried and true D'Amato family capo.

Mafia royalty by birth.

Father of Alex Passarelli.

Last but not least, the man who'd threatened Amelia's life, forcing her out of Chicago when she was only eighteen. He had no doubt learned of her return to the city, as well as her current profession.

Had Luca found out about Amelia and Alex's interactions over the past few months? Had he discovered that Alex had provided her with intel pertinent to the Bureau's takedown of a Leóne prostitution and sex trafficking ring? The Leónes were the D'Amato family's mortal enemy, but involving the FBI in the ongoing feud was still taboo.

Even with access to the vast databases of the FBI, Amelia couldn't find the answers to her queries without personally reaching out to Alex. After their last interaction, to say she wasn't keen on the idea was a grave understatement.

For god only knew how many years, Alex had kept his family's relationship with Trevor Storm a secret. Amelia's older brother had been on the D'Amato payroll and had laundered the funds through his wife's hair salon. He'd taken any specifics about the arrangement with him to the grave.

Allegedly, Alex and his father had reached out to Trevor for help with the cold kidnapping case of Gianna Passarelli. Alex hadn't admitted as much, but Amelia wasn't naïve enough to believe that Trevor's involvement with the D'Amatos had ended at Gianna.

Despite the love Amelia held for her older brother, she was pissed that he'd kept such a volatile secret. Worse, she was more than a little disappointed.

If Trevor hadn't fallen in with the D'Amato crime family, he might still be alive.

Amelia tried to ignore the fact that she was playing the same dangerous game, but Ben Storey's murder was a pointed reminder that she'd never truly leave behind her ties to the D'Amatos.

Just because she hadn't found any bad blood between Ben

Storey and the D'Amatos didn't mean Luca's hands were clean. The seasoned mafioso was a vengeful prick. Amelia didn't doubt that he was capable of killing Ben in cold blood. But why target him?

Amelia had little interaction with the councilman. It was a pretty big leap to think that killing him would score any points against the girl who'd attempted to steal his son. Though if Young was tied to the Leónes, it did stand to reason that Young could have ties to the D'Amatos. And that still pointed to potential mafia involvement. Which kept Luca at the top of her suspect list.

Three shots fired from a silenced rifle in the distance was consistent with a mafia-style hit. *Was that a warning?*

Any shooter worth their salt would not have attempted to aim at her shadow through the curtains. Too many variables to miss the target. The bullets might not have hit her, but they'd come close.

Too damn close.

Gritting her teeth, Amelia rubbed her eyes to clear away the fog in her vision.

Zane emerged from behind the wall that separated the foyer from the living area, and his impassive expression warmed. "Hey. You're still awake?"

Amelia wiped her fingertips on her black leggings to displace the smudged eyeliner. "It's not even nine o'clock yet. I slept until noon."

"Must have been nice. I think I got about two hours of sleep last night." As if to emphasize his point, he yawned.

"Stop it." Amelia tried to wave away the contagious gesture, but her effort was in vain.

He chuckled as he draped his suit jacket over the back of a chair next to the kitchen island. "Sorry. I can't really help it at this point."

Amelia scooted to the side to make room for him. "Did

you guys find anything?" She could guess the answer but was obligated to ask anyway.

Letting out a sigh, Zane loosened his shiny blue tie. "Not much. Spencer and the CPD canvassed the apartments across the street. One resident thought they ran across a woman they didn't recognize around the time of the shooting, but they couldn't remember much about her. They'd been busy wrangling their five-year-old at the time, and they just remembered that she was blonde, and she was carrying a guitar case."

Amelia sat up a little straighter. "A guitar case? She could have hidden a rifle in it, easily."

Zane paused beside the couch to untuck his dress shirt. "That's what we were thinking. But the resident we talked to really couldn't remember much more about her than her hair color, the guitar case, and that she was dressed in dark colors."

"I'm guessing there aren't any security cameras?"

"Nope. Ballistics says the trajectory of the bullets puts the gunman, or woman, on the roof of the building across the street." He dropped down onto the couch cushion, and Amelia caught a whiff of the product he used to style his hair, mingled with his woodsy cologne.

"That rooftop is perfect for a sniper to set up and stay comfortably for a long while." *The perfect place for a mafia contract killer.*

Zane dipped his chin. "Exactly. There were no shell casings, so whoever they were, they policed their brass. They would've had to leave in a hurry, though. The CPD officers who responded were pretty close by, and they got there within minutes."

"The shooter knew the area." The more Amelia learned about the would-be assassin, the more she realized she was lucky to be alive. If she hadn't immediately dropped to the floor, the second shot would have hit its mark. She brushed off the thought before the bout of unease could manifest as a pit in her stomach. "They must have staked out the neighborhood. I could have *sworn* someone was following me today. I can't believe I didn't see them."

"Well, like you said, they knew what they were doing." He unfastened the top button of his shirt. "But I think the big takeaway we've gotten so far is that we might be searching for a woman."

Amelia wrapped her arms around her legs and rested her chin on her knees. "Do you think Ben might have actually had a mistress? That explains where the messages came from. The ones planted on my laptop."

Zane rubbed a cheek heavy with stubble. "That could be. We were thinking more along the lines of a contract killer tonight, but I suppose we don't know much about Storey's *actual* personal life, do we?"

Amelia let herself fall back in her cushioned seat. "I guess not. That might explain why I didn't notice anyone following me when I was out today. I would've been watching for a man, not a woman."

Narrowing his eyes in feigned indignation, Zane waved a finger at her. "Sexist. Women can kill people just as well as men can."

Amelia flipped him the bird. "Shut up."

He flashed her one of his showstopping smiles. "Anyway. I took a different route home and did a few laps around the apartment before I parked, just to make sure no one was tailing me. Spencer would be disappointed by anything less, I'm sure. Which reminds me. I have something for you."

A flurry of sarcastic comments, plenty of which were dirty, ran through Amelia's head, but she bit her tongue as he dug in the pocket of his slacks.

As Zane reached out to her, he opened his hand to reveal

the slim, silver band of a ladies' watch. "Here, I picked this up for you on my way home."

Amelia liked the style, but she wasn't sure how the accessory would help her against a hidden sniper. Not unless Zane had acquired it from James Bond. "Um, thanks. It's cute."

His shoulders shook as he lapsed into a fit of laughter. "I'm sorry. Your face." He covered his eyes, and she could tell he was fighting back another round of mirth. "You looked confused, but you were still trying to be polite, and it was just…it was funny."

"Sure." Amelia dragged out the word for an extra three syllables.

"Okay, okay. Sorry." Zane gestured to the watch. "On the back. There's a switch that you can use to turn on a GPS tracker."

As Amelia flipped over the face, she spotted the button beside a tiny screw. "Oh. So, it's like Life Alert, right?"

When she looked up, Zane had donned another of his charming grins. "If that's how you want to think of it, sure."

The good humor was infectious. Neither of them had smiled or laughed much lately, and the moment of levity was like a cool breeze on a stifling summer day.

"Well, thank you." She slid the band onto her wrist. "It'll go great with my pajamas because I'm not leaving here for the next few days."

A pang of concern dampened his smile, and Amelia wished she could vacuum up her sarcastic comment.

She waved a dismissive hand. "It's okay. Hup would probably lose her mind if there wasn't someone familiar with her all day. She's six, but she still acts like a kitten. I cleared everything with SAC Keaton. I'm just going to work from home…err…from your apartment for the next few days."

For a beat, he seemed lost in thought. Almost as if he was about to reveal a groundbreaking truth or a deeply buried secret. But as soon as the expression appeared, it was gone. "That's a good idea, actually. There were reporters camped out down the block from the office this morning, but they were gone by the time we got back from RCN."

"Oh." Amelia snapped her fingers, Zane's strange expression all but forgotten. "Real Chicago News, that's what I wanted to tell you. Here, check this out." She tucked a leg under herself and scooped the laptop off the coffee table.

"Did they post something else?" The seat at Amelia's side sank as he moved closer.

"Kind of. It's good, though." She touched the trackpad to bring the screen to life and typed in her password to reveal...

Shit. It was her most recent query into Luca Passarelli.

How did I forget about that?

The thud of her heartbeat reverberated throughout her entire body as ice-cold dread snaked its way up her back. She fought against the abrupt urge to slam the laptop closed and throw the computer across the room.

"Luca Passarelli?" Zane's curious voice cut through the whirlwind of anxiety that roared in Amelia's head.

"Um, yeah."

"He's a D'Amato capo, right? Why were you looking at him?" His tone was amiable enough, but she could have sworn she caught a hint of suspicion in the words.

Amelia had two choices and little to no time to consider her options. She could break down and admit the truth. She could confess her four-year high school romance with Alex Passarelli and all the baggage that went along with such a connection. If she told the truth, mentioning Trevor's involvement with the D'Amatos would be inevitable.

She'd have to face reality, and she wasn't sure she was ready to step into the proverbial light.

There was Emilio Leóne and the Leila Jackson kidnapping. Alex had helped her crack the case wide open, and she'd come close to an outright lie when she'd told the Bureau that the tip had come from a confidential informant.

What would Zane think of her if he knew she'd cooperated with a mob boss to catch another mob boss?

Would his opinion of her involvement in Ben Storey's death change? Would he take her connection with the D'Amato family to Spencer in hopes that the relationship was a new lead?

He'd have to. He'd have no choice.

They'd rip apart Amelia's past, just like they'd ripped apart her home. She kept those skeletons buried for a reason...she wasn't that person anymore.

The Cinderella story of a poor girl from Englewood finding true love with the wealthy son of a mafia kingpin was bullshit, and she was ashamed that she'd ever thought otherwise.

Her second option was to lie.

Despite the secrets that followed her like phantoms, Amelia had never been dishonest with Zane. She liked to think that the sentiment was mutual and that he held their friendship in the same high regard.

A single lie could end the delicate trust. One moment of untruth, of weakness, and the relationship that meant so much to her would come undone.

But if she told the truth, she risked everything. Zane would be obligated to investigate the new lead, and gradually, the FBI would unearth all the secrets.

Like dominoes, the ghosts of her past would topple everything she held dear. Beginning with her career and ending with...well, she didn't want to know.

Amelia cleared her throat, but the gesture did little to chase away the lead weight in her stomach. She'd been quiet for too long, and she knew firsthand how observant Zane could be.

"Um, would it be okay if I told you it's something I don't want to talk about right now?"

Or ever.

She knew the question would only heighten his curiosity, but she couldn't lie to him. She just couldn't.

Zane's stare was like a pair of laser beams on the side of Amelia's face, but she didn't dare look him in the eye. Not yet.

"Sure." He was clearly disappointed and more than a little concerned, but his respect for her won out, which nearly brought fresh tears to her eyes. "What did you want to show me?"

She'd almost forgotten the reason she'd opened the laptop in the first place. "Right, that." A couple taps brought up the homepage of Real Chicago News and their newest post. "They just published this a couple hours ago. It's a revision from their article earlier."

As Zane leaned forward, he seemed to maintain as much distance between them as possible. "No pictures. And this version says that the photos they shared might not have been real."

"Right. Those pictures are still out there, but they're definitely harder to find now. Real Chicago News was by far the biggest site that had posted them. Which is just in time because Storey's in the national news now."

Zane dragged a hand over his face and slumped back in his seat. "Great. That's *exactly* what I wanted to deal with tomorrow."

Amelia eased the laptop closed and rolled her aching shoulders. "Yeah, it's a mess, isn't it?"

"In more ways than one."

The remark could have been a passive-aggressive jab at Amelia's unwillingness to share her history with Luca Passarelli, or it might have been a genuine comment about the sinkhole that Ben Storey's murder investigation had become.

As Amelia turned to meet Zane's intent gaze, she wasn't sure.

All she could do was hope that she hadn't just sabotaged the first real connection she'd made with someone in the last decade.

22

As the car slowed to a stop in front of a two-story gray stone house, Zane locked the screen of his cell and pocketed the device. To his side, Spencer Corsaw propped his arms atop the steering wheel as he studied the residence.

In an effort to catch Iris Storey before she started her day, Zane and Spencer had set out to the Storey residence bright and early. They'd even called ahead to ensure the trip wasn't a waste of time.

Tall elms and oaks stood in neatly manicured lawns, and despite the impending morning rush hour, the street was quiet. In the side mirror, Zane watched a mother a few houses down herding two children into the back seat of a Land Rover.

The upscale portion of Chicago was far enough away from lower-income areas to maintain its image as an upper-middle-class neighborhood while close enough to the heart of the city to retain its character.

Zane had half-expected the Storey family to reside in a cookie-cutter suburb forty-five minutes away from the FBI office, and he'd been pleasantly surprised to learn that the morning drive would only take twenty. Which was more than enough time for his mind to wander to Amelia's bizarre behavior the previous night.

He couldn't help but be curious about Amelia's reasons for researching Luca Passarelli, especially after the near heart attack she'd had when she realized the man's information was still on her computer screen.

Amelia had always perked up at the mention of the D'Amato family, and her sudden interest in Luca made the behavior all the more peculiar.

So far, there was no indication in the Storey investigation that pointed in the direction of the D'Amatos, so he couldn't quite figure out why she would have been researching that mafia family in the first place.

What secret was she keeping from him?

Even if the topic hadn't pertained to a powerful mob boss, her inability to trust him with the truth still would have stung. But the fact that she'd refused to talk about researching that same mafioso in the midst of a murder case —a murder for which she'd been framed—had given him pause.

As Spencer killed the engine, Zane pulled himself back to reality. He rubbed absentmindedly at the tattoo on his shoulder. A tattoo that Amelia would undoubtedly recognize.

What would he have done if she'd caught a glimpse of the nautical stars on his shoulders? Or the matching stars on his knees? Would he tell her that he'd spent most of his CIA career so deep undercover that he'd almost forgotten who he was?

Maybe she'd be impressed by his lofty standing in the Russian mafia. By the stars on his shoulders, signifying the position of authority he'd held, and the stars on his knees, which meant he'd bow to no man.

If Spencer hadn't been at his side, he'd have scoffed at himself. He already knew the answer to his stupid question.

He'd lie. He'd make up an undercover operation he'd worked with the FBI. The tale would explain his reluctance to go into detail, and he'd be absolved of any expectation to share specifics.

That's different. I can't *tell her about what I did in the CIA. I can't tell* anyone *about that.*

But just because he wasn't permitted to discuss his time in the CIA didn't mean the betrayal was any less significant. There were ten entire years of his life he couldn't even mention. That decade had defined him, and Amelia would never know.

At the absolute least, Amelia deserved the benefit of the doubt. She'd always been honest with him, and he'd done his damnedest to return the favor.

He knew he *should* trust Amelia, but the caveman part of him didn't want to. Despite his desire to think rationally, Zane struggled to reconcile the double standard.

The realization came with a stone in the pit of his stomach, and he was suddenly glad he'd missed breakfast. Why was it so hard for him to accept that some secrets must not be told? Maybe, in time, they could eventually confide in each other. But if Zane ever hoped to get to that level, he had to stop the Neanderthal part of his brain from distorting his perception.

Spencer's voice was a merciful reprieve from the spiral of what-ifs.

"Iris Storey is a State Supreme Court judge." The SSA still rested one arm on the steering wheel. "I think it'd be worth asking her if she's had any risky cases lately, you know? Anyone threatening her about something that she ruled against them, that sort of thing."

"Yeah." Zane's tone was so confident, he could have tricked himself into thinking he'd paid attention. "That's a good idea. We've been looking at this from Ben's perspective, but it's certainly possible for a judge to rack up a few enemies."

Spencer unfastened his seat belt. "Exactly. All right, you ready?"

"After you." Zane mentally crossed his fingers as they stepped out into the crisp November morning.

Though Cassandra Halcott had submitted a subpoena to Real Chicago News the day before, the Bureau wasn't likely to receive the original copies of the photos for days, maybe even a week. If the discussion with Iris Storey yielded no new information, they'd be stuck beating their heads against one dead end after another while they waited.

Tree branches rattled overhead as the wind whipped its way down the street. The sudden cold was a much-needed slap to the face. By the time they reached the end of the sidewalk, he was wide awake.

Zane clenched his jaw to keep his teeth from chattering. "Wasn't it, like, eighty the other day?"

"Welcome to the Midwest, buddy." Spencer shot him a grin. "Just be patient. It might be eighty again next week. Who knows?"

A grin? Since when was Spencer Corsaw so damn jovial in the morning? Or ever?

Zane made a mental note to ask the SSA about the cause of his apparent good spirits once they'd wrapped up their interview with Iris Storey.

A few cement steps took them up to a covered porch, complete with a woven welcome mat. As Spencer raised a hand to knock, the heavy wooden door swung inward.

Iris Storey stood just beyond the threshold. She was a

striking woman with porcelain skin, bright green eyes, and vibrant red hair. Most of the redheads Zane had met throughout his life used dye to achieve the uncommon hue, but Iris's color appeared natural.

She knelt down as a Welsh corgi trotted up to her side. "Agents. Sorry, I didn't mean to surprise you." She scratched the pup's head and waved them inside. "Friede hardly ever barks, but I saw your car pull up. I'm honestly surprised I haven't heard more from the FBI before now. I gave a statement to the man who...who gave me the news. But that's been it so far."

Zane recognized the corgi's name from a popular video game franchise and guessed one of Ben's kids had named the dog.

Though Iris was already aware that Zane and Spencer were federal agents, Zane flashed his badge out of habit. "Morning, Mrs. Storey. I'm Special Agent Palmer, and this is Supervisory Special Agent Corsaw. We're sorry we haven't been around to speak to you sooner, but it's been...busy. Thanks for meeting with us so early."

Once the door was closed, she flicked the deadbolt into place before turning to face them. "It's no problem. I'm not expected in court for another week, but I'd rather get this done with early. Dylan and Janis are with my sister for the next couple days, so I guess it's a good time for this. Do either of you want anything to drink? I just brewed a pot of coffee."

Zane usually declined when a witness offered him a beverage, but he was running on a grand total of six hours of sleep over the past two days. "Yes, coffee sounds great. If it's not too much trouble."

Iris offered him a strained smile. "No trouble. I'd feel bad drinking it in front of you guys without asking."

A somber moment of silence trailed after them as they

left the foyer, broken only by the clack of paws against hardwood. Dealing with a bereaved widow was never an easy thing to do, but Iris's lack of tears confused Zane more than anything else.

Dark circles under the eyes, flushed cheeks, and the slight smudge of eyeliner hinted toward a haggard woman who had been in the throes of an emotional breakdown, but in the moment, she presented herself with polish and control. Maybe that was a practiced skill, honed from years as a judge. But the effect it had on Zane was off-putting.

Glancing over at a handful of family photos that lined the walls of a short hallway, Zane was struck with a sudden realization. He'd been so focused on tracking down clues to point him toward Ben Storey's killer that he'd almost forgotten about the man's family.

They emerged into the expansive kitchen, and Iris poured him and Spencer each a steaming cup of coffee. After thanking their hostess, he and Spencer followed Iris to a sunny breakfast nook tucked to the side of the kitchen.

Zane set a notepad and pen beside his mug. "First and foremost, I just wanted to extend my condolences to you and your family. I know how hard this is, so thank you for helping us out this morning."

Spencer dipped his chin. "Yes. I'm sorry for your loss. We'll do everything we can to find out who's responsible."

Swiping at her nose, Iris's knuckles turned white where she grasped the handle of her mug. "Thank you, Agent Palmer. SSA Corsaw."

Though Zane was taken aback by her use of the abbreviation "SSA" at first, he reminded himself that Iris Storey was a judge and a former lawyer. During her tenure with the justice system, she'd undoubtedly crossed paths with plenty of federal agents.

Interviews with those who had close ties to law enforcement tended to either go well or turn into a complete disaster. In Zane's experience, there was no middle ground.

Bracing himself for the worst, he cleared his throat. "Mrs. Storey, some of the questions we're going to ask might be somewhat uncomfortable. I just want you to know that we're aware that you were in court at the time of your husband's death, and currently, the Bureau doesn't consider you a suspect."

Iris straightened. "Of course. I'm here to help."

So far, so good. Now for the true test. "I appreciate it. To start with, I don't mean to imply anything, but we have to ask. Do you know if your husband was having an affair?"

Zane was fully prepared to jump in to reassure the grieving woman that the question in no way meant Ben had cheated on her, but the need never arose.

"Yes." Iris wrapped both hands around her mug. "He was."

"He...was? You knew about it?" He hoped he'd kept the disbelief from his tone, but his brain was still struggling to catch up to Iris's nonchalance.

"Yes, I've known about it. About them. He's been sleeping with other women since a couple years after our daughter was born. Seven years in total. I've lost count of how many at this point, but it has to be over ten. Those were just the drawn-out ones, though. I'm sure he had plenty of...*flings* that I don't know about."

Zane bit down on the tip of his tongue to keep from parroting the words back to her. "Did you know any of these women? Any of their names?"

As her gaze shifted to the table, she twisted the white gold wedding band around her ring finger. "Some. I kept track of them in a journal. I can give you a copy of the page before you leave."

"That would be helpful." Zane dug deep to salvage his

composure. "With all due respect, Mrs. Storey, why did you stay with Ben if you knew he'd been cheating for so long?"

Iris let out a weary sigh. "I asked myself the same thing every damn day, Agent Palmer. It's...complicated, I guess. We're both public figures with very busy lives. And there are the kids too. Divorce is more painful for them. And, well... we didn't argue or hate each other. And I guess I just figured that as long as we got along well enough, we could stick it out until they were grown and moved out on their own. Honestly, that's the only reason I'd have filed for divorce."

His heart ached for the woman in front of him. Iris held herself with the poise and dignity he'd expected of a State Supreme Court judge, and he doubted anyone knew the hardships she'd endured. All the while, she maintained an outlook that was surprisingly positive.

She let go of the ring and returned her grasp to the mug. "Ben might not have been a good husband, but he was a great father. I still loved him, but it's the same type of love you might hold for your alcoholic father or an old friend who's become addicted to painkillers. You love them at a distance. We had a decent arrangement. No one was fighting. The kids were loved. There was no reason to insert drama into the equation."

"Do you know if there was anyone recently?" Spencer's tone was gentle, and Zane knew if anyone could understand Iris's marital struggle, it was the SSA. "Anyone who might have been angry with him or might have harbored a grudge when their relationship didn't pan out?"

Iris worried at her bottom lip. "I could always tell when he was...*serious* about someone. He'd become even more distant with me. Like he could only share so much of himself, and he was busy giving it all to her. Honestly, I welcomed the freedom it brought. I could use the time to focus on myself and the kids. I'd just pretend I wasn't married and that Ben was my roommate."

"I'm sorry you had to go through that." Zane wished he could come up with a more profound statement, but he was at a loss.

"That's just how it goes sometimes, I suppose." Her forehead wrinkled as she took a long sip of her coffee. "I do remember the last serious relationship he had. He wouldn't normally tell me about any of it, but this one was different."

Zane scooped up his pen. "Different in what way?"

"It seemed more meaningful, I think. I never learned the woman's name, but he was seeing her for more than a year and a half."

Spencer folded his hands atop the table. "How did you find out about it?"

Rubbing one pale cheek, Iris turned her distant gaze to the SSA. "We used to have a cloud that would back up all the pictures we took on our phones. I've always been a little more tech savvy than Ben, and I don't think he knew how the cloud system worked at first. One day, I logged in to go through the pictures to find some for a calendar I wanted to make for my parents. And, well…"

As Zane scrawled out a few notes, his pulse picked up at the prospect of the new lead.

"There were pictures." Iris sighed. "Pictures of her, and of him with her. Even a video."

Zane's blood froze in his veins.

"Are they still accessible?" Spencer's voice was distant and tinny.

"No." Iris cupped her mug. "He deleted them all. They've been gone for a long time. I'd never caught him with photos like that before, and I never did again after that."

"Could you identify the woman again if you saw her?" Spencer asked.

"Yes, without a doubt. That woman has…" Iris swallowed hard. "I've had dreams about her ever since I saw those damn pictures. Ben had mistresses before her, but like I said, she was different. I'd even talked to a lawyer because I thought he was finally going to ask for a divorce, and I'd wanted to make sure I had everything together. But, by that time, he'd gotten rid of all those pictures. That's how I know that there's no trace of them left. I *tried* to find them, but I couldn't."

Zane had his cellphone in hand. With a deftness he didn't think possible, he unlocked the device and pulled up a picture of Amelia. Time slowed to a crawl as he slid the device to Iris. "Is this the woman from the pictures?"

Iris peered down at the glowing screen, but she shook her head almost immediately. "No. I don't recognize her."

Though he was tempted to sag with relief, Zane maintained his professionalism. "Could you describe this woman? Was there anything about her that stuck out?"

"There was one thing, yeah. She had a tattoo on her lower back, one of those tribal designs."

Another strike against Amelia being the mistress.

Thank God.

Zane had never seen Amelia's lower back, but she'd told him about all her tattoo experiences over the years.

Of course, when she'd asked if *he* had any tattoos, he'd done his best to sidestep the answer and subsequent explanation. At the time, he hadn't known Amelia well and doubted they'd ever be faced with a situation where she might catch him shirtless.

"What else could you tell us about her appearance?" Zane clicked the pen a couple times to keep his thoughts from wandering.

Iris fidgeted with the end of her sleeve. "From what I could tell, she was taller than average. Probably taller than me, and I'm five-seven. She was white, and she had dark hair and brown eyes."

Zane scribbled out a few more words on the notepad. "Do you know if they were together recently? If they'd maintained contact or if he was still seeing her?"

Despite Iris's nonchalant tone from only minutes earlier, the sorrow on her face told Zane the wound had cut far deeper than even she acknowledged. "I don't think so. Ben ended things with her about six months ago, and he swore it wouldn't happen again. Normally, he wouldn't tell me about that sort of thing. He'd just try to act like none of it had ever happened. But this time, he said he wanted to make our marriage work, and that he was willing to rebuild the trust he'd destroyed. I told him he'd never be able to put those pieces back together, but he was adamant that he'd try."

How in the hell Ben had intended to prove himself after seven years of infidelity was beyond Zane's understanding. Iris had endured countless lies and betrayals from her husband and *still* cared for him. Perhaps Zane had a thing or two to learn about rushing to judgment.

Iris's voice cut through the uneasy silence. "I'm sorry. You probably didn't need to know all that."

"It's okay," Zane reassured her with his trademark smile. "No need to apologize. We've had a development recently that indicates we might be looking for a female suspect, which is why we're asking these questions. Now, do you know if Ben had been seeing anyone new lately?"

She reached for her coffee. "If he did, I didn't know about them. Either he was actually trying to follow through with what he'd promised, or he'd just gotten better at hiding it."

If Zane had been a betting man, he'd have put his money on the latter.

With each new tidbit of information he gleaned, Ben Storey's personal life turned into more of a mess. When Zane had been introduced to the man a few months earlier, he'd never have guessed that someone so outwardly successful had hidden so many skeletons.

That was the point, though. The darker the secret, the deeper it had to be buried.

And if Zane wanted to catch Ben's killer, he had to follow the rabbit hole until the end.

23

A s I stepped onto the cracked asphalt, I tightened the collar of my coat against the cold wind. The ramshackle parking lot behind an abandoned convenience store was a far cry from the peaceful lake where I'd met Stan Young the day before. There were no ducks, just debris and cigarette butts that had been swept into drifts against the sun-bleached building and rusted gas pumps that hadn't seen use in close to a decade.

Was this what I'd become? I'd gone from ridding the world of scumbags to meeting with a senator who had connections to some of the worst of the worst.

And why?

Because Ben Storey ruined your life, that's why.

As my father had liked to say when he was still alive, "Don't get mad. Get even."

Ben was dead. I'd gotten even with him for sure.

But what about Amelia Storm?

The woman simply wouldn't die. I'd missed my chance twice now, and I'd begun to wonder if I'd get another opportunity to take the woman down.

Fury raged through me when I thought about the leaked photographs of a very nude Amelia. I hated her, almost as much as I hated him. She was making a fool out of me, and that was something I couldn't tolerate.

All that was on a personal level, of course. There was still the professional issue of eliminating the agent. Stan Young's "guy" was apparently obsessed with her, and Stan wanted her gone too.

I reminded myself that I was here because Stan was a gateway to more money and power than I'd ever imagined I could achieve. The senator was useful to me, and I to him. That was all. I didn't have to like the man. I just had to keep my wits about me.

A car door thudded, and I turned toward the source of the disturbance.

Right in time for Stan Young's shrewd stare to meet mine.

The senator could have been an attractive man, but the scheming glint in those gray eyes made the hair on the back of my neck stand on end. I might not have considered myself a psychopath, but I couldn't say the same for Young.

I ignored the sudden uptick in my pulse. Straightening to my full height, I circled around the front of my car to where Stan waited. "Morning, Senator."

He dipped his chin in a curt greeting. "Morning. I assume you know why I asked you to meet with me on such short notice."

Tightening my jaw, I jammed both hands in my pockets. "Amelia Storm."

"That's right." To my side, he leaned against the car and scratched his forehead. "What the hell happened? You realize she's going to be ten times more difficult to reach now, don't you?"

"I do." I let out a mirthless chortle. "Believe me, I do."

"What's your plan to deal with it? How are you going to

fix this?" Stan pinned me with a look that would have sent most men and women running for the hills.

I wasn't most men or women. "I have a plan. She might be on high alert, but I can still get close to her. She trusts me." I hesitated before I posed my own question. "What about the pictures? When were you going to tell me about those?"

He waved a hand as if the unexpected release of fake, explicit photos of Amelia and Ben wasn't worth noting. "It's to help bolster the motive. It's part of my contingency plan, in case planting the murder weapon and the messages didn't work, which they didn't." His gaze grew frigid. "They're good fakes, you have to admit. I made sure of it."

If I was honest with myself, I didn't believe his explanation. I trusted Stan Young as far as I could throw him, and I suspected there was more to the images than his casual dismissal let on.

For the time being, I'd keep the suspicion to myself. I wouldn't put my faith in Stan on a personal level, but our working dynamic was based on a far more predictable virtue: the pursuit of power. Seeing Amelia Storm take the fall for Ben Storey's murder and wiping our hands clean of the entire situation was a mutual interest, and I'd take a shared goal over blind trust any day of the week.

As long as our motive was the same, Stan was on my side.

"Okay." I was careful to keep my tone agreeable and nonaccusatory. "Is there anything else I should know about? Anything in the arsenal that I might be able to use?"

He rubbed his chin. "Right now? Not that I can think of. I'll let you know if that changes."

I put forth an unmistakable air of confidence, but in the back of my mind, I knew I was a fish out of water.

I had experience planting evidence and setting the stage for murders to be ruled as accidents, but I'd never framed another person for a crime I'd committed. The core concept might have been the same, but the execution was much, much different.

When a person was dead, I could control the narrative. But when they were alive, they had a tendency to cause problems.

Once she's dead...

I'd be back in familiar territory. If I made Amelia's murder look like a suicide, I could tie her to everything.

I shifted my attention back to the senator. "What do you know about fast-acting sedatives? Something that's in and out of a person's bloodstream fast enough that it won't show up on an autopsy?" I had a vague familiarity with such substances thanks to my career in law enforcement, but the specifics still eluded me.

Slowly, a smirk crept to Stan's face. "Plenty, actually."

I returned the devious expression. "Perfect."

I gathered up all my hesitancy, stuffed the discomfort into a box, and shoved the box to the depths of my mind.

Amelia was collateral damage. Stan was intent on killing her no matter my involvement—her fate was sealed.

One shot to the temple would do the trick, and since she'd be sedated, she wouldn't feel a thing.

I was doing her a favor, really.

At least if I was the one to deal the final blow, I'd know she wasn't raped or tortured.

Woman to woman, it was the best I could do.

Joseph leaned forward in the driver's seat to catch one more glimpse of Stan Young and his companion. For the past day, he'd followed the senator's movements like a shadow, and his diligence had just paid off in spades.

His mission had been simple. He wanted to know who in the hell had killed Ben Storey.

The task was supposed to have been Joseph's, and Joseph had been fully prepared to follow through with the hit before he'd learned that Storey was already dead.

To his further surprise, an unknown gunman had taken three shots at Amelia the day before. Joseph knew damn well that the two events weren't a coincidence.

Stan had hired someone else, and he'd tasked them with killing Ben *and* Amelia.

But why?

After Joseph had accompanied Zane Palmer to respond to the shooting at Amelia's apartment, he'd put the pieces together in short order. Stan's hired gun had tried to take out Amelia from a distance. A nice, safe distance.

But they'd failed. And if Joseph knew Stan half as well as he liked to think, then the senator would want a word with his contract killer as soon as possible.

All Joseph had to do was wait.

He had to admit, Stan's co-conspirator was a good choice. One most people wouldn't have pointed a finger at.

Joseph wasn't that surprised. He just wondered if the woman was working with the senator by choice or if he held something over her head, forcing her to do these dirty deeds.

It didn't matter. Not really.

What mattered was that Joseph was pissed.

Joseph still wasn't sure what he intended to do with the newfound information, but he had no intention to sit idly by as someone else carried out Stan's bidding.

He wasn't through with Amelia, and he'd be damned if anyone finished her off before he had his fun.

24

A fter only three hours *on the job* at Zane's apartment, Amelia concluded that she was ill-suited for working from home. She understood the appeal, but after catching herself dozing off twice, she knew she needed the structure. At the absolute least, she'd need a home office. Somewhere she could associate with productivity and not ten a.m. naps.

Maybe if I had more to do than fill out paperwork and look through old Leóne files, I'd be more than half-awake right now.

Leaning against the kitchen island, she lifted a soup-bowl-sized mug of coffee to her lips. The steaming liquid was one step below scalding, but she sipped it anyway.

Today was only Wednesday, and she had a long week ahead of herself.

As she took another sip, her cell buzzed in the pocket of her zip-up hoodie. Amelia pulled out the device to check the caller's identity.

"A Wisconsin area code," she muttered to herself.

Lainey had been arrested by the DEA two days earlier, the same day Ben Storey was killed, and Amelia almost went to prison.

Gritting her teeth, Amelia swiped the screen to answer. "This is Agent Storm." The call wasn't work-related, but she'd made an ass out of herself the last time they'd spoken. For this conversation, she wanted to ensure Agent Menendez regarded her as a peer and not another stressed-out family member of a defendant.

"Good morning, Miss...I'm sorry, Agent Storm. This is Agent Pablo Menendez with the Drug Enforcement Agency. Do you have a minute to talk?"

"Of course." She'd rather discuss Lainey's charges with a DEA agent. After the events of the last two days, she didn't trust herself to refrain from biting her sister's head off.

"Good. I'll try to make this quick so you can get back to your day. This call isn't exactly protocol, but considering your position in the FBI, I'm reaching out as more of a professional courtesy. Your sister has been...obstinate."

Amelia bit her tongue to keep from snorting. "That doesn't surprise me. What's she being charged with?"

She swore she heard a muffled sigh. "The DEA, and our office, in particular, has been under some pressure to crack down on drug smuggling in airports. Now, we don't have any reason to think that your sister is connected to any sort of trafficking ring, and the amount of heroin that was seized from her was relatively small. But..."

Why did there always have to be a damn "but"?

"Let's hear it." Amelia's voice was flat.

"During our usual review, we looked through her phone and her recent online communication. You said on Monday that she was flying to Chicago to attend rehabilitation, is that correct?"

Amelia wondered for a split-second if she was being interrogated. "That's correct. Why do you ask?"

This time, the agent's sigh wasn't muted. "She'd been

using an application called Hushed. It's a secure messaging app, and—"

"All the data sent and received is encrypted." Unease prickled the back of her scalp. "Which is why a lot of people use it over some of the traditional messaging outlets. I'm familiar." She wasn't about to reveal *why* she was familiar with the stupid app.

"Well, she was using Hushed to communicate with someone who appeared to have been in Chicago. I suppose another reason I called you today was to ask if you might have an idea who that was."

"No." Amelia's reply was terse and immediate. "She said she was leaving that dipshit…excuse me…boyfriend, and that she wanted to get clean. At least, that's the story she told me, Agent Menendez. Trust me, she's just as likely to lie to me as she is to the federal government. Maybe even more likely." She stopped herself before she began ranting.

"That answers my next question."

As Menendez went on to explain the charges that the DEA had brought up against Lainey, Amelia only committed about half the man's words to memory. She should have known that her sister was using her to get to Chicago and that Lainey had zero intent to get clean when she arrived in Illinois.

She'd been hopeful about the future of her and Lainey's relationship. Amelia had failed Lainey by fleeing Chicago and leaving her little sister to the wolves, but she'd let herself believe she could make up for the past.

The notion was laughable to her now.

No matter what she did, the ghosts always had a way of catching up to her.

25

By the time Monday morning rolled around, Zane wondered if he ought to just move into the FBI conference room. He'd spent most of his waking hours that weekend at the field office.

The expansive whiteboard was covered with names, locations, and dates. Most had been crossed out, but a select few remained. They'd worked their way through the list based on the potential for each person, place, or time to result in a viable lead.

Unfortunately for Zane, the process meant that each new search was less relevant than the last.

Resting a hand over his tired eyes, he slumped back in his chair. A couple hours earlier, they'd *finally* received the documents in response to the subpoena Cassandra had issued to Real Chicago News. The "news" organization had fought the subpoena hard, but nearly a week later, they had the images in hand.

The tech lab's digital image specialist had been knee-deep in a review for another active case, but he'd assured Zane and Spencer that they wouldn't have to wait long.

He'd considered texting Amelia to advise her that they'd finally gotten their hands on the pictures, but he'd decided to wait until after the lab gave him something to report. If their roles were reversed, he'd rather wait for all the information than deal with the anxiety of being fed one tidbit at a time.

After tediously reviewing Ben's life, Zane was convinced he could have filled out a mortgage application for Ben Storey. He and Layton Redker had dug into any facet of the councilman's personal affairs they could find—his military service, his tenure practicing law, his political career, every damn thing. Spencer helped when he was available, but he still had Supervisory Special Agent duties to attend. The Storey murder wasn't the only active case in the Organized Crime Division, though it *was* the most publicized.

Ben's murder was so publicized that Zane hadn't bothered to leave the FBI building during his shift.

The Bureau made sure reporters didn't camp too close, and the field office was surrounded by a tall iron fence. Zane was grateful for the barrier, but he didn't dare drive to a nearby café for his afternoon caffeine fix. For breakfast, lunch, and dinner, he suffered through the breakroom coffee. The sludge-like brew had most likely shaved at least two years off his life expectancy. For the sake of his stomach lining if nothing else, he hoped the scattered news vans would disperse sooner rather than later.

SAC Keaton was scheduled for a press conference in the afternoon. Jasmine Keaton had a way about public speaking that tended to quell the anxiety of her audience. She was a master of providing sufficient answers without revealing pertinent details. There was a reason she'd been put in charge of the Chicago Field Office.

With a frustrated groan, Zane pushed his chair away from the circular table and stood. Potent breakroom coffee or not, if he sat in the dark for any longer, he'd fall asleep. He stretched both arms above his head, joints popping and crackling as he forced his limbs to move. He'd been sitting for so long his ass had just about gone numb. His legs protested with a dull ache as he forced them into action.

Halfway through his short trek to the light switch, the door swung open, and Spencer Corsaw burst into the room.

The SSA's chest heaved as if he'd just run up ten flights of stairs. "Palmer, there you are."

Zane blinked. "Where else would I be?"

Spencer seemed to ignore the rhetorical question. "I just got a call from the tech lab. Keith was analyzing those pictures of Amelia and Ben about twenty minutes ago. He says he's already got results."

The announcement chased away Zane's lingering fatigue. "He does? What are they?"

"I'm about to head down there to get the details." Spencer waved for Zane to follow him. "Come on."

Scooping his phone off the cluttered table, Zane all but shoved Spencer back into the hall. "Well, what'd he tell you so far?"

A ghost of a smile passed over Spencer's face. "They're fake. Something about the concentration of pixels being different from the background image."

Though Zane wanted to throw a victorious fist in the air, he tempered his reaction down to a curt nod. "Any idea where the pictures came from?"

"That's what I'm hoping to find out." Spencer was on the move before he finished the comment.

As they neared the turn in the hall that led to the elevator, Glenn Kantowski suddenly emerged from behind the corner. Her honey-brown eyes were fixed on her cell, and in his rush to get to the lab, Zane came within an inch of bowling her over.

Glenn snapped a hand to rest over her heart as she took in a sharp breath. "Oh my god. I'm so sorry."

Zane took a swift step to the side and out of her path. "It's okay. That was my fault. I damn near run into someone around this corner every week."

Pushing up her glasses, Glenn smiled. "Me too. You guys look like something just happened. Was there a new development in the Storey case?"

Spencer jumped in before Zane could answer. "There is. We just got confirmation that those pictures we saw on Real Chicago News are fakes."

For a beat, Glenn's eyes popped open wide. "Wow, that's…that's good, right?"

Zane thought that was an understatement. "Yes. Very good."

A worried expression crossed her features. "How's Amelia holding up?"

A wreck, but Zane wasn't going to let anyone know that. "She's good. Been pretty busy looking for leads."

"Right, gotta find that sniper." She chuckled. "I won't keep you. Just wondered if she had checked in today. You know, not sleeping on the job. Working from home and all. I'm not saying I want a sniper to take a shot at me, but I wouldn't mind reviewing casefiles in my pajamas."

Her statement wasn't far from the mark. More than once during the past weekend, Zane had found Amelia snoring on the couch with her laptop.

"I'll be sure to let her know you asked about her." Zane tilted his head toward the elevators. "We're headed downstairs to see what else the lab says about those RCN photos."

"No worries. I'll be wading through casefiles all day." Glenn waved him off like a mom watching her kid run toward the school bus. "Good luck with those images."

Zane was itching to get to the lab, so he didn't have to be told twice. "Good luck with RICO."

She groaned. "I need all the luck I can get."

As Zane and Spencer took off down the hall, he silently agreed.

They all needed a bit of luck.

As I slid into the driver's seat of my car, I closed the door and reached for the glove box. Buried beneath a pair of mittens and the registration papers was the prepaid cell I used exclusively to communicate with Stan Young. I hadn't heard a peep from the senator since our meeting the week before, but as I powered on the device, I crossed my fingers.

He'd been responsible for submitting the doctored images of Amelia and Ben to Real Chicago News, not me. I'd been assured that the fakes were high quality and that their purpose was to throw doubt on Amelia's rendition of the night Ben had been killed. And to also screw with her personally.

Why oh fucking why hadn't she been killed that night?

None of this would be happening if Amelia hadn't been on a freaking video call with Zane Palmer instead of standing over Ben's dead body like she was supposed to have been doing. That one little fluke had caused everything else to unravel, and everything we'd done to pin Ben's death on the agent hadn't been even close to enough.

I knew who'd take the fall if I couldn't pin the crime on Amelia, and it sure as hell wasn't Senator Young.

The dinky screen flashed to life, but I'd received no new texts. No missed calls.

I spat out a series of obscenities and tossed the phone back into the glove compartment. I could reach out to Stan, but he'd been due to return to D.C. for his congressional duties today. I doubted he'd answer.

I was on my own.

My first attempt to eliminate Amelia had been premature, but I'd had the past several days to come up with a new plan. I didn't want to rush, but Stan's oversight had just forced my hand.

Today was the day Amelia Storm would finally die.

26

A melia leaned back in her seat at Zane's dining room table, shielding her eyes against a shaft of sunlight that seemed determined to blind her. No matter where she moved, it found a way through the window blinds, either hitting her full in the face or washing out the colors on her laptop screen.

The overstuffed sectional was far more comfortable, but when her task was to sift through old Leóne cases, she didn't want comfort. With hard, wooden chairs that matched the dark finish of the table, Zane's dining room suited that purpose to near perfection.

Closing out of the digital scans she'd perused that morning, she blew out a sigh and reached for her cell.

She could hardly believe only a week had passed since she'd discovered Ben Storey's lifeless body on the floor of an abandoned house in Englewood. The past seven days had lasted a lifetime.

No matter how many times Zane assured her she was welcome to stay as long as she needed, she couldn't help but feel like an intruder. Before last week, the man had lived alone with no pets. Now, he was stuck with a pseudo-room-mate who never left the damn house and a cat that had shed on everything and clawed at the backside of his couch.

The twinge of guilt about Luca Passarelli still nagged at the back of her mind, especially when she considered how distant Zane had become. Not that he was ever home. He left for the office before she woke, and when he finally returned, she was ready for bed.

Amelia massaged her temple and tapped out a short message to her fellow agent, Glenn Kantowski. She and Glenn had waded through Leóne documents together. Their main goal was to search for a significant event they might have missed on the first go-around. SAC Keaton had given them until Wednesday, but at their current rate, Amelia figured they'd be done before the end of the day tomorrow.

And so far, they had nothing to show for their efforts.

After double-checking the text, Amelia pressed send. *Any new developments for RICO?*

Three dots at the bottom of the screen indicated that Glenn was composing a reply. The ellipses disappeared, reappeared, and vanished again.

Amelia hated when her phone showed her another person's typing activity. She'd spend minutes watching them stop and start their message, and her anxiety would mount with each second. If they had to pause to think about their reply so many times, surely they were about to send her a novel. At least a paragraph.

Just as she was about to lock the screen and stand up to stretch, Glenn's response appeared: *That's so weird. I was JUST about to text you! I think I might have found something big we can use, and I was wondering if you could come to my place so I don't have to deal with bringing everything with me.*

Amelia blinked down at the message a few times, as if she expected the words to change. She'd nearly lost all hope of resurrecting the RICO case. Had Glenn really unearthed a crucial piece of information they'd missed before?

"Only one way to find out," Amelia muttered to herself.

But leaving the safety of Zane's apartment to do so? He would absolutely kill her if she left by herself.

Still...she was going nuts, and she would only be outside for a few moments, so it wasn't like she was walking into a lion's den or anything like—

Bam. Bam. Bam.

The memory of the bullets sinking into her wall made her jump, almost as if it was happening in real time once again. The flashback was so real that her fingertips tingled from the surge of adrenaline that jolted through her system.

"Pull it together, Amelia Nicole Storm."

She was pissed at herself but also thankful that her subconscious had given her that reminder. As bored as she was, she needed to be smart if she wanted to live another day.

I'd love to come to you, but I can't leave protective custody.

She felt like a baby as she hit "send," but it was what it was.

Her phone buzzed quickly. *Poor you. I bet you're going crazy.*

Amelia didn't have to hesitate this time. *Yes! Bat shit nuts.*

The three dots jumped and danced for longer than Amelia had the patience for, but the moment she set the device down, it indicated a message: *I have an idea that will kill all the birds with one stone. How about I arrange an escort for you, then you'll have me for protective custody the rest of the day. I can drive you back later. Would that work?*

Amelia only needed to tap three letters: *YES*

A laughing emoji was followed by: *Hang tight, and I'll let you know the plan.*

Less than a half hour later, the plans were in place.

Glenn's message said: *Someone from CPD will be by in fifteen minutes to get you at the back. I've given them your number so they can text you when they've arrived. Good?*

Amelia was already stuffing her feet into her favorite canvas shoes. *Perfect!*

Fifteen minutes later, she was ready when the promised text arrived. *Black Mustang at the back door.*

On my way.

Pulling up the hood of her sweatshirt to cover her hair, she shouldered her handbag, double checking that her service weapon was tucked inside. The Bureau was no closer to locating Amelia's would-be assassin, but she was pointedly aware of the fact that someone was trying to kill her. She wasn't willing to go out in public, but a trip from one FBI agent's apartment to another FBI agent's house was about as low risk an endeavor as she could imagine.

In fact, spending the afternoon with Glenn was even safer than staying cooped up at Zane's place by herself. The only risky part of the journey was the trip itself. A CPD escort should mitigate that risk a great deal.

Before she left the apartment, Amelia flipped the tracking switch on the GPS watch that Zane had given her. With all the crazy that had happened in the last week, she figured it was better to play it safe. And with that thought, she grabbed her phone and sent a quick message to him as well.

Glenn has a lead on our RICO. I have CPD escort to her place. Don't wait up.

They'd been so quiet with each other the last few days. Amelia hoped that checking in with him and using the silly but very thoughtful gift he'd given her might help patch some of the tension Zane had been showing. She had to be more honest and open with him, even if there was one secret she couldn't divulge.

That thought weighed heavily on her heart. He'd done so

much for her, showed her so much more than the kindness between friends. Could she ever trust him with her darkest secret?

While at the moment she knew the answer was uncertain, deep down, she wanted to trust him. She connected with Zane on a wholly different level than anyone else. Maybe she should. On the off chance her theory was correct, better it be Zane leading the investigation than SSA Corsaw, or god forbid Cassandra breathing down her neck. She'd already had enough of a taste of what it was like to be on that lawyer's bad side.

With that thought and one last glance around the apartment to ensure she hadn't forgotten an important item, Amelia threw the deadbolt and stepped into the hall, every sense on high alert.

On the balls of her feet, she made quick work of the stairs and then paused just inside the metal door leading out the back. Opening it only a couple inches, she spotted the black Mustang just a couple feet away, the passenger door open and waiting for her. Two steps and she'd be inside.

Without giving herself time to think too much, Amelia was out the door and inside the vehicle before a sniper could have even lifted a gun. Even so, she scanned the tops of buildings and the surrounding area to be sure.

"I secured the area before I contacted you."

Too focused on the surrounding area to pay much attention to her escort, Amelia did a double take at the sound of the familiar voice.

"We're going to have to stop running into each other like this."

Cynthia McAdam winked. "Third time's a charm."

The officer's arm whipped out like a snake, her fist coming down on Amelia's leg. Even as the sharp sting of a needle penetrated her skin, Amelia struggled to reach into her handbag, going for her gun.

McAdam's arm came up, and the officer's elbow connected with Amelia's jaw. The world burst into a kaleidoscope of stars she fought against, even as the sedative took effect.

Drowning in darkness, Amelia fought to stay awake.

It was a battle she was destined to lose.

27

The scent of car exhaust registered in Amelia's brain as she clawed from the depths of unconsciousness. She started to reach for her throbbing temple, but her hands wouldn't budge.

A hard band dug into her wrist, but the scrape of plastic was nothing compared to the pain in her head. With every beat of her heart, she felt as if a blacksmith was driving a hammer into her skull.

The pain was excruciating, but a sudden wave of fear pushed aside the agony.

Where am I? Come on, Amelia. Get your shit together. Focus. Figure out what the hell is going on, and deal with the damn headache later.

Cynthia McAdam. The needle.

The memory rose up like a slap to the face. The officer had jammed a needle into her thigh. The world had gone black, and now she was…wherever the hell *here* was.

Darkness. Motion. Car exhaust. C'mon, Amelia. Open your eyes and put it together.

She struggled through her cloudy mind to grasp the

answer. The rumble in her ears wasn't the sound of an HVAC system, and the swaying and bumping beneath her wasn't a floor. She was moving, and all she could smell was...

A trunk! This is a car. And it is going somewhere...fast.

She tried to grumble a four-letter word, but she couldn't force her tongue to make the shape necessary to speak in anything other than a guttural growl.

Her eyelids felt like sandpaper as she forced her eyes to open. Tears slid along her cheek, but she gritted her teeth at the discomfort. She blinked until the scratching sensation was gone, but she was met with only darkness.

Because I'm in a trunk.

She groaned again. McAdams was only slightly larger than her. Had the officer had help transferring her unconscious body to the trunk? Was Amelia now facing two foes instead of one?

She forced the questions from her mind. She needed to deal with one thing at a time.

Both arms were behind her back, and the ties that bound her dug into skin that already felt raw. Zip ties. And not just one. McAdam had done it right. Instead of circling both wrists with a single tie, she'd braceleted both and then tied both strips of plastic together.

Crap.

Wriggling her fingers, she tried to see how much give she could get. The answer was immediate. Not much.

She'd had the foresight to wear the watch that Zane had given her after she'd almost been shot. She just needed to free her hands enough to push the panic button he'd shown her.

Though she didn't have the first clue where she was, at least Zane would know as soon as he got the alert.

Provided he was paying attention to his phone, anyway. She had no idea if he had seen her earlier message, and she reminded herself that she needed to plan to make her escape without the aid of backup. Relying on someone to swoop in to rescue her was as good as a death sentence.

Still, she had to try. She closed her eyes and imagined where the small panic button was located. Twisting her wrists until they surely must be bleeding, Amelia rotated her thumb until it touched metal.

The car hit a bump, and Amelia bounced inside the trunk. She lost her breath on the landing, and tears pricked her eyes as she fought to inhale a lungful of air.

Had she pressed the right button? And if she had, had she held it in long enough to make the electrical connection?

She didn't know.

The car slowed and turned a sharp left, tossing Amelia around the space like a rag doll. She cursed and was able to brace herself enough for the next turn. Where were they? Not in the city still, that much she could tell.

Amelia knew how to escape zip ties...if she were standing. Trapped inside a small trunk as she was, her ability to get enough leverage to chicken-wing her arms was nearly impossible. But she had to try.

Using all her force, which wasn't very much, she attempted to pop the plastic lock.

It wasn't happening.

Think.

Mind still foggy from the drug she'd been given as well as who knew how much carbon monoxide was penetrating the trunk space, she forced herself to be still and consider all her options.

As the panic ebbed away, her thoughts crystallized a little more. *Her shoes.*

Years ago, one of the special forces members she'd served with told her to carry a razor blade in her shoes at all times.

Whether a person's hands were tied in front of them or behind their back, they could most likely reach their feet.

It took a little maneuvering, but she managed to wiggle and pretzel herself enough to access the right shoe. Slipping it off, she pried the insole up. Wrapped in duct tape, the end of which was doubled over for easy access, was the blade. Now, she just needed to get it turned in such a way that she could cut the plastic.

"Easy peasy," she muttered to herself.

Easy had been wishful thinking because her numb fingers dropped the razor before she could strike the first blow. Refusing to give up, she blindly searched for her only method of escape. That was when the car began to slow again.

No. Not yet.

They couldn't be at their destination yet. She needed a few more minutes. That was all.

Before she could brace herself, the vehicle turned right, and Amelia was thrown headfirst into the metal side of the trunk. Stars burst in her vision again and nausea burned her throat, but she managed to stay conscious. Just barely.

Dammit, wake up, Amelia. Stay awake. Think. Focus.

Still sick to her stomach, she began searching for the blade again. Wriggling like a fish on the shore of a lake, she searched the carpeted space until her fingers touched duct tape.

She nearly sobbed in relief.

You can do this.

The plastic scraped Amelia's wrist as she repositioned her fingers. Sweat beaded on her temples from the exertion and intense focus it took to saw the plastic instead of her wrists. Each bump in the road only exacerbated her splitting headache, and the urge to give up and let herself go limp was like the temptation of a mirage to a traveler stranded in the desert.

No. I won't let it end like this.

She shut out the sense of blind panic that threatened to consume her. Each time her focus threatened to drift off to the discomfort of her surroundings, she turned her thoughts back to the zip ties.

She pushed down with the blade, and her finger slipped. Whether the moisture along the band was sweat or blood, she couldn't tell, and at that point, didn't care.

As she positioned the blade for another attempt, the thrum of the tires against pavement slowed, and they began to roll over what appeared to be gravel. Desperation burned through her veins.

Refusing to be defeated, she focused all her energy and pushed against the plastic with every ounce of strength she could channel.

Her heart leapt as the plastic loosened a bit as the car came to a stop. She began to saw at the plastic harder, faster, managing not to cry out when the sharp edge of the razor hit skin.

If she had the use of her hands, she could surprise McAdam. She'd have to time her movement well, but if she could daze the woman enough, it might give her the precious seconds she needed to escape.

With the after-effects of the sedative still swimming through her system, she couldn't be sure of how much control she'd have. Still, she had to try. She had no other option.

The thud of a car door slammed her right back into the moment.

Her hands weren't free. She needed more time.

But time was now her enemy.

Deep in her heart, Amelia knew it was too late.

ZANE LEANED back in his chair as he punched in the code to unlock his phone. Though sunshine streamed in through the wall-spanning windows of the conference room, the blinds had been drawn, and the overhead lights switched on.

For the first time in the last week, he felt he finally had good news to share.

The tech department had run the images of Amelia and Ben through a handful of different algorithms. The younger analyst explained how the process worked, but most of it had gone in one of Zane's ears and out the other. All he remembered was that the program searched for differences in the concentration of pixels.

So far, they'd established that the two people in the images had been composited. Neither had matching pixel depth, though they had been color blended to appear from the same shot. The graphic artist had done a very good job of matching perspectives as well. To anyone who didn't know better, the two appeared to be seamlessly joined.

Based on the mismatch on the pixels, it had been determined that Amelia's images had been sourced from video footage as still images. Her images had much more depth and density. The image of Ben appeared to have been taken on a camera phone. Satisfied with the determination that the pictures were fake, the lab shifted to its next analysis.

Unfortunately, the second algorithm didn't guarantee success at the same rate as the first. Rather than searching for pixels or alterations, the code was designed to pick apart the *source* of the picture. Digital images were often encoded with information about their origin, including servers to which they'd been connected. Any graphic artist could alter the so-called "source code" to erase their virtual footprints, but most reputable ones wouldn't erase their digital signature on any piece of art.

The tactic had been rare when the Bureau's image analysis was first developed, but as with most aspects of technology, advancement made the capability easier to obtain. Layton Redker had advised them not to let their expectations exceed reality.

Zane stared down at the message indicator on his phone. How had he missed Amelia's earlier text? He narrowed his eyes. She was going to Glenn's about the Leóne RICO? When did that happen? Hadn't he just seen Glenn on his way into the tech lab? And why the hell was Amelia going to Glenn instead of the other way around?

Even with a CPD escort, it was a stupid risk to take.

Frustrated to his core, he opened the app to locate Amelia's position.

If she's even wearing the damn watch.

As he tapped the screen, his phone buzzed and screamed an alarm that wasn't familiar. The sound scared him so damn bad that he nearly threw the device against the wall. Heart hammering, he managed a quick glance around the room to ensure no one had snuck in to witness the split-second of panic before he unlocked the screen.

The smile slid off his face when he realized what the alarm meant.

He hadn't recognized the notification sound, and now he knew why. The bell didn't belong to a text message, an email, or even a weather alert.

It was the panic alert on the GPS tracker he'd given Amelia. And according to the latest update, Amelia was about forty-minutes west of the FBI office.

"Shit!" He was on his feet before he realized he'd stood. "Corsaw, we need to leave. Now!"

28

F *igure it out. You can do this!*

Keys jangled at the back of the car, and with no better options at hand, Amelia let her body go limp. Eyes closed and ears ringing, Amelia struggled to make out the sounds just outside of the vehicle.

The lock clicked, and daylight rushed into the darkness, bringing with it a cool blast of fresh air and retina-piercing light, even through her eyelids.

Wait for it.

McAdam expected her to be unconscious. If she were a smart woman, she wouldn't have brought Amelia out here, wherever here was, to just kill her in the trunk of the car. Too much blood. She'd have had some plan.

Not yet…

Struggling to keep her breath slow and steady, Amelia fought against the panic that had her heart trying to punch a hole through her chest. A wrong move now might be her last. She just needed to play dead long enough for McAdam to do the heavy lifting and provide the opening she needed to make her break.

Not yet...

As a pair of hands clamped down around Amelia's calves, she called upon every ounce of discipline in her mental arsenal to keep her reflexes at bay. She wanted nothing more than to lash out at the dirty cop, but her hands were still bound behind her back. She had to wait for an opening to land a kick.

If she didn't make her moment of opportunity count, she was as good as dead.

McAdam gripped her legs and dragged Amelia halfway across the trunk in a single forceful tug.

The rough fabric liner was like sandpaper against the side of her face, but Amelia forced every muscle in her body to remain limp. She hoped her hair would obscure her face enough and keep her pained expression from being seen.

"My god," McAdam muttered. "You're heavier than you look."

For a split-second, Amelia was certain the officer had noticed her reaction, and she wasn't sure if she should lash out now before the chance slipped away for good. Just as Amelia was mentally prepping to fight, she was dragged a few more inches.

McAdam hadn't noticed Amelia's wince. There was still hope.

Almost. Just a little closer.

As if she could sense Amelia's silent plea, McAdam pulled until Amelia's legs dangled over the lip of the trunk, then rolled her over onto her back.

"It's about damn time!"

The new voice came as such a surprise that Amelia very nearly startled and opened her eyes.

With her hands tied behind her back, she had believed herself capable of taking down Cynthia McAdam, but could she escape from two?

"Traffic in this city is hell." McAdam's response held such a note of whiney petulance that Amelia could almost imagine that the woman had reverted back to a thirteen-year-old.

"That's not what I meant."

The newcomer's voice was closer now...familiar.

McAdam made a snort that was half laugh and half angry bull. "Then what did you mean?"

Daring to open her eyes the barest of slits, a second shadowy form joined the first. "I meant, it's about time you did the job right."

Amelia couldn't contain the small gasp that escaped her as Glenn Kantowski lifted a gun...

Bam!

Blood and gray matter exploded from the back of Cynthia McAdam's head. The officer crumpled out of sight, and Amelia could no longer pretend to be unconscious.

When Glenn turned the gun toward the trunk, Amelia knew she was out of time.

Now.

Summoning all her energy, Amelia braced both arms beneath herself for balance and bent her leg to the side. Glenn's eyes widened as Amelia's heel met the bumper.

With a gasp of surprise, Glenn tried to jump back. "What the f—"

Amelia kicked up with as much strength as she could manage, sending her canvas Vans straight into the woman's cheekbone. An audible crack accompanied the blow, and the force of the collision reverberated along Amelia's shin.

Glenn's head jerked to the side as she staggered back a couple of steps, then crumpled forward against the rear quarter panel of the car.

A potent combination of disgust and dread coalesced in Amelia's stomach as she pushed herself the rest of the way out of the trunk. Her legs were rubbery, but adrenaline rushed through her veins, giving her the strength to move.

Though she badly wanted to run away, she needed a weapon more.

But as she moved toward the FBI agent, Glenn began to stir and open her eyes.

Abort. Abort. Abort.

Before Glenn could sight the weapon, Amelia took off in an unsteady sprint toward a cabin at the end of the rounded driveway. Each pounding footfall echoed in her already aching head. Zigging as much as she could, she waited for a bullet to pierce her back.

Like some miracle, she reached a covered porch. She'd never seen this place before and had no idea where she was.

Deal with that later. Get to cover.

Her kick would have dazed Glenn—maybe even given her a concussion—but the seasoned FBI agent wasn't down for the count. Amelia had bought herself thirty seconds. A minute, if she was lucky.

As she rounded the end of the porch, she kept close to the wood siding to obscure herself from Glenn's view.

Her mind raced as she came to a stop in front of an addition that jutted from the side of the cabin. The sunroom was only about six feet wide and ten feet long, but Amelia would be more vulnerable as she made her way past the obstacle.

She peeked out to what she could see of the driveway, but only a sliver was visible, none of which included Glenn or the car. Keeping herself out of Glenn's line of sight was a double-edged sword.

Hunching her shoulders to make herself a smaller target, Amelia gulped in enough precious air to appease the burn in her lungs.

She couldn't stay here. She had to keep moving, no matter what.

With a burst of speed that should have eluded a person in Amelia's physical state, she darted out from her relative cover. As a twig and a clump of dried leaves crunched beneath her feet, Amelia winced.

Might as well have used an airhorn to tell Glenn where I am.

Her breath came in pants by the time she ducked into the corner where the sunroom met the cabin. For a moment, at least, she was out of view.

And she was fully upright.

Lifting her hands as high as she could, chicken winging her arms, she brought them down toward her ass. Snap. One side of the zip ties came free, but that was all she needed. The hard plastic peeled away a layer of her already raw skin, but her relief at the sudden freedom of motion outweighed the stinging pain.

She dropped the zip tie to the brittle grass and stretched her arms to restore circulation. One problem was solved, only a hundred more to address.

First and foremost, she gave the panic button a proper press. If Zane hadn't heard the alarm before, surely to all that was good and holy, he would now.

Next, she needed to know where the hell she was. Sunlight glittered off the surface of a body of water that was barely visible through a stand of trees on her left, but at the distance, Amelia didn't have the first clue if she was next to a river, a rural northern Illinois lake, or Lake Michigan itself.

Based on the position of the sun, she hadn't been unconscious for long. It wasn't quite midday.

Wait. I have a watch that also tells time.

She raised one battered, bloody wrist. Despite the beating she'd taken from jostling about the trunk of her car, the silver hands still ticked.

One in the afternoon. Glenn couldn't have taken her far. Could she?

The gravel driveway and wooded area suggested she was in a remote area. If she made it off this property, she could go for help. As long as she ran in one direction, she'd come across civilization eventually.

But getting away from Glenn's watchful eye was easier said than done. The wooded area that surrounded them might be unfamiliar to her, but Amelia could assume the landscape was known to Glenn.

She flexed her tingling fingers and crept to the end of the cabin.

Inhaling to steady her nerves, Amelia peeked around the corner. She retreated almost immediately in case Glenn had looped around to the other side, but she'd spotted no movement.

Maybe the woman was already lying in wait. She'd kicked Glenn pretty hard, but unsteady as she'd been coming out of that trunk, Amelia couldn't be certain.

Either way, Amelia had to keep moving. Glenn was armed, and if she spotted Amelia at this point, bullets were sure to follow.

Resting one hand on the siding to steady herself, she inched forward to take stock of the backyard. A set of steps led up to a wooden deck, on one side of which was a picture window and a sliding glass door. The space was complete with a large, round table, a sleek stainless-steel grill, and a couple lounge chairs scattered about. Across from the outdoor living space, not far from the tree line, was a shed roughly the size of a single-car garage.

Her mind moved quickly as she took stock of her options.

If she went inside the cabin, she could search for a phone to call for help, or a weapon to defend herself. However, she doubted she'd find a loaded handgun, and anything less would be bringing a knife to a gunfight. Literally.

And the phone? No one had landlines anymore. She

wasn't willing to bet her life that the property's owner was in the minority.

Which brought her to the next question mark.

Who *was* the owner? She'd never heard Glenn mention a vacation house, and Zane hadn't included the detail in any of his recollections about the woman from the Public Corruptions Unit.

Rather than killing Amelia outright, Glenn had gone through the trouble to have a fellow officer of the law drug her with a syringe, tie her hands behind her back, and load her into the trunk of a car to bring her to this place.

Whatever waited inside was almost definitely part of Glenn's plan. She'd either driven Amelia here to stage the scene of her death or to make the disposal of her body easier.

Bodies, Amelia reminded herself. Cynthia McAdam made that a plural.

So…murder/suicide? Was that what Glenn had been thinking?

No matter the agent's plans, the cabin was a death trap. Amelia risked being cornered or ambushed, not to mention the possibility of an accomplice. Glenn might have taken a blow to the head, but Amelia was still no match for her.

She had one choice left. Run to the cover of the woods, find the road, and flag down the first person she came across.

Run through an unfamiliar wooded area. What could go wrong?

Had she not been reliant on stealth, she would have snorted at the thought. Her plan to make a break for the trees was riddled with flaws, but she had to take the risk.

The muffled thud of a car door sent a sudden rush of adrenaline throughout her tired body.

She had to move quickly. Her window to escape was about to slam closed.

29

I couldn't believe that bitch kicked me. Damn near knocked me on my ass too. If her strength had been at full capacity, I'd have likely lost consciousness.

Senator Young had messed up yet again.

First, the idiot had assured me that nothing could go wrong when he first decided to set up Amelia for Ben Storey's murder. Of course, at the time, Cynthia McAdam was supposed to shoot Amelia as soon as she entered the abandoned house, but that video call had sullied that plan.

Then there was the half-baked Plan B that I should have refused to follow through with. Planting the murder weapon. The messages. The nude pictures. They had all muddied the water but hadn't been the quicksand needed to drown Amelia Storm.

And now…damn him. Stan had assured me that the drug I'd used was potent enough to last for an hour—more than enough time to drive to Ben Storey's hidden vacation home northwest of Chicago.

I'd been careful to measure out a dose of the sedative that matched the weight on Amelia's license, but apparently, I'd been off by about twenty minutes. Or maybe Cynthia hadn't pushed the plunger all the way in.

I'd planned the perfect murder/suicide scenario, but now, everything was screwed.

As pissed as I was, and as much as I wanted to lay the blame solely at Stan's feet, I'd have to conduct a thorough search into what in the hell had gone wrong before I confronted the senator.

I'd tried to take off after her, but dazed as I had been by the cheap shot Amelia had taken, my body wouldn't obey my brain.

With one elbow resting along the bumper for support, I heaved, emptying my stomach of the granola bar I'd had for breakfast. The puke mixed with Cynthia McAdam's blood and brains, making me need to puke again.

The bitter sting of stomach acid coated my throat, but I had no time to find water to help extinguish the burn. Wiping my mouth with the back of one gloved hand, I swallowed in a vain attempt to eliminate the foul taste on my tongue.

What stung worse than a direct hit to the cheek was that Amelia had made a run for it. I should have seen that coming.

As soon as I was satisfied that the last wave of vertigo had passed, I used the Mustang to steady myself and stood.

Run while you can, Amelia. I'm still going to kill you.

Gritting my teeth, I retrieved the FBI-issued Glock from the holster beneath my arm. The weapon was Amelia's, and I'd intended to wrap her hand around the grip after I'd dumped a half-bottle of vodka down her throat. Between the booze and the heartfelt suicide note I'd typed up the night before, I'd been certain that the Bureau would rule her death a suicide.

Glock in one hand, I pulled the key fob out of my coat pocket and locked the vehicle. I wasn't sure if Amelia knew how to hotwire a car, but I wouldn't make it easy for her to get in.

As I turned to the cabin, the familiar sight jabbed a phantom blade at my heart.

Ben and I used to spend weekends here, making love all night and greeting the dawn in each other's arms. When we were thoroughly exhausted, we'd sleep through the afternoon so we could do it all over again.

The time away from our lives in the city, our respective spouses, careers, and responsibilities had been the happiest of all my memories. Even now, I could still remember the warmth of his body next to mine.

This wasn't how we were supposed to end. I wasn't supposed to divorce my husband of twelve years and break up my family. Ben, the damn chicken, shouldn't have bailed on me in the last second.

Lenny Kantowski, my now-ex-husband, was a man of means. He'd known I was cheating and dragged me over the coals when the time came for custody proceedings. Though I liked to tell my fellow agents at the FBI that I was leaving the office early to pick up my son from school, I left out the fact that collecting him from band practice was just about *all* I was able to see of my little boy.

His father had made sure to twist the knife in deep as payback for daring to betray him. And every time I dropped my son off at his house, he made damn sure to parade his new fiancée out for me to see. She was a real piece of work too. A pretty redhead seven years my junior, whose parents commanded a respectable hotel business in Chicago. Naturally, when they passed, she'd inherit their fortune.

Despite the combined wealth of Lenny and his fiancée, the pair still didn't hold a candle to Stan Young. With the corrupt senator in my corner, I'd planned to level the playing field and take Lenny back to court. Show that bastard what it feels like to have his heart ripped out of his chest. And I'd make damn sure the only time he saw his son was through supervised visitation. Lenny had been unfaithful long before I'd met Ben. It was thanks to Stan's connections that I'd found proof of it.

Even if I couldn't prove Lenny's infidelity, I'd find another way. I'd blackmail him. I'd frame him for embezzlement. I'd rip away his livelihood like he had mine.

Playing by the rules was a fool's game. And I'd lost one too many times. Meanwhile, those who were successful broke the rules with almost reckless abandon and profited, so why shouldn't I?

Here I was. Back where my downward spiral had started, it would end.

The best lies ran parallel to the truth, and I'd selected the peaceful cabin for more than just its relative secrecy. I'd planned to copy my own experiences with Ben Storey and paste them into Amelia's life.

I tightened my grasp on the nine-mil.

Amelia was collateral damage. Unfortunate, but that was the way of the world. It was me or her.

I'll be damned if it is ever me again!

Taking in a lungful of crisp November air, I exhaled and counted to five. Renewed determination rolled over me in waves as I headed toward the backyard. With hurried strides, I ate up the distance, only pausing when I reached the end of the cabin.

I lifted the nine-mil to peer down the sight as I stepped out from behind the corner. My muscles tensed, preparing for an ambush, but I was greeted by only the undisturbed deck.

She could have gone inside.

Perhaps she'd thought to arm herself or even make an emergency phone call. I swung my aim over the yard to double-check that she hadn't hidden behind a shrub to bide her time.

The area was clear. My shoes thudded against the wooden stairs as I trotted to the sliding glass door. I couldn't recall if I'd bothered to lock the damn thing when I'd stopped by the night before. No one wandered around out here searching for houses to loot, and I'd kept any items pertinent to the plan close to my person.

As my gaze settled on the handle, the hairs on the back of my neck rose to attention.

Against the white plastic, there was a smudge of crimson, plain as day. In the receding daze of the sedative, Amelia must not have noticed the mark as she'd rushed to get inside.

To ensure she wasn't crouched on the other side of the glass, I leaned in to watch through a crack in the blinds.

Before I was satisfied that I was safe to enter, a flicker of movement on the glass stole my attention. The motion hadn't come from inside the cabin but from the reflection.

Spinning around on my heel, I leveled the handgun as Amelia sprinted out from behind the shed. Her steps were erratic, swaying as if drunk and making a valiant effort to run home from the bar.

I inched my finger closer to the trigger and held my breath. From the distance, I couldn't rely on a headshot.

With each passing heartbeat, Amelia grew closer to the tree line. Her wobbly route made her slower, while also rendering her a far more difficult target.

I followed her unpredictable pace for another couple feet as I drew a bead on the middle of her back. With a steady exhaling breath, I eased my finger back.

A raucous report split the air like a lightning bolt, and the force of the Glock's recoil vibrated up my arm. I'd been prepared for the kick. My aim didn't waver as I squeezed off two more shots.

Bark exploded off a birch tree in the distance. My second bullet went wide, but just before Amelia slipped into the woods, I caught a flash of crimson on her light gray hoodie.

I'd hit her.

Now, I had to finish the job.

30

————

B lood soaked through the side of her sweatshirt. With each movement, her clothes rubbed against the gaping hole the bullet had torn through her skin. She couldn't stop to assess the true damage, not that she wanted to. Seeing it would only send her into shock. As long as she could keep moving, adrenaline would do the rest, allowing her to stay on her feet.

In the distance, Amelia spotted a building with gray siding. Unsure of how much distance she'd put between her and Glenn, she knew she needed to find shelter, safety, maybe a phone to call for backup. She used the searing pain to keep her grounded in the moment. One foot in front of the other. She couldn't think of unknowns. Wouldn't assume anything about Glenn.

Focus, Amelia. Get to that house. That's an order, soldier.

She gritted her teeth, biting back the cry of pain desperate to explode from her lips. Digging into all her energy reserves, Amelia sprinted from the cover of the woods and made a beeline toward the cement steps of a screened-in front porch. Though she'd detested all the running she'd done in the military, the experience was paying off.

Casting one more paranoid glance to the woods, Amelia reached for the door handle. She couldn't tell if the owner was home, nor did she care. She just wanted to get out of the open.

The door didn't budge.

She balled one hand into a fist and banged against the wooden frame. "Hello? Is anyone home? I need help, please. I'm hurt, and there's someone chasing me."

With each desperate breath, fire spread beneath her ribs. Her heart struggled to maintain the frantic pace that kept adrenaline pumping through her body. In just the few moments she'd stood waiting at the door, she'd felt her legs weaken. How long would it be before they gave out?

Blood continued to ooze from her wound. Her hoodie was ruined, but even as Amelia pressed her hand harder against her shredded skin to stem the flow, she knew it was a futile effort.

She needed a proper first aid kit. She needed time. She needed *help*.

"Please!" Her voice cracked as she pounded her fist on the door. "Hello? I can see your truck parked in the driveway! All I need is a phone, please!"

Panic rose in her chest. Amelia sent a frantic glance back toward the woods, checking the trees. There was no movement, but Glenn could emerge at any second, and Amelia was a sitting duck. She was losing the battle and running out of options.

The creak of hinges jerked her attention back to the cabin. As a middle-aged man opened the interior door, his entire body stiffened.

"What the hell's going on out here?" His words were tinged with a faint Southern drawl.

"Someone's trying to kill me." As if to emphasize her point, Amelia looked over her shoulder to the backyard. "Please, I just need to call for help."

Though his face was blurred by the screen that separated them, his hesitancy was obvious. He scanned her up and down, and Amelia was convinced he was about to shoo her away.

At the last possible second, just before Amelia was ready to force herself to resume the treacherous run, the man sighed.

"All right." He flicked the lock and opened the flimsy door. "That wound of yours don't look too good. Come inside, I'll find you something to help with the blood."

"Thank you." Amelia wheezed as she limped forward. She cast one last look at the trees before she followed the man inside.

She tried to ignore the onslaught of horror movie flashbacks as he led her through a living room with furnishings reminiscent of the seventies.

Though the plaid couch and matching loveseat could have been pulled from a Sears catalog circa 1973, as they rounded a corner into a kitchen almost as large as the living and dining areas, Amelia noted that the appliances and electronics were sleek and state-of-the-art. Apparently, the man's affinity for the past ended at aesthetics.

"You said there's someone out there tryin' to kill you, is that right?" He eyed her with understandable suspicion.

Swallowing the invisible cotton balls that filled her mouth, Amelia clutched her side a little tighter. "Yes. She... she shot me, but I don't think it hit anything vital." If the bullet had clipped her lung or her liver, she'd have bled out or suffocated back in the woods. "Do you have a weapon? In case she finds me here?"

The man rubbed his salt and pepper beard before he

opened the door of a tall cabinet beside the refrigerator. "Here. I usually save these for cleaning, so don't worry about getting blood on them. Name's Miles, by the way." He held out two bleach-stained tea towels. "And don't have no need for no gun out here. Peaceful living...normally."

"Thank you, I'm Amelia." Without her badge, she knew better than to reveal she was an FBI agent. Chances were good that Miles would think she'd lost her mind if she tried to claim she worked for the Bureau. "Do you have a phone? Can you call 911? My phone is...I don't know what happened to it."

His expression softened, though the change was slight. "My cell's over at the computer desk. Let me go get it, and I'll call for you. Just so you know, though, the cops take a minute to get out here."

"Where is *here*?" Amelia blurted the question before she could think it through. Wiping her bloody hand on one sleeve, she jammed the towels against her side.

A mixture of befuddlement and suspicion took over his expression. "You're about ten minutes north of Millington, in Illinois."

"Millington?" As a chill came over her, she wasn't sure if blood loss or fear was to blame. She'd never heard of that place before, but her knowledge of the rural side of Illinois had always been limited. "How far away from Chicago are we?"

He scratched his cheek. "Probably an hour, or thereabouts."

Amelia's stomach clenched. She blinked to steady her wobbly vision. "Please, call 911."

"Right. Hold on." As Miles neared the oaken desk in the neighboring dining room, a series of knocks cut the eerie quiet like an ax splitting firewood.

Sucking in a sharp breath, Amelia jumped.

"FBI, open up!"

Glenn's voice sent sheer dread to gnaw at the back of Amelia's thoughts, threatening to swallow her whole.

Miles shot her a suspicious glance as he picked up his phone. "Who in the hell are you, girl? You runnin' from the Feds?"

"I'm the Feds. Just call 911. Let the police sort it out." Her words weren't a request anymore. They were a plea.

He hesitated, and if she were closer, she swore she'd have heard the gears grinding in his head.

"Whoever's inside, I need you to open the door," Glenn called. "I'm Special Agent Glenn Kantowski with the Federal Bureau of Investigation."

Miles jabbed a crooked finger at Amelia, his blue eyes wild with fear and anxiety. "Stay right there, you hear me? Don't you touch nothin', either. I don't know who the hell you are, and I don't want to."

Amelia damn near burst into tears as she watched the older man pocket his cell and head for the door.

Of course Glenn had her badge. And *of course* she'd taken Amelia's. She wasn't even sure she could blame Miles for choosing to answer the door over dialing 911 for a bleeding, suspicious stranger.

Never mind that I wouldn't ask him to call 911 if I was running from the cops.

Pressing the makeshift bandage tighter against her ribs, Amelia crept to the wide doorway between the kitchen and dining room, looking for anything she could use as a weapon.

Careful not to leave behind a bloody handprint, Amelia crouched to take cover behind a tall china cabinet—another relic from decades past. Heart clamoring against her chest, she held her breath. That's when she heard the *thwup-thwup-thwup*. She listened harder. A helicopter?

"Afternoon, Mr. Peters. I'm Agent Kantowski with the FBI's Organized Crime Division. Have you seen anyone on your property this afternoon? I'm afraid—"

That was Amelia's cue to get the hell out of dodge.

She rubbed her sticky hand against her jeans and hobbled toward the back exit she'd spotted when they'd arrived in the kitchen.

Each movement diligent and measured, she flicked the deadbolt and twisted the knob. As she used her fingertips to push open the door, a wave of chilly air struck her like a physical blow.

After all the running she'd done, she shouldn't be this damn cold.

Blood loss, which had no doubt been exacerbated by her desperate run through the woods, had caught up to her.

Time was not on Amelia's side.

She wouldn't give up. Even if she didn't make it far, she'd go down fighting.

Easing the door closed behind herself, she swept her gaze over the backyard.

Into the woods we go. Again.

With one hand on her ribs, she used the other arm for balance as she forced her hurried walk to a jog. Glancing to the house to ensure she hadn't been followed, Amelia ducked behind the shed.

Her shoulders shook as she gasped for breath. She was already winded. If she didn't have speed, she'd have to rely on stealth.

After locating a tree with a trunk large enough to conceal her frame, Amelia headed toward it.

She made it three steps.

"Amelia Storm, stop! Don't move!"

Amelia spun around to face the speaker. As she spotted

the matte black Glock in Glenn's hand, terror sank its claws into her heart.

The woman wouldn't shoot her in front of a private civilian, would she? Miles was nowhere to be seen, but he could easily be watching from the window. Amelia could still have an opportunity to escape.

Glenn took a step closer, her aim unwavering. "Drop your weapon, Ms. Storm."

"What? I...I don't have a—"

"Drop your weapon, or I'll shoot!"

Bile rose in the back of Amelia's throat as she spotted the hilt of the hunting knife tucked in Glenn's waistband.

Glenn wouldn't shoot her in front of a witness unless she could prove that Amelia was armed. In the hands of someone with a decade of military experience, a six-inch hunting knife would be more than enough justification. And the fact that Amelia was partially concealed by the shed would give Glenn the chance to plant the evidence.

This was the end.

Amelia was too weak to run, much less try to fight. Glenn had clearly mapped out her plan well enough to bring a weapon to plant on Amelia's body.

"What the hell did I do to you, Glenn? I thought you were my—"

The crack of a gunshot shattered the eerie, serene quiet of the woodland air.

Had Amelia not caught the spatter of blood and brain matter that exploded from the side of Glenn's head, she'd have been sure the shot was meant for her.

As Glenn's body crumpled into a graceless heap, Amelia's mind devolved into a whirlwind of paranoia.

Maybe Miles *was* a psychopath. A creep ripped straight from an eighties slasher or a modern thriller, perhaps both.

He could have decided he wanted to torture and kill Amelia, so he'd murdered Glenn to get her out of the way.

When Amelia spotted the shape of a familiar man at the edge of the cabin, tears of relief prickled the corners of her eyes.

Spencer Corsaw.

Lowering his weapon, Spencer advanced a few steps closer to Glenn's still form. "You okay, Storm?"

Teeth chattering, Amelia managed a nod. "I-I-I'm f-fine."

Spencer didn't seem convinced. He holstered the nine-mil and turned back to the house. "Palmer, she's back here. She's hurt."

Amelia spotted Zane jogging from the other side of the house. He didn't seem that far away, but as Amelia tried to focus on him, his form distorted. Light began to dim around her as if sunset had come early. And then everything went sideways. The ground came up hard to greet her as darkness stole her vision.

"Stay with me, Amelia!" Zane's frantic voice tried to saw through her brain. "Don't do this, Storm. You're not leaving me with all the paperwork. C'mon. Hang in there." His voice sounded so very far away. "Guys, we're losing her."

31

With a deep breath to steady his frayed nerves, Zane pressed down on the stainless-steel handle, tucked a stuffed cat in the crook of his elbow, and pushed open the heavy hospital room door.

After Spencer shot Glenn, Amelia had to be emergency airlifted to a hospital on the outskirts of Chicago. The paramedic, who'd arrived alongside the sheriff's department, had been concerned about her making it to the hospital in time. Her blood pressure had dropped to dangerously low levels, and she couldn't keep her eyes open.

Zane had been beside himself with guilt for not checking his messages sooner. If he had gotten there just a little earlier, maybe he could have prevented her from being shot. As it was, they'd been damn lucky that there was a chopper available and ready to go. Things could have ended up much differently if Spencer hadn't been able to commandeer it based on their emergency.

Thankfully, a couple blood transfusions and one minor surgery later, and Amelia was awake and stable. Though the usual hours for visitors had passed, the hospital staff made an exception when Zane had shown off his badge. They'd run the request by Amelia, and she'd given the green light.

As Zane stepped into the dim, sterile room, he wondered if he should have waited.

Locking the screen of her phone, Amelia shifted her tired gaze to him. Dark circles rested beneath her eyes, and her cheeks were even paler than usual.

"Are you sure I should be here right now? You look like shit." He pressed his lips together as soon as he finished.

Though he worried his joke had offended her, Amelia set her cell to the side and smiled. "So do you. I just got out of surgery a bit ago. What's your excuse?"

He blew a raspberry as he pulled a chair closer to the bed. "My excuse? I spent the last few hours wondering if one of my closest friends was dying."

She dropped her gaze. "I'm sorry."

"No." He held up a hand. "You're not supposed to apologize for that. That was all Glenn's fault."

Amelia stroked the sterile white sheets like a child would stroke their favorite blanket. "I guess. But I shouldn't have left your apartment. If I'd stayed there..."

"None of this would have happened...*today*." His voice was stern on purpose. She needed to not blame herself. "But it *would* have happened. And if it'd happened on a different day, the outcome might not have been the same. We might not have caught Glenn, and you might've been hurt a lot worse. Here." He held out a stuffed calico. "I know you miss Hup. I stopped at a gas station on my way here, and I saw these stuffed cats. This was the last calico they had."

Her eyes turned glassy as she held the plush cat to her chest. Swiping beneath her nose with one hand, she sniffled. "That's sweet. Thank you. I...I do miss Hup."

A phantom hand squeezed his heart. He hated the part of himself that had doubted her so much over the past week.

The guilt was so pervasive that he could hardly look her in the eyes.

Instead, he cleared his throat. "Is something wrong?"

"You mean aside from someone I thought I could trust having a law enforcement officer stab me with a syringe and load my unconscious body into the trunk of a car so she could frame me for a murder that she committed...before she killed me in a way that made it look like suicide?"

He opened and closed his mouth a couple times before he could conjure any coherent words. "Yeah, I guess that about sums it up, doesn't it?"

In all Zane's experiences with the CIA and the FBI, he'd never been trapped in the trunk of a car. Nor had he experienced the displeasure of a colleague attempting to frame him.

He'd been betrayed, stabbed in the back—literally and figuratively—and used, but he'd never been *framed*.

For the first time since he and Amelia had been partnered, he couldn't imagine how she must feel.

"What did you guys find?" Amelia's voice cut through his mental rant before it could start.

Zane straightened. "A storage unit. That's where she kept all the tech she used to try to frame you. On a laptop hard drive, we found copies of those Photoshopped pictures that she sent to Real Chicago News. That computer also had access to the cameras that were hidden in your apartment. That footage deleted itself on a rolling twenty-four-hour basis, though, so we aren't sure how long the cameras had been in your apartment."

"Wow. That doesn't make me very excited to go home." She stroked the stuffed cat's head. "Thank you again for letting me and Hup stay with you. I know that Hup can be kind of a dick sometimes. She did claw the back of your sofa and left hair all over your furni...." Her voice cracked.

Before he could consider the action, he reached out to clasp her hand. "You'd do the same for me. I know you would, even if I had a jackass cat that knocked over your shit and clawed up your couch. You can stay for as long as you need. I mean it."

Amelia swallowed and tightened her grip on his hand. "Okay. Okay. Sorry. I don't know what's wrong with me right now. Maybe it's the morphine or the lack of morphine. I don't...um...what about Iris Storey? Did she recognize Glenn?"

"She did." Zane was happy for the subject change. And for the opportunity to deliver good news. "She confirmed that Glenn and her husband had an affair that lasted almost two years. As best as we can tell right now, Glenn met him through work. She and the Public Corruption Unit were investigating a law firm where Storey practiced when he first moved to Chicago, and they consulted with him about it."

"So, we think that her motive was revenge? A crime of passion."

"Yeah." With one last squeeze, he released her hand. "We searched that cabin. Which, by the way, Storey owned."

Amelia pulled the white knit blanket up over her lap. "Do I even want to know what was in there?"

Reading Amelia's forged suicide note had been surreal. Zane didn't want to add to her obvious stress, but he knew she'd eventually find out. "As you already know, Glenn wrote a letter intended to make your death look like a suicide. Autopsies don't test for the sedative that she used to knock you out, and, well...you already know that she had your service weapon."

Amelia snorted. "Yeah. Bitch shot me with my own gun."

Zane couldn't help his laughter. "Sorry. I don't know if you meant for that to be funny or not, but...it was."

"I didn't, but it was funny."

In the silence that enveloped them, Amelia seemed lost in thought as she twisted a piece of blonde-tipped hair around her index finger. "How didn't we notice that? We'd been working with her for how long?"

Zane rubbed his unshaven cheek. "I don't know. Some people are just good at hiding who they really are, I suppose."

Amelia set the stuffed cat in her lap. "Yeah. I guess."

Another spell of quiet followed on the heels of the first. As Amelia stifled a yawn, Zane took his cue. "Well, I should let you get some rest. And I could use some myself, honestly."

"Do you think I'm one of those people?"

Her question struck him like a slap to the face. "What?"

She bit her lip, and he could tell she hadn't intended to speak the words aloud. "I can tell you've been looking at me differently since you asked me about that search I did on Luca Passarelli. You're not the only one who's observant, you know? I just...I want to make sure that you don't think I'm someone like *that*. Someone like Glenn, who's going to turn around and stab you in the back."

He swallowed past the tightness in his throat. "No. Of course not." Rare were the moments when Zane was rendered speechless, but he couldn't craft a remotely eloquent response.

She rubbed her nose with the back of one hand. "There're things about me you don't know, but please believe me when I say that none of it defines who I am. I'm *not* like her."

"I know you're not."

Even though I let myself think you were. But that's just because I'm an asshole.

He wanted to offer her more reassurance, but he'd wallowed dangerously close to hypocrisy.

Rather than stumble over himself to expound, he rose from the sparsely cushioned chair, leaned forward, and wrapped Amelia in a tight embrace. As she slid her arms around his shoulders, she tucked her face in the crook of his neck.

He wasn't sure how long they'd have stayed locked in that position if a light knock hadn't pulled their attention to the door.

Clipboard in hand, a nurse peeked into the room before she pushed the door the rest of the way open. "Hi, Amelia. I'm just here to take your vitals and check on how you're doing."

Zane touched Amelia's shoulder as he offered her a tired smile. "I'll send you a picture of Hup when I get home, okay?"

Amelia blinked repeatedly, and he could tell she was fighting back tears. "Okay. Drive safe. I'll talk to you soon."

He was damn close to tears himself as he offered her a gruff, "You will."

32

Joseph was halfway through unwrapping a fun-sized Twix when the door at his back swung open. He didn't have to pull his gaze away from the early morning Chicago skyline to know that his visitor was Stan Young. After all, he was in the senator's office. Young had returned from D.C. the day before, and Joseph saw his opportunity.

He knew Stan had more than a few questions burning in the back of his head.

Popping the candy into his mouth, Joseph leaned back in his seat and propped his elbows on the leather armrests. "It's almost Thanksgiving. Why do you still have bowls of Halloween candy on the executive floor?"

Stan's expression might as well have been carved from marble. The man was clearly tired, but his poker face held firm as he closed the door and took his seat behind the polished desk. "It's Thanksgiving candy, Joseph. Look at the wrapper."

Joseph opened his hand and peered down at the gold plastic. "Huh. Turkeys. I didn't even notice them."

"Mm-hmm." Stan dragged a hand over his face, his

dispassionate façade finally breaking. "You want to tell me why you're here? Or how in the hell you got in here in the first place?"

With a snort, Joseph pulled out his badge and flipped open the leather case. "I'm an FBI agent. I go wherever in the hell I want."

Stan's eyes narrowed. "So, you're telling me that you came into my building and waved your badge around for everyone to see?"

"That…" Joseph lifted a finger as he pocketed the badge, "I did not do. I actually didn't have to show my badge to anyone other than the receptionist out in the lobby. Honestly, considering she's the only one who gave a shit that a stranger was up here, you should probably promote her to your head of security."

"Thanks. I'll take your expert advice into consideration." Stan crossed both arms over his pricey suit jacket. "Now, was there anything else you wanted to talk to me about? Believe it or not, I've actually got a lot of shit to do today."

Waving his finger, Joseph leaned forward. "Yes, actually. I'm glad you mentioned it. I was just curious about how your hired gun worked out. You know, the *two* women you paid to kill Ben Storey *and* Amelia Storm. Except, oh, right." He held both hands out to his sides. "Agent Storm isn't dead, is she?"

Stan inched closer to his desk as he pinned Joseph with an unimpressed glare. "I hired her…them…to do a job you couldn't. Period. End of story. It just turns out that *she…they…* couldn't do it either, but for a different reason. I swear to God, Larson." As Stan paused to take in a breath through his nose, Joseph was surprised steam didn't shoot out of his ears. "You're *obsessed* with Amelia Storm. Did you think I wouldn't notice? Why the hell else would you have wanted to frame her for Storey's murder?"

Joseph lost his hold on the feigned nonchalance as the

first hint of indignance prodded at the back of his mind. "Like you're one to talk. How many people did I have to *take care of* after you went off the rails and kidnapped Gianna Passarelli?"

A muscle in Stan's jaw ticked. The man maintained his intense stare, but he didn't speak.

"And that wasn't the end, was it?" Joseph slid back into his seat. "Remember two years ago? You thought that Detective Storm was getting a little too close to your secret. Who took care of him?"

"Yes, well, that doesn't mean it gives you license to lose your mind over this woman." Stan's voice came through clenched teeth. "If anything, you should learn from my mistake. I let Sofia Lettiero, Sofia *Passarelli*, get to my head, and you see where it got me. Don't let Amelia get in your head, Joseph. Brian and I need you with your damn wits intact."

As many times as Joseph had mentally run through this moment, he hadn't imagined Stan providing genuine advice.

The senator had a point. Back when he'd met Amelia at the FBI field office in Boston, he'd been a grand total of six months removed from shooting her brother in the head. For reasons he still didn't understand, he'd been drawn toward her like a moth to a flame.

And he knew damn well what could happen. Just like Icarus. His wings would melt if he flew too close to the sun. And that ended with a deadly fall from grace.

Joseph let out a sigh as he massaged his temples. "You're right. But what in the hell were you thinking, hiring Glenn Kantowski?"

"I was thinking about making another ally in the Federal Bureau of Investigation. She was in Public Corruption. Her position would've been invaluable, especially with the election coming up next November. This senate seat isn't a guarantee. I like to hedge my bets."

"I get it." Joseph lifted his hands in a sign of surrender. "But she didn't make the cut. Fortunately, *someone* had the foresight to plant all that evidence in her storage unit."

"That someone sure is humble this morning." Stan's tone was flat.

It pissed off Joseph that the senator didn't acknowledge his smart thinking, but he waved away the remark. "Whatever. Don't worry about Amelia Storm. I've got another sweet piece of ass to keep me company."

"An Assistant U.S. Attorney, I know." Stan snorted out a laugh. "You sure like to play with fire, don't you?"

"I've got enough practice by now that I like to think I know what I'm doing."

Stan's amused look turned grave. "Don't get cocky, Joseph. Take it from someone who's been there."

"I won't. I'm not." He didn't have the same resources as his benefactor and knew all too well that a Sofia Passarelli situation would ruin him. But he wasn't about to reveal his trepidation to Stan. No. He needed to give off an air of complete confidence. "Just...have a little faith in me, okay?"

Stan flattened his palms against the desk. "Don't give me a reason not to."

When it came to loyalty, Joseph wouldn't give Stan a reason to doubt him. As for Cassandra Halcott, Joseph was confident he had plenty of opportunity to play without the risk of being burned.

If he couldn't have Amelia, Cassandra was more than suitable as her substitute.

For now.

The End
To be continued...

Thank you for reading.
All of the Amelia Storm Series books can be found on
Amazon.

ACKNOWLEDGMENTS

How does one properly thank everyone involved in taking a dream and making it a reality? Here goes.

In addition to our families, whose unending support provided the foundation for us to find the time and energy to put these thoughts on paper, we want to thank the editors who polished our words and made them shine.

Many thanks to our publisher for risking taking on two newbies and giving us the confidence to become bona fide authors.

More than anyone, we want to thank you, our readers, for clicking on a couple of nobodies and sharing your most important asset, your time, with this book. We hope with all our hearts we made it worthwhile.

Much love,
Mary & Amy

ABOUT THE AUTHOR

Mary Stone lives among the majestic Blue Ridge Mountains of East Tennessee with her two dogs, four cats, a couple of energetic boys, and a very patient husband.

As a young girl, she would go to bed every night, wondering what type of creature might be lurking underneath. It wasn't until she was older that she learned that the creatures she needed to most fear were human.

Today, she creates vivid stories with courageous, strong heroines and dastardly villains. She invites you to enter her world of serial killers, FBI agents but never damsels in distress. Her female characters can handle themselves, going toe-to-toe with any male character, protagonist or antagonist.

Discover more about Mary Stone on her website.
www.authormarystone.com

Amy Wilson

Having spent her adult life in the heart of Atlanta, her upbringing near the Great Lakes always seems to slip into her writing. After several years as a vet tech, she has dreams of going back to school to be a veterinarian but it seems another dream of hers has come true first. Writing a novel.

Animals and books have always been her favorite things, in addition to her husband, who wanted her to have it all. He's the reason she has time to write. Their two teenage boys fill the rest of her time and help her take care of the mini zoo that now fills their home with laughter...and yes, the occasional poop.

Connect with Mary Online

facebook.com/authormarystone

goodreads.com/AuthorMaryStone

bookbub.com/profile/3378576590

pinterest.com/MaryStoneAuthor

instagram.com/marystone_author

Made in United States
Troutdale, OR
06/29/2024

20906536R00179